The Protein Bomb

a diversion

Edwin Ahearn

2002

I.

Things, regrettably, just don't run straight for me. For writers, whether making fiction or recording actual events, who work to a plan and know right from the first indent where they're going, so that even digressions behave integrally, I have an admiration bordering on awe — not necessarily an affection; the inept wafflers are often more likeable with their "that reminds me" technique of cheerful inattention to the larger view, but dangerous, like some of our childhood friends, who were fun to be with but horrible as examples.

My tale, no quarrel, could use a shot of paprika here at the outset; unfortunately, the only episode which has any connection to my main theme consists of something I decided not to do. In the summer, as a result of a lengthy interview with a retired and anonymous operative from French intelligence, I was launched almost inadvertently on a short series known (though not to the public) as "The Spooks," a rather hit-or-miss and inherently inconclusive look at the aims and methods of secret government as maintained and quite lavishly financed by far too many countries. I do syndicated television in Brussels.

Brief focus and certainly propellant was that hackneyed classic, the unexplained disappearance, a few years ago, of Feyd Mirré, prosperous Moroccan businessman living in Paris, sometime arms broker, shadowy intermediary in various cases involving hostages and other dealings with demons where pious western governments wished to preserve deniability. *L'affaire Mirré* has had more esoteric and unlikely explanations than Jack the Ripper, marshalling an excess of inconclusive evidence; a headless, handless corpse of about the right size and age fished, à la Simenon, from the Seine and never positively identified, conflicting "eyewitness" accounts (one from a handsomely compensated prostitute) of how Mirré spent his last known evening in Paris, various subsequent sightings of him in anywhere from Aspen, Bogota or Canberra to Xian, York or Zeebrugge, three or more definitive but mutually incompatible scenarios based on alleged inside knowledge of operations by everything from German intelligence to Islamic extremists, with the inevitable C.I.A. as lurking *deus ex machina*; there is even an earnest theory implicating extra-terrestrial abductors (no arrests are anticipated). Amusingly, Mirré's absence was first signalled by the inconsolable yapping, in his upscale flat, of a famished Ayr terrier: beam me back, Scottie.

A selective and tendentious cross-section of all this was served up by my French canary, and only hours after the interview was broadcast I had a demand for rebuttal from another contributor wishing to preserve anonymity, a former (allegedly former) officer in Israeli intelligence, later with large trepidation taped in the eerie noontime shadows of a cellar jazz-club in Gstaad (how I could spin this all out if I had no scruples about its relevance; silent string bass leaning like a sinister, adipose drunk against the silent piano, ghost feet flickering overhead, across the greenish glass bricks of a skylight, small unexplained creakings and rustlings. We had coffee.).

My informant (I call him, though he did almost anything but) deployed a pre-emptive technique of simple disassertion, offering no evidence but repeatedly citing a self-defined "common sense" as the proper test of credibility. A man with whom nothing went unplanned, not excluding the cumbersome negligence (whoops!) with which he let slip the name of Willem Zuylen as one who had more to tell about more subjects than Mirré. After our taping, he gave me, with a token simulacrum of reluctance, a number in Amsterdam where Zuylen could sometimes be reached. I left with the feeling of a slight, unnegotiable advantage; Nameless thought I didn't know I had been played.

Zuylen answered when I tried, and, equally jolly in French or English, briskly agreed to come down to Brussels. A stocky, muscular, coral-cheeked cherub of almost seventy, with no conscience, an engaging chuckle, and an insatiable addiction to foul little black cheroots, which happily he sucked and gnawed at more often than lighted. For over thirty years, I had no impulse to doubt, committed to no nation or system, cheerfully unrepentant about profit that often came from both ends of a transaction, he had been a kind of freelance broker for prized and mostly classified information; the Americans, he asserted, had been fully aware that he was also selling to the Soviets (and vice-versa), but each of the then major players had been convinced that what they got from Zuylen was infinitely more valuable than what Zuylen got from them; everyone was happy, even the British and French, who, for a relatively modest outlay, were given a Zuylen-eye-view of what both the Russkies and the bloody Yanks were up to now.

    I wish there was room for Zuylen in my real story; he kept all of us in Brussels entertained with his outrageous anecdotes, mainly turning on the endless stupidity of intelligence operatives, and after all the backlighting and electronically disguised voices, his barefaced television appearance was refreshing; he insisted there was nothing he wanted to hide, and that no one had any motive to have him silenced — the last was debatable once you brought embarrassment into the sums, but I believe he went on the principle that having survived far longer than might be expected, he was, as gamblers say, playing with house money. Though comfortably fixed, he is not, by the way, fabulously wealthy, as might have been (he said) but for his amiable vulnerability to a hard-luck story or a set of long, slender legs. His drifts into a lubricious nostalgia with the last category — what I suppose might be called Bondage — were overly graphic for general consumption, and largely edited out before airing.

    Otherwise he was allowed, encouraged, to range as far and as luridly afield as his relish and memory (invention, sceptics might maintain) would take him. My original purpose in turning to him was nearly buried in the avalanche, but he did reiterate his belief that Mirré, whom he had tipped off about a planned assassination (source not revealed), had contrived his own disappearance, and was probably still alive somewhere. That was on tape, and in private he in turn gave me the name of a woman living in Paris I should talk to.

    A woman from the far American west, once a dancer (modern), now the exiled ex-wife of an oil-rich hypersheikh, emir, imam or sultan, who had set her up in the Grands Boulevards with remarkable generosity considering that her unwillingness to yield a millimetre to Islamic precepts in either costume or behaviour had almost led to his deposing. Let's miscall her, as a divorced royal consort, Katherine of Oregon.

Knowing the history I expected either an airhead or a bitterly self-defeating militant, and was sweetly surprised; she was youthfully thirty-eightish, unaggressively stylish, bright, witty and deftly balanced between tough and charming; after some initial sparring I invited her to dinner. She twitted and outbid me, OPEC took us both to storied regions of gastronomy and price, and even stood us a bottle of '78 Latour without noticeably blinking. Somewhere amongst our entertainment Katherine did record that neither by police, barring a brief, routine interview and briefer enquiries to confirm minor details, nor by press (till now) had she been closely interrogated about Mirré's disappearance, an amazement, since she had been dogged by papparazzi for most of that year, after being snapped in close conversation with him at Champs d'Auteuil, and in fact had seen a good deal of him; indeed, one theory had him snuffed by agents of her ex-husband, who remained intermittently proprietary. Western investigators evidently adopted an Islamic view of her purely passive importance, as a possible motive, like some inanimate but coveted treasure.

She, however, agreed with Zuylen in believing Mirré still alive; she wouldn't specify just why, but in languorous morning, before I returned to my unused hotel-room, kept the chain intact by telling me of a man (not in Paris) I might ask about it — it was clear by this time that for many reasons, including her continued safety and my tender personal regard, I wasn't going to put my hostess on the air, or make any attributable use of what she had to say.

But here is the really important thing I didn't do: expose the one she identified. I did make the journey to see him; happy with an excuse for a couple more *dolce far niente* days with Katherine, I even waited for a colleague to come down from Brussels with very portable videocam. We set out together (in the wrong direction, with the thought we might be tailed, Katherine having warned me she was often watched), but just where our confusing route was about to turn definitively towards its eventual goal, I recognized my quarry would never talk to me on camera, and neither was I going to do a snoop piece that might blow, as they say, his cover, perhaps bring about his death. So, sending my cameraperson on to the Gulf of Genoa, where a spectacular oil-spill was being spectacularly bungled, I continued alone for an off-the-record chat with — well, we might call him Ariosto, though his real name is very ordinary, and the man himself, though he lives and dresses well, is extrinsically notable only for a lack of any memorable characteristics. A note from Katherine and my solemn vow his invisibility would be preserved (in which, intended or not, coming from a journalist, the threat of the converse inevitably lurked) won me several lengthy, fascinating conversations, filled with semi-revelations.

Ariosto was and is a virtuoso manufacturer of new personalities, producing not merely skilfully forged credentials but entire, almost-verifiable biographies, backed up with medical and dental records, well-thumbed heirloom snapshots of spurious relatives, odd newspaper clippings, whole lifetimes of ostensibly checkable milestones and trivia. He would never admit to any dealings with Mirré, but I don't doubt they occurred; Ariosto's elaborate services are priced beyond the range of all except the very wealthy individual, besides large criminal enterprises and governments — he was sardonically amused that none of the agencies of law and intelligence who hired him had ever known anything about the mid-level civil servants in their own countries with whom he had "arrangements" — which I took to mean, had bribed to supply him with documents indistinguishable from the authentic, perhaps to create entries in various official records. As he, bewilderingly and at some level distressingly claimed, you can reach a point in documentation and manufactured memory where the distinction between a real and a forged past becomes meaningless; none of us can actually revisit those places we say we came from, all lives are uncheckable words, fakable papers, fading photographs, what we choose to believe.

At this point in his confessions, I began to read in his mild eyes a new weighing of options, as if he was wondering whether the greater risk would be to trust my promises not to expose him, or to kill me — have me killed, I'm sure it would be; Ariosto's own weapons are telephone, fax and computer keyboard, and in the fairly small-scaled way of forgery, transferred funds, or, as it might be, murder, he can swiftly cause things to happen at widely-spaced points on the earth's surface.

Gradually, not willingly, I acquire the proper currency for these transactions; the man-to-man reassurance is necessary tender, but buys nothing without the hard, metallic backing of perceived power, which is to say, latent threat — there's no offence in this; it is simply the syntax of business in Ariosto's world. It was a warm Saturday evening; we were in our shirtsleeves, and reflected lights bobbed in the dark waters of the long lake, the broad river, the placid bay. We had met twice earlier in the week, and I made plain if not quite explicit that lengthy reports of our talks had been transmitted to my private files in Brussels, to which I alone could have access while alive, but whose passwords, deposited appropriately, would become public domain in the event of my death or unexplained absence. A trifle surprised (I think) by such toughness, he congratulated me, quite genuinely, on my prudence, warned me against even inadvertent leakage, and we parted on cordially wary terms.

My mini-series had moved to topics more generic, but I did wrap up the Mirré business with the conclusion that "according to reliable inside information" he was still alive, present whereabouts not known. When the French police duly came to question me, I covered my known tracks with bumbling inefficiency, leaving the impression my sole source was the tip from Zuylen, and won myself a large helping of ineffable French disdain, they having interviewed the man about ten times. It's still a wonder that Zuylen would on brief acquaintaince supply me with a lead — Katherine of Oregon — that he had adamantly denied the lawmen, but possibly I was more generous than they in keeping him supplied with his favourite cherry-brandy. Perhaps, too, he wanted to go on enjoying the spectacle of French police repeatedly traipsing up to Amsterdam when the answer they wanted was within shouting distance of the Palais de Chaillot.

Had I been able to, with the nanograin of help supplied by Ariosto, I would never have tracked down and identified Mirré to elicit the reason behind his self-exile; if I had it might make a better story than the one I have to tell, but as is it's going to have to remain as a tiresome opening flourish, with neither antecedents nor consequences. The real beginning comes later, beyond summer, when Ian Gossbrooke, in Brussels on some European business, rang to ask whether I'd have dinner with him. I didn't know him, knew of him only vaguely as a superior sort of ministerial aide, whose international trade views carried some weight, though his affiliation is to the F.O. rather than the Treasury or Economic Development. On the phone he was unforcedly friendly and strikingly confident, and his vowels had that faint alien injection of flat-hat diphthong which the nobs, especially Tony's nobs, use nowadays for protective colouring; I recollected there's an earldom from which Sir Ian is no more distant than nephew or so.

The address he gave me was in a quarter where the Eurocrats now cluster, and he was indeed borrowing the flat in which the taxpayers of Colchester or Monmouth, Macclesfield or Exeter maintained an inaudible Continental presence in appropriate splendour. Tall, affable, slightly stooped, faintly paunchy, wavy hair visibly receded (though he is no more than forty-two or three), he apologized for the absence of his wife, who had so much wanted to meet me, but was, as always at this time of year, in Scotland with her people for the shooting (with guns, I believe he meant; Lady Iona is no maker or star of films).

Gossbrooke had read both my books, commending particularly the second, where I had interleaved collected occasional pieces with a kind of running and cumulative commentary on the struggles for stability and development in the disintegrated Soviet empire.

He was flattering me, and redoubled flattery by regretting (however) that I was, at least for now, lost to print, and to my old Eastern European stamping grounds; he even assured me there would certainly be a government job for me in that field, if and when I tired of the circus.

All fine, as was the dinner, tournedos, which he served from the pan, though the real cooking and salad-making was done by a small, anxious-faced Belgian girl who scuttled like a gecko, and vanished as effectively when she was not required, and an irreproachable Savigny-les-Beaune. Finer still was the cognac, originally bottled, Gossbrooke claimed, for Kaiser Wilhelm in Dutch exile, but he did not strike me as a man who used time, blandishment or rare brandy unthriftily, and there was the distinct sensation of having at last come to the point when he asked, ever-so-offhandedly, whether I had heard of Lydia Solyitnova, *née* Losen.

I had not, though from the names she must be — and here again, apologetically, I must resort to exasperating anonymity, this time of an entire country, not a small one (ex Warsaw Pact, yes and no, former constituent republic of Soviet Union, probably); Solyitnova's nationality must be left indefinite.

She was, Gossbrooke told me, a bio-chemist, widow of the better-known physicist, Andrei Solyitnov, who died in a car-crash a few years ago.

"The cloak-and-dagger types," Gossbrooke said, not altogether convincingly distancing himself from them, "Believe it was suicide, and so, I gather, does his wife. There's a child, too, incidentally, eleven then, fifteen now, I suppose." He added that it had been, by all report, a devoted alliance of devoted parents, which left, as he evidently intended, a large *why*? attached to the suicide theory.

"It appears," he said, then checked himself. "What I have to say is not merely off the record, but tremendously confidential, not only not for broadcast but not for sharing with anyone, ever."

I failed not to grin. "Why pick a journalist?"

"Not any journalist. With that Dusatian business you were involved in, there was at least one aspect you decided to sit on, though it could have been a biggish story for you."

"On rare occasions we have to respect the public's right not to know."

"I think you'll find this, perhaps even more so, one of those occasions."

His improbably cold eyes regarded me for a steady eight seconds, and then, evidently taking silence for assent, he resumed. "Several months before his death it seems Solyitnov happened to browse some of his wife's work — on ribonucleic acids, very possibly, since at about that time she published a paper on that subject. Whatever it was — and it may be germane that Solyitnov himself acquired an advanced degree in organic chemistry before he switched to physics — we know that what he saw dovetailed in some way with his own current preoccupations, and he suddenly perceived, or was convinced he did, the potential for what you might call a cross-disciplinary weapon of unimaginable destructive power — nothing to do with bacteriology, so I understand — some unholy alliance between fission and proteins."

"According to chronic rumour," I put in, unaware why Gossbrooke thought I should know all this, and more than ever mistrusting his implied divorce from Smiley's world — "weapons of unimaginable destructive power are already in existence."

His sweetest smile. "One gathers this protein bomb, as I've heard it called, is something altogether new, and quite special. I'm no scientist, but as our scientific types point out, if we could make an intelligent guess as to its nature, we could proceed logically to the same point, but this must have been some sort of sudden revelation for Solyitnov, a theoretical leap. Whether it could ever be translated into reality is mere conjecture, but we do know that it put the wind up Solyitnov so badly that he swore never to make any reference to it — to unthink it, if genies ever could be stuffed back in the bottle. Lydia may not actually have grasped the principle he'd — well, divined might be the *mot juste*, but he must have made her promise not to tell anyone about it; she had certainly witnessed his reaction to the idea."

"Evidently — " I prompted, he having paused.

"Yes. Well, unfortunately, Solyitnov was a bad drinker — not a drunk, quite the opposite, bad like the chap in *Othello* — "

"Cassio. One sip and he's sozzled."

"Cassio, of course. It seems they were winding up some sort of government project, and Solyitnov was obliged to have a glass or two — as you know, they're great ones for toasting tournaments — and at some point he confided his gratification that the government had no idea what he had up his sleeve. Unfortunately, the ear he chose belonged to Galek."

"Harry Galek?"

"Ah. You know him?"

"I've met him, briefly; I wanted to talk to him about translating his novel."

"Into English? It's been done; *Nevertheless*? I've read some of it. I can't see what all the fuss was about."

"The translation is particularly poor — " very straightforward, deadpan English; all wrong. Galek, an ardent admirer of James Joyce and Nabokov — the latter must have been tricky to sustain under the Communists — writing in standard Russian streaked with various dialects, has a style baroqued with word-play and veiled allusion, most of it, in any strict sense, untranslatable, and the authentic, often hilarious flavour could only be conveyed by finding appropriate English equivalents for the puns and echoes, along with the faintly sinister tone. The difficulty, as I tried to tell Gossbrooke, was that Galek, who speaks, genially enough when I met him, a wildly unidiomatic English, imagines himself a complete master of our tongue, and saw no flaws in his inept translator.

Gossbrooke jutted a lower lip, sign that this literary excursus was over. "It is in other capacities, of course, that we have been concerned with Galek."

"He has those — " placing him somewhere between curiosity and chimera; a pistol shot and equestrian up to international standards (he has ridden for his country at the Olympics), an authority on early coins — but I suspected none of that was of urgent interest in Gossbrooke's sphere; novels and horses and firearms and numismatics swept to the margins, Galek had been something like a colonel in the old secret police, emerging in the post-communist era as a xenophobic nationalist politician.

"At the time when Solyitnov was indiscreet, Galek was simply hanging on — he was with their Ministry of Defence, but his influence was minimal; the westernisers were in control, and trying to keep Uncle Sam and the World Bank happy; where weapons were concerned, disposal was the priority, not development. Just the same, and all by himself, he kept the pressure on Solyitnov to tell all. You wouldn't think so, but it apparently got worse when Galek resigned from the government to stand for parliament himself — when he became a leading spokesman for the New Nation party. They were still very much a minority then, of course, but we believe Solyitnov saw them as the writing on the wall. At any rate, it was on his way back from another grilling by Galek that he ran his car over a cliff."

"Not, you say, an accident — "

"It's what they ended up calling it, of course. Certainly, Galek didn't have him removed — not that he isn't quite capable of it, but — " a shrug, largely of his lower lip.

Understood; if you want information, you don't silence the only possible source — well, a miscalculation might happen, no doubt has happened, while applying torture, but you certainly don't arrange a driving-accident.

"There are some other farfetched scenarios, mainly entertained by, and involving rival factions. Not my bailiwick, but I do get briefings from the intelligence side, and a bloke I have no reason to doubt tells me we have in our possession what may well be the last letter Solyitnov wrote, to one of his old college cronies, speaking in a veiled way of being subjected to intolerable pressures, which threatened to involve his wife and child. Together with the timing of the car-smash, it leads to a strong presumption of suicide. There's no way, naturally, to know how much of this persecution was in his own imagination, but it seems certain he believed that would be the end of it, the only way to end it."

"But it didn't." The conclusion was obvious enough.

"As you say. The widow, assuming she has anything to tell, would be even more reluctant than he was; she got herself in trouble signing human rights declarations and so forth in her single days — Solyitnov was always more patriot than pacifist, which gives us a measure of how terrible he believed his weapon might be, if he chose death rather than be forced to develop it. Quite possibly Galek would have gone straight after Solyitnova, but, as you know, he was one of the deputies booted out of parliament in their `ancestral estates' scandal, and the New Nation people had to keep him at arm's length for a while."

"He was in the wilderness when I met him." And clearly saw his disgrace as only a transient setback, irrepressibly cheerful, very ready to pontificate on his country's future.

"Now, of course," Gossbrooke threw out, once more designedly flattering my knowledge of the region. And he was right, I saw it at once. Early in the year, the economy floundering and after a series of international humiliations, Galek's country had dismayed Washington and worried anyone by choosing for president Kvitka, the crudely outspoken leader of New Nation, provoking in Strasbourg another round in that surreal debate amongst the righteous apostles of self-determination on how to rebuke an electorate that freely chooses what is plainly wrong.

The transgressors have a hybrid governing system, with a directly-elected president, on the American model, and Kvitka's proclaimed programme of flag-waving militarisation and diplomatic intransigence had been somewhat curbed so far in that his party enjoyed nothing like a majority in parliament — which, however, he was confident of attaining in next year's elections. In the mean time, though I no longer kept detailed watch on the day-to-day doings of the eastern European countries, I had no doubt Galek's fortunes had seen an upturn.

"He apparently enjoys something like ministerial rank," Gossbrooke confirmed, "Although he has no published title, or officially acknowledged portfolio. As a matter of fact, most of the ranking ops from the old Communist secret police seem to have gone over to the right wing. A characteristic of the species, I suppose — back in 1945, I believe, quite a lot of the Gestapo hardly blinked before they signed on with Moscow."

"Or Washington," I said, "Even Whitehall, according to whether they were captured by the effete western democracies or the godless Bolshevik hordes. It goes beyond a lack of any real convictions, I think — they're people with a servile lust to be within smelling-distance of power."

Gossbrooke nodded with actually signalling agreement, and for probably adequate reasons let the speculation drop. "Be that as may, it's quite clear Galek still believes Solyitnova can help them develop the weapon to make them into a super-power on the cheap — possibly the dominant world power in terms of deliverable terror — and that she still declines to have anything to do with it. Cripes, Mark," (not for the first time the attempt at a matey tone only measured how far we were from any real human contact; Gossbrooke was too rehearsed for that) "The woman should have left the country years ago, after she lost her husband; now it's doubtful she could — Galek has made her his personal project; she was always a very private sort of person, and they seem to have succeeded in severing the few personal relationships she had. Not that there's open persecution, or anything of that kind; her teaching contract was terminated, but she has been installed in a brand-new laboratory with a staff of assistants, ostensibly to work on government food research — but where they've put her looks uncomfortably like exile, or an undeclared house-arrest. One would suppose Galek began with appeals to her patriotism, but from all we can gather, neither that nor the prospect of wealth would cut much ice with her; the next stage would be threats, but you can see the inherent weakness there — they no doubt believe her continuing cooperation would be needed in translating theory into a practical weapon."

"One of the inherent weaknesses," I amended, with the abrupt sensation I was listening to doomsday fiction from 1960, or possibly 1910. "You're not talking about a police state, not yet at least. I don't much doubt Kvitka would like to control the press and muzzle the opposition, but he can't so far. I could ring one of the people I know at State Television, and there would be a news-magazine segment on Lydia Solyitnova in a week. Or tip off the newspapers that an eminent scientist is being intimidated. The Liberal Democrats are still the largest parliamentary party; get the premier to demand some answers. Failing that, there's Amnesty, or even the United Nations; this is a country, no matter who's in the presidential palace, that's going to be dependent for a long time on western goodwill. Or — " now a possible reason for this entire narration came to me — "Do you want me to do a story about it?" But that didn't square with his insistence on secrecy.

Head bowed, Gossbrooke sadly shook his head. "The worst favour we could do Solyitnova is to turn her into a *cause célèbre*. Look at it, man. Inevitably, the reason why she's being hounded by Galek would come out; she'd never know another day's peace in her lifetime, only there would be a whole international pack of hounds chivvying her. So far, her possible access to her husband's breakthrough, whatever it was, is known to, at most, a dozen people; it's only by chance that we heard about it — one of Solyitnov's young assistants, if you must know — " my eyebrows having risen — "did a year at Cambridge, and our intelligence types recruited him to keep an eye on the nuclear situation back home. So far as we can tell, the Americans haven't a clue about this — most of their people on the ground there are warhead-watchers — or else doing what they can to discredit Kvitka's lot, one supposes. Actually that's awkward for them; quite a number of the older New Nation people lived a good part of their lives on C.I.A. money, becoming what they are with C.I.A. support and encouragement — "

Gossbrooke's evident pleasure in the discomfiture of an ally struck me as undignified, but, "That's what the C.I.A. is for isn't it? Whenever America dislikes how a country's being run, Cuba, Iraq, Ecuador, anywhere, they spend a lot of time and money training and arming to the teeth so-called nationalists, drug-runner nationalists, religious fanatic nationalists, terrorist-nationalists — who invariably turn out more brutal and more dangerous than the gang they were created to displace. But they still keep doing it; it's part of their Demon-of-the-Month policy."

"Speaking of which," Gossbrooke offered, "Lord knows how, some very dangerous people may know or guess something, I can't say how much, about the Solyitnova business — we know they've been poking about in that part of the world — " and he gave me their nationality, here withheld; an Islamic country whose four-letter name, rendered in English, begins with a vowel.

"Are they included in your dozen or so?" — tartly, resenting this obvious and manufactured appeal to fashionable fears.

As rapidly abandoned. "You know the Yekhalets district?" abruptly enough.

"By repute; I've never been there. It has quite a history." An oddly discrete region in the northwest of its country, not lofty enough, perhaps, for a plateau, but adequately inaccessible; the entire upraised dome, about the size of Gwent, was for centuries a barony or something similar, nominally at various times (after the Avars evaporated) a province in such principalities as Novgorod, Vladimir, Volhynia, an absurdly overblown Lithuania, Poland, with a scimitared interlude under the Khanate of the Golden Horde, but always arrogantly near-autonomous, as befit its defensibility — at least until central authority acquired the nutcracker artillery to humble its ancient baronial castle. Even after that, it was a refuge for bandits with warlord pretensions, for counter-revolutionaries in the civil wars of the 1919-22 period, and for partisans (not always distinguishable from either of the foregoing) during the German occupation. As late as 1947, a small remnant of those opposing Stalinist rule (an episode till recently kept carefully from the pages of history) held out there till starved into surrender and promptly exterminated.

"Galek's ancestral lands are there," Gossbrooke told me, letting in a hint of the hallmarked laird's disdain for the parvenu. "He laid claim to the entire damn' plateau — had it, too, for a month or so, till the scandal erupted; when they booted him from parliament, he still managed to keep the château, and what used to be the monastic estates — on the basis of his name, he claims descent from the old ruling family."

"That's absurd — " but to report accurately what I said here would oblige me to give correct versions of *Galek* and *Yekhalets*, both altered in the interests of discretion. I'll just say that if your name was Merlborough or Marbrow, it would certainly not suggest you belonged at Blenheim, where the family name, as distinct from the title, is Churchill.

"In any event — " Gossbrooke — "that's where they put up Solyitnova's new lab, that's where she is now, and heaven knows what pressures can be used against her; Galek is spending most of his time up there. It's not a happy situation. There may of course be nothing in this magical protein bomb, but if there were, its destabilising potential is disastrous, not only for the region but for the world. If not, that's still a disaster for Solyitnova; she can say so as often as she likes, they won't believe her, and she'll never have any peace."

To ask what, then, he proposed would obviously have been superfluous; after waiting in vain for me to do so, he resumed: "Speaking informally, I think I can say we would be prepared to offer her asylum — "

"In exchange for — "

"No, no, no — " prepared, he pounced on that. "I'm assured we have no interest in any new super-weapon — none beyond ensuring that it is never developed. We might have to tuck her away in East Dereham for a year or so, but I've been assured she can have a post at a major university as soon as the diplomatic dust subsides. Galek's lot will go orbital, of course, but they can never risk letting on why they want her so badly."

"Has the offer been made to Solyitnova?"

A lengthy pause; Gossbrooke had hold of an unsharpened, an unitiated pencil, and began studiously turning it over and over by placing it upright on the table and sliding thumb and middle-finger down till it toppled. "There was a do in Berlin last week, the opening of the new film starring a friend of yours, Christa Rasch. Astonishing creature, isn't she."

Not liking this new tack, I gave rote assent, and forbore to expand.

"At the party, she was telling us, my wife and me, the story of how she was rescued last year — I'd heard the outlines of it before, of course, but it was interesting to hear the inside detail. She has enormous respect for your — aah, your resourcefulness, and it gave me an idea. You must understand that here, not in any sense am I speaking officially as a part of the government."

"Oh? — " on the edge of irritation; my dipcorps father was trained to respond correctly to such disclaimers.

"Christa Rasch says, when you turned up at that place where they were holding her, your cover story, if that's the term, was that you were seeking an interview with her — I don't know if it would be unfair to say your television credentials give you a weapon — "

"Potentially," I agreed, if uneasily. "Where people, and even governments, are made by image, and know it — "

"It occurred to me — " another theme he didn't want taken to its conclusion, and for excellent reasons — "that if you, with your reputation, happened to be doing a series of interviews with Nobel laureates — "

There in one short step, I had to laugh. "My international reputation, such as it is, begins with the Christa Rasch affair. That's especially true for the former Warsaw-pact countries; it's the first thing that would come to Galek's mind if I turned up wanting to interview Solyitnova." That Gossbrooke, a full professional for all his old-boy camouflage, could never have missed this point worried me more for just that reason, and I began speculating on games within games; was I being enlisted less as a messenger than a message?

"Perhaps. But even so, could they risk turning you away, knowing the power you have?"

"I have no idea. If what they hope to get out of her is important enough, I suppose they might risk it. She's not a Nobel laureate, by the way, is she?"

"Solyitnov was, in 1986."

"In any event, I'm far from clear what good it would do for me to meet with her; if she has decided to cooperate with her government, she isn't likely to tell me so, and if not, I have no means of helping her."

"You could tell her she can have sanctuary in the UK. Even quite moderate pressure can be made intolerable by the feeling of inescapability. Your friend Galek has a great deal of experience in eliciting information."

"She can only have sanctuary in the UK if she can get there."

"I had in mind you might help us set up something. So that we can get her out without creating an international incident."

A swift, ill-informed review of possibilities. Were the constraints on Solyitnova purely psychological, and could she be freed simply by driving her to the airport and putting her on a plane, or would such an attempt merely lead to her formal arrest (and mine)? Could Galek, then, be intimidated into allowing her exit, with a hint that we knew what he was up to? But if he was shrewd enough, which, as I told Gossbrooke, I didn't doubt, he would go public with an account reversing the roles, his own people protecting and the perfidious Brits attempting to suborn a distinguished scientist — a version he might even be able to sell to Solyitnova herself. I myself found it hard to believe in London's deep, disinterested solicitude, as conveyed by my host.

"Christa Rasch," he harped, "implied that the hardest part of your first contact was convincing her she was in fact a prisoner, when she believed she was holidaying with friends. `Mark,' she said, `is someone it's hard not to believe' — " a chuckle. "Innocent blue eyes, she said, but frankly, that's what gave me the idea of asking for your help here; we need an envoy Lydia Solyitnova will trust."

Yes (I did not comment), but if Christa could trust me it was at least in part because I was acting on my own, out of what I knew for myself, not conveying promises I couldn't see kept, on behalf of professional shaders of the truth, with a story I had no means of verifying.

None, that is, except to go and see for myself. Cautiously, "What sort of support would I have, if I did go?"

"Nothing official," promptly. "You would have a contact in the capital, outside the embassy, whom you could call on for some help. We can cover all your personal expenses, and any reasonable amount that might be required to grease the wheels."

"Reasonable?"

"Twenty-five thousand pounds presents no major problem. A larger amount would require additional authorisation." A self-deprecating laugh. "'Course, I would have to have some results to show, if it went up into six figures."

I tried not to betray astonishment, having expected five hundred or so as the answer; whether I was ready to accept the improbable bio-nuclear super-weapon hardly mattered; feasible or not it was certain that someone in London believed in it, and at a fairly high level.

"You're going to help us out, then."

"Not with the hand you want to deal me — " and I proposed an alternative, one which would not trumpet in advance its purpose. Sometime soon, I was expected to take a week or ten days off, and could make the journey, not with a camera crew and Lydia Solyitnova as my proclaimed target, but alone, to meet with Galek and reopen the question of an improved translation for his novel. Once up in the Yekhalets district it ought to be possible to find where Solyitnova was, and visit her on the quiet.

"If Galek agrees to see you on that basis. You say he was not interested before?"

"I was no one in particular then; a couple of books in print make all the difference — " books, moreover, I was certain Galek must have at least browsed. No less vain than authors generally are — than me, for instance — he might well be flattered to discuss it, even if he had no intention of authorising any new translation; vanity, we are habitually instructed, creates blind spots, and it seemed possible he would accept my ardent desire to redo his novel as reason enough to bring me to that remote region of his country.

Gossbrooke nodded. "Bear in mind that with all his oddities he is by no means stupid. He must not be allowed to guess that anyone — any other government, particularly — could have cause for the slightest interest in Solyitnova. When you see her — " and here I disconcerted him by holding up a hand.

"Until I see her, I absolutely decline to give any assurances about what more I'm willing to do."

"There's not much point to the exercise, if you're just going to drop in to say hello — " spoken lightly, but brittly so.

"Don't misunderstand me; I'm willing to deliver your message, that she can expect a sympathetic welcome in England. But as a responsible journalist I'm not entitled to accept any story that I'm told, without some sort of confirmation, and I'm certainly not getting myself permanently barred from the country unless I'm very sure it's worth doing."

"Understood, understood — " still masking an annoyance that must be almost instinctive in one accustomed to issuing incontrovertible orders — but there were reasons why he couldn't dispatch an obedient paid underling on this quest. "But you in turn must understand I require your assurance you will not reveal British interest in Solyitnova — that we are aware, that is, of the reason behind Galek's interest. Not to anyone over there, of course, but again I must emphasize, there is never going to be a story for you in this. I am relying on your — discretion."

Once, without shying, he would have said what he wanted to; my patriotism, my honour, but fashion was against him.

"Certainly," I said, while thinking, I don't know — forty or fifty years along, when Gossbrooke is in the family vault and an ancient, anglicized Solyitnova expires in the peaceable obscurity of Cambridge or thereabouts, I might do a cobwebby Now It Can Be Told. As you can see, we were both wrong.

"I hope you don't mind if I do." Gossbrooke lighted a long-delayed cigar, I having for about the eighth time declined one.

"Christ, what for?" Nimrod demanded, when I told him where I was going. "Nothing is happening there. Go see Colombia, they got a war on."

"This is supposed to be a break. So I don't go stale — " I quoted out of his own mouth.

"Yeah, but ten days playing with yourself and you will be getting crazy." He dropped some of his chins to ponder. "You don't much ski — well, too early, anyway, my place in Innsbruck will be like the British Museum, except there might be some starlets, modelets, wenchlets working on their tan, you would hate that. You like sailing? My boat is doing nothing down in Quiberon, I can make a call, it is waiting for you; there's a very nice girl, blonde, Mado, in Brest, and those are real nice, too, Mado's crewing is great, yeah, both."

I thanked him, and gave him the story about translating Galek's book, an ambition he respected but did not understand. Jacob Niemenraat was and still is director of the Brussels news operation, a principal investor, not much past forty, blunt hands, a winning manner, a pudgy face; had made separate fortunes in electronics and, what? *flower-seeds*! before interesting himself in television production. This biography should be a clue that beneath the often inconsequential verbiage lies a patiently orderly mind, like the Bach *Inventions* apparently capable of keeping several separate strands in parallel or intersecting play without confusion.

He enjoys the nickname I conferred (now generally adopted), a reference not to prowess in the chase, but to Nimrod as first ruler of Babel. The establishment in Brussels is peopled by a Euro bunch, young, the technical side Belgian, Dutch, German and Brit, the reporting staff I nominally direct a similar muddle of nationalities, with French and English the dominant social modes, though we tape or do voice-over translations in several more languages. Nimrod likes to convey, as most short-term visitors have received, the impression of an easy-going kind of fun factory, meeting multiple deadlines and maintaining our standards as a breezy adjunct our to polyglot badinage and good-natured competitiveness.

A benign camouflage, except that Nimrod also pretends to deceive himself — my words are carefully arranged; I didn't and don't believe his experience piloting international enterprises could leave him so naive, but his preference for regarding dire personality-clashes as the harmless squabbling of mettlesome colts and fillies threw — and was near-certainly calculated to throw — all such energy-draining questions back in my lap. Oh, if I insisted stridently enough, Nimrod would offer his single all-purpose solution, "You wanna get rid of him?" — or her, or them, where a feud was fully bilateral — which, as he knew it would, made me seek some resolution short of decimating our cohort.

He may have been right; we're all tape, not a minute of (or transmitter for) live programming, so the opportunities for actual mutual sabotage (far from unknown among the broadcast giants) are limited, and if it came to the Nimrod answer, there are at any time several dozen people looking for work in television news; for every slot available I had four wide shelves crammed with audition tapes, quite a number of them reasonably competent, a few very good; no one was actually indispensable. But Nimrod knew our success was kept up by offering the eventual viewer a fairly stable cast; for all his testy disdain of "frigging prima donnas," he was aware we had to ignite and sustain at least some minor stars.

I was about to say the hothouse atmosphere of television reporting, the hurry and harry, the evanescence of its product — not to say, the lack of any visible audience to applaud and reassure — seem to foster sulks, hair-trigger jealousies, a ruthless rivalry far beyond anything encountered with its print ancestor — but that might be both unfair and unscientific; a career in politics, for example, doesn't create a liar; rather, it offers an attractively remunerative line for those with no particular adherence to the truth, and the ones who lie most adeptly and live most comfortably in a world without fixed facts tend to rise; similarly, the electronic media, and especially news, may have a special attraction for those seeking a way to make their paranoia work for them, actually help them claw their way into prominence — not every journalist can stumble into the politically-driven abduction of an international ikon.

A side-benefit of my holiday was to leave Nimrod to deal with round one thousand or so in the turf-battle between Ada and Ketil, two young and attractive reporters, with no conceivable overlap except when it came to allotment of those coveted seconds of exposure, twenty-eight of which, lopped from one of Ketil's segments so that Ada could finish a sentence and say goodnight, had precipitated the newest crisis.

Ketil is an Icelander, tall, blondish, likeable when unmiffed, our nearest approach to a sex-symbol on the male side, adept in three languages, with a bloodhound nose for governmental corruption and mismanagement (he could fill his allotted span six times over without ever stirring from Brussels). The spirit of the sagas surges in his veins — in a magazine puff piece, that could stand as unqualified praise, but having actually read *Laxdaela* and *Njal*, I mean that with all his manly virtues he is peacock-proud, touchy about his standing, fatally quick to take offence, moodily addicted to the principle of retribution. He is twenty-four.

Ada Boyle is two years older, Irish; her violet eyes and curling tease of a voice have caused youthful hormones to surge and somnolent middle-aged glands to stir anew, though motherly women and identifying girls adore her too; she conducts a neat interview, and the lilting innocuousness in which she sheathes her steel has allowed her to make a speciality of complicated corporate stories and a meal of glib, self-contradictory spokesfolk; there was a brief fling with Ketil when first he came to Brussels (I believe Boyle went off the Ketil, rather than the other way about), and by now she was technically insane and atypically blunt on the subject; perhaps some race-memory of proud Keltic princesses carried off as Viking concubines fed the flames of her rancour, but she had told me more times than I could count that I had to choose between them; Babel just warn't big enough for both. Ketil, meanwhile, charged and perhaps believed I took Ada's side (I was, after all, obliged to defend the editor who stole his twenty-eight seconds) because I wanted to sleep or was sleeping (not his phraseology) with her.

Which I certainly was not — the other is immaterial; with

any of our volatile talents I've been sane enough to restrict extramural contact to lunch, the odd glass of beer when there's something to celebrate — this ban applying only to jostling personalities with names and images; the writers were safe enough, and I was in fact seeing quite a lot of Carina, who in tranquil young anonymity did voice-overs in rippling Spanish and purling Italian, while I had from the first counted as a confidante Lise, who operates a remote camera (she was the one I dispatched to Genoa before going on to meet with Ariosto), and is full of good sense, resigned good humour, and survival instinct. She is Danish, past forty and therefore an old-timer by the standards of Babel, long but not now married to a Scot, from whom her English acquired a lingering Glaswegian lubrication. Technically irreproachable, had worked for Thames and RTDF; a stringy, vague-eyed, athletic son of fifteen at school in England. I should add that there has never been anything sexual between us, aside from the occasional intentionally grotesque verbal lewdery, and that she has an almost entirely separate friendship with Carina, largely based, maybe, on the natural community of women with wrecked marriages to compare, though Carina's, which occurred before she was twenty, lasted fewer months than Lise's had years.

Lise told me earnestly to keep an eye on my arse; without violating my implied word to Gossbrooke — by which I mean there was nothing said about super-weapons or who, specifically, had asked me to go — I had told her something of my real motive for the journey, by now thrice-postponed for a garland of reasons, most lately the off-year American elections, for which I was content to let others do the leg-work in Washington, New York and California, but could not absent myself from analysis and commentary. We had stopped after work in our usual hangout for sandwiches and a cold beer.

"I don't see any particular danger in it for me. It's unlikely I'll do anything more, once I find the woman and give her a brief message."

"Uh — " Lise nodded glumly. "When I was in Paris, we were going off to do a piece on Lebanon, this was when they were all killing each other, an American chap gave me a hundred dollars just to shoot some footage of a house outside Beirut his people were interested in, all very innocent, eh? I never did find out what it was in aid of, but my hotel room was turned upside down, they nicked my camera and all the tape I had, and some snot-faced little scut from the Christian Militia *advised* our producer it wasn't safe for us to stay — no lie. I had a car for the week, and when we pulled out early, there was a nice kid at the hotel, I gave him the keys, he could use up the last two days, impress his girlfriend. Couple of weeks after, I heard they had to scrape him off the ceiling of the underground garage with a fish-slice."

"A bomb?"

"I tell you, boyo, watch your arse. You start doing simple little favours for these 007 types, what do they care, it's not like losing someone they've got an investment in."

I nodded, but pointed out that `who will this one annoy?' was the first, most persistent question with any news story, and one it was our professional duty to ignore. "Once you start thinking about all the things that can kill you, you might as well switch to selling corn-flakes."

"Aye," she almost said, "But sticking your neck out for a story is not the same as running an errand for some spook buzzard." A spook buzzard today impatient enough with my delays to use an insecure phone to confirm, pettishly I judged, that this time I really was leaving.

Lise said brightly and as if relevantly, "Why not get married? But with a wife and family to think about — " as I failed to follow — "You get a different perspective — blokes do, generally, not Ken, he was just a bachelor who got hooked, poor sod, ran after me till our wedding day, then ran away from me for eleven years. You could marry Carina, be good for both of you."

"Carina thinks marriage is *una bestia da quattro zampe --*" and for adequate reason. Her own too-early experience of the beast had resulted indirectly from the loss of her father; she was of French-Italian parentage, but born in Bilbao; he, the French half, being some sort of broker for olive-oil. He died quite suddenly when Carina was fifteen, and her mother moved the family (there is a younger sister) to Livorno, her first home. A while later — it must have been a couple of years, but not long enough for Carina — her mother remarried, a man now conceded to be both *simpatico assai* and *homme bien gentil*, but at the time bitterly resented out of loyalty to her father. To the extent that Carina ran away, fetched up in Lyon, and very shortly married Léon, who just as rapidly turned into a swine.

The breakup and a new escape precipitated her career; short of other marketable skills, unwilling either to work indefinitely at the waitress level, or to slink home to mother (with whom, however, she was back in touch), blessed with a melodic voice, Carina turned her fluent and literate command of three languages (her English is improving, too, but we're quite comfortable together in French) into the work she now does very well. Though as I'd quoted to Lise, she was left with a sour opinion of marriage as an institution (this had not been any sort of issue between us), that was cool-headed opinion, and she had recuperated from the experience with no detectable bitterness or lingering mistrust; she could be gritty when arguing for a more idiomatic or more euphonic phrase than one she'd been given to read (and was usually right), but was generally — I don't think loved puts it too strongly — for her unfussing competence and unfailing smile; that she is very pretty in a large-eyed but small and slender idiom does nothing to hurt her popularity.

"Another?" I asked Lise, the bartender hovering meaningfully over our drained glasses.

"Okay — no, let's go mad and do a Tuborg, I've had my anaemia treatment for today." As often, she wondered that the rusty tang of Belgian beer had actual admirers, and while not quite sharing her Nordic condemnation, I observed that it was the way of habit to turn residual adulterants into prized peculiarities, as with a delicacy she knew well, lye-fish, where all Scandinavia had addicted itself to the linger of a harsh preservative.

"You've got taste," she pronounced. "What's a really good wine?"

Wine, yes, turpentiney Greek wines were another case in point. "Red or white?"

"Doesn't matter."

I had enjoyed plaice for lunch. "Wehlener Sonnenuhr, in a good year."

"Would you know it by taste?"

What was this? "Perhaps," I temporised, having been led astray before by the subtle shadings of rieslings.

"What's a really good wine you would know right off?"

"Oh — '78 Latour — " at about three quid a teaspoon, I ought to remember it.

"But somebody who didn't know Latour from Guinness, somebody who was just thirsty, they'd still know this was something special, uh?"

"What the hell are you talking about?" It was unlikely she'd gone from dead sober to squiffy in one grateful gulp of Tuborg.

"Wouldn't they?"

"Good is good, it's not all label snobbery. Anyone who'd ever had wine before would know '78 Latour was great stuff. What are we talking about?"

"Carina, you bleeding moron. 'Scuse me, boss, but you're thick as a brick about Carina."

"No I'm not — " Good God, don't take offence; Lise practically defines well-meaning, but these — the plural stands, though I had never had exactly this experience before — are awkward moments for me; some unsought intensity in my nature puts the jocular, unoffending insult eternally outside my functional repertory. There are those who could cheerily tell Lise to mind her own fucking business and leave friendship unrippled; not me. I laboriously say, "You don't have to tell me how lucky I am, but what there is between Carina and me is what it is for the absence of — oh, you know, promises, plans, all that possessive clutter."

"Christ, show me a man who's not possessive, I'll find you a cock that sings like a lark. Okay, Kearns, let's say you're the only man in Brussels, in all Europe if you like, who can really appreciate Carina, and you think that, what is it, '78 Latour has to belong to poobahs like you who know what it is. Listen to me, there's plenty of blokes in the offing who know Carina's pure gold, even if they can't tell why, she's not going to be on the market forever."

"All right," I said, and for that moment, really meant.

"You are a bloody fool. No," answering the one question I was determined not to ask, "She hasn't said a word to me, she always says the same as you, she likes it like this, no ties, course she does. I'm talking about the world, the way life works. You know Léon is in Brussels?"

Léon from Lyon, Carina's ex, the inadequately-known quantity. "No, I didn't. What for?"

"What do you think for? She has no clue how he tracked her down — now don't go all testosterone on me; why hasn't she told me, we don't have any secrets — nasty young plook, he struck me, but like she says, he was there when she needed him — "

"You've met him?"

"For about five minutes — " she did not expand on when or in what circumstances, and I, while invaded by a gloom, would not ask any question to betray concern. Dismaying how easily Lise had ignited the petard to blow my cool.

"Don't fret, she's got the brains not to go back for another helping of bloody Léon."

"I know that — " or believed I should. "I'm just surprised that she hasn't mentioned it."

"Why? If one of your old flames drifted by, that Rasch babe, you'd have to see her, and you wouldn't necessarily discuss it with Carina, would you? If you say `that's different,' I'll smack you one."

"I don't want to keep her locked away — " feeling, evidently, the need for some defence.

"Course you do. Course you do. You're a bloke, and you're in love, only too damn canny to admit it. You should tell Carina, look, no more song and dance, we're getting married."

"When did you become such a cheerleader for matrimony?" Or for Carina, who is, I concurred, pure gold, though I wouldn't have expected world-worn Lise to notice.

"Aw, shut up. I'm dead sentimental — " wiping a fictitious tear, and I was startled and faintly horrified to see the spoof gesture was camouflage for the genuine swimming brightness in her eye.

Marriage. My car was all right where it was, and after seeing Lise on her way I walked home through dappled dying-autumn light, the sky a pale greeny-blue still after rain layered with contrasted clouds, puffy white, streaked grey and looms of sombre indigo. Marriage, a state or perhaps an institution that persisted with an unreasonable tenacity, along with the trappings that decked its portals; brides, often enough in this time attended by their own offspring as gleeful maids and sullen ringbearers. still draped themselves in the lily symbols of treasured inexperience, and with their grooms still fled to a purely notional orgy of carnal acquaintanceship (about which bawdy jokes once convulsing Ur of the Chaldees pathetically persisted) — where in sobering fact, the rite that formerly proclaimed the beginning of *all that* often enough, what with the kids and what with the jobs and what with the routine, now trumpeted the beginning of its end, at least as a shared observance; it never has been easy for a sole man, confronted with thrice-familiar stimulants, to match the appetite of a yearning woman, nor for a woman to divert and channel a man's addiction to whatever's freshly enlivening; a failure to make peace with these anti-romantic data is the source of much bitterness and estrangement. Yet if I were to marry it would be by the Book of Common Prayer, and neither as speaker nor auditor could I take for sonorous but empty verbiage that *forsaking all other*.

The great, gloomy advantage of futile loves — unreciprocated or only part-reciprocated, yearnings for the married, spoken-for or otherwise unclaimable — was their painful perfection; age could not wither nor custom stale a state that existed almost entirely in the mind and guts; what was true and wondrous at first sight was obliged to remain that way, without any disappointments, ruptures, patchings-up, omitting all the mess that real life brings with it. Not a camouflage for mere male vacillation, that, I was sure, was approximately Carina's belief as well; there was about our undefined attachment a large measure of carefully preserved unreality, if that isn't putting it too strongly — say, then, we were both in our own ways and not by accident declining to lock ourselves onto a consequential path; while inevitably we became more intimate we did not let ourselves *depend* on that growth, and nothing that happened yesterday was allowed to extend any claim on today.

Rare, prized and not indefinitely sustainable, such a matching of pleasures and expectations (or chiefly their absence), the sweeter for me in that Carina, up close and with (for example) her tights drying over the shower-rail, was still a gasp of wonder; attained to the extent that she was, still made me disbelieve my fortune and doubt that I could ever have done anything to merit it. These, for however long they could remain, were a goodly treasure, not thoughtlessly to be staked on a roll of the dice. Marriage.

There are more occasions to inform against me; not long ago, having some time off, Carina came to London, where I was nagging my way through a maddeningly complex scandal to do with the fencing of stolen art (and wishing I could tell it all in print, far better to deal with its subtleties than the fitful and ephemeral idiom I was stuck with). We spent a long week-end at my parents' place, near Sevenoaks, at its leafy and blooming best in unreasonably good weather, and Carina was a hit with the ancients; my mother still sees any woman on my arm as a candidate for daughter-in-law (though recently she had been more single-mindedly pushing for Stephanie Forbes, an accomplished neighbour I've known since she was an annoying brat), but with Carina it was Dad's turn, too; he adored her on sight, and relished the opportunity to air out his highly literary Italian, largely picked up from opera librettos, a dialect in which it's easier for him to declare undying love or remorseless vengeance, to conspire at murder or seduction, than to order a sandwich or report a lost umbrella. He also showed her (which he seldom does) his small but quite spiffy collection of early stamps, and indulged in some amazingly uncharacteristic name-dropping about his diplomatic years; at any moment I expected him to stand on his head, or offer to shinny up a tree for Carina's admiration; she was amused, but not derisively, and on our way back to town told me my father was a strongly admirable type, *anglais à outrance*. That was after he'd confided at parting, again unprecedently, that my "lady friend" had won my mother's unqualified approval. Which of course meant, mainly his — an oddity now glossed by Lise's surprise offensive. Consensus; I ought to marry Carina — but Lise notwithstanding, she might in any case continue to mean *no ties*, whereupon I would have dropped a large stone into our clear, unwrinkled pool, with unpredictable effects. No, no, calculus and counterpoint are easy; it's the infinite variables of pairing that resist all learning.

II

    It is prematurely wintry, bright but with a gnawing chill, on the day when I arrive in — the capital, anyway, of Solyitnova's country, entirely to the eastward of, say, Berlin, where, though adequately fluent in the language, I could never pass as native. Not very ancient pictures and footage of this place and others like it in what was once the Eastern monolith possess a graininess beyond their actual age, a sort of shabby thirties quality with hats and head-scarves and quaint-looking cars, persuading me that it could not have been long before my first visit here, a decade or so back, that it quite suddenly began to look like everywhere else, the imitation-America we now expect on all our urban travels, the sterile airport on the stalk of stark *autobahn*, the rectangular building blocks and streets made sclerotic by, chiefly, Germany and Japan, the bright sweatshirts, the jeans, the overpriced, overdesigned canvas-and-rubber footwear.

    The contact Gossbrooke has given me is Dominic Minghela, a Lithuanian, naturalised here, who runs a car-rental business and speaks fluent, not to say copious, American. A small, narrow-shouldered, mid-fortyish man in a tight, dark suit, who hails me with a "Hi, buddy," meant to be breezy, though there is a disturbing mismatch between the brooding, closeted Baltic unease of his origins, and the what-the-hell accents and snappy sunglasses of Southern California. We have met for an early lunch, at what I suppose is the closest local imitation of an American diner, vaguely modelled on a Pullman from the palmy days of rail travel on that spacious continent, the illusion somewhat spoilt by the unreformed Eastern European maternalism of the thick, plaited, embroidered waitress who seats us, and the dingy, mistyped bill of fare — all the *cartes* I can recall from my one brief revisit of the U.S. were glossy affairs with seductive photographic illustrations of glamorous hamburgers and lush salads, *viandes fatales* looking back in sultry invitation over, as it were, a bared shoulder.

    "There's a place out Sepulveda," he proudly informs me, "They put a slice of cucumber in your ice-water, free, basically. Here, you should try the Chicago club sandwich, it comes with sauerkraut, the whole deal."

It does, but I doubt the gastronomically proud Illinois metropolis would acknowledge attribution of the double-decked sandwich on coarse bread, stuffed with what seem to be slices of sausage, onion, beetroot and courgette in a mildly mustardy sauce, perfectly edible, decidedly not American.

Minghela, with a conspirator's glance behind him, says he knows what I'm here for, but when I sound a sceptical, "Oh?" modifies that.

"Basically, Sir Gossbrooke says, take care of the guy's needs, that makes it a big deal, always, he's my main man, you know?. Listen, I can easy give you guys, one, two. three, five guys, no problem, basically. they do what you say, no questions asked, doesn't have to be legal. Two hundred a day each guy. Basically, a bargain."

"Two hundred what?"

"Dollars, U.S.," he rebukes me; only hopeless outsiders ever think in any other currency. "Naturally, any special stuff you might require, weapons, explosives, faked documents, any of that, that would run you extra, but this is still a great deal, basically for your own major-league team, home-grown."

Gossbrooke's problem-free twenty-five grand is rapidly losing its munificence (I haven't mentioned that a couple of days after our meeting there was, hand-delivered to my place, a thick envelope containing 1200 euros, mixed denominations, the notes all used and carefully non-sequential, an unsigned "*to cover expenses*" written on the outside), but the mere idea that I might be blundering into a scenario where bombs and assault-rifles are incidentals fills me with nervous repugnance; I tell Minghela I had better get the lay of the land before recruiting any "team," no matter how slavishly devoted.

"I give you one guy, top class, good driver, good shot either hand, two-fifty a day."

"I'll be driving myself." It seems to me hugely unlikely that any of this assistance has been discussed with Ian Gossbrooke; Minghela is panning ore of his own.

And beginning to lapse into a practised resignation. "In the old days, you know, with the Sovs, money was basically no problem when you guys wanted shit done — the Americans, everybody. Sure, you had to be more careful then, but basically I always know who needs to get paid off. I can make you a very attractive deal on a Porsche, like noo, a real honey, basically."

I counter by enquiring about a VW, and at last let him rent me a Volvo, also basically a real honey, like noo, for which I am charged the usual rate — or so I assume; he may have inflated his price assuming that H.M. Government is footing the bill; there is certainly no fellow-conspirator's discount.

Minghela wants me to have dinner with him, basically, and the hand-picked girls he offers to supply, like his guys, are eager to comply with my weirdest and most extravagant whim (only functional questions asked?), but I have already spoken with Galek, and am expected in Yekhalets, at least six road hours away, for an evening meal. Indiscreetly, perhaps, I say this, and am not encouraged at the change worked on Minghela; he blinks, checks another glance behind, and echoes the name with a wholly manufactured offhandedness. "Old Harry Galek, huh? I'm sure basically Sir Gossbrooke tell you — " Minghela's command of English is paling, too — "My name must be left out whenever you talk with government guys. You don't know nobody here, basically, okay?"

"There's no reason for it to come up."

He chuckles unconvincingly. "Sure, but — "

"Don't worry." A wasted injunction; he does, most of his waking life.

The drive, mainly in sparse traffic over dull roads, with interludes in uninteresting towns and skirting one grey major city, allows plenty of pondering time. I initially made contact with Galek from Brussels, and as foreseen, new standing as published author lent weight to my renewed talk of translating his book; he was dubious but not dismissive, and snapped at the bait when I suggested my visit — I say, bait, but with small idea how I could further Ian Gossbrooke's objectives, it seems possible I might end up really doing the translation, for which a sample half-chapter is with me, and actually not bad at all, an episode concerning a suddenly inexplicably popular minor official, whose title and name pronounced together became something very rude in Galician dialect; the existing English version merely transliterated him and lost the pun, but I changed him to Dalore (rhymes with *galore*), chief executive of a small town, elected to a stirring chant of *Mayor Dalore! Mayor Dalore!*

All right. There is not much visible hope in the mission I have half-undertaken, but what there is shrinks and vanishes like a dying candle-flame unless I can locate Lydia Solyitnova, and do so without warning Galek; vanity might sustain his belief in the reason for my visit, but any mention of her name must awaken the slumbering ogre; he even made jocular reference to the Christa Rasch business in our brief earlier talk. But Yekhalets, though the size of a small county, isn't impenetrable forest or trackless desert, and a new-built government lab ought to be identifiable.

Until that can happen, any more anxious speculation is disproportionate to the available information, but Lise's unexpected outburst has set another problem beside Case Solyitnova, and it is not long before I am worrying away at Case (in ominous German, *Fall*) Carina. I made love to Carina last night with, because of Lise, an undesired watchfulness, which she interpreted as preoccupation over my mission to Galek's lair.

Conjectured, analysed and set aside, the m-thing still haunts, but added to those autonomous doubts about my aptitude for something so defining, I remain relatively certain she'd say no if I suggest it; her flight from dependant daughter to dependant (and oppressed) young wife has made her emergence into self-supporting functionality very sweet; she has occasionally taken me to dinner or a concert, which has given her great pleasure, and even in my absence (which sounds more presumptuous than I feel) thoroughly relishes her life.

That isn't to reject Lise's implied scenario; enfranchised, women are still persuasible, and someone more assertive than I could breeze along and insistently claim Carina for his own. So it might have to be; I am not prepared to head that off with pre-emptive bullying of my own, like rescuing a country from aggression by annexing it.

But it would be a pity to let these new considerations bring about the birth of things till now — as seldom with lovers — refreshingly absent between Carina and me, strategies and secrets, calculation, however benign. When it was time to leave for the airport, I said lightly, "You know, I stopped for a beer with Lise last night. She thinks we should be married." A slip of litmus-paper.

"Ah, Lise — " after an eye-widening moment. "In the end, I think she is a true puritan. She sees us *living in sin* — " the last in parodistic English (We in fact still maintain separate addresses).

"She says she is a sentimentalist."

"One may be both, no? Like Puccini."

"Has she said anything to you?"

"Oh, no — perhaps; I'm not sure. She is always telling

me how different you are from men — men in general, you know. Perhaps she wants to marry you herself. She says she has never known a man with so little need to dictate to women, who remains a real man. How would she know that part?"

Licenced teasing, good for an embrace. "Someone's been talking."

"But she says, that makes you into a fatalist with women."

"A *fatalist*?" For a moment I suspect a lapse of translation, but French is the only language (of about seven or eight between them) which Lise shares completely with Carina, and must be what they were using.

"Yes — you know, *chè sarà, sarà*. But that's me, too, that's what we want, isn't it? We can talk about marriage when you're bored with me."

Matrimony, then, as a sort of dead-file for expired interest — but that kind of hint, like "Let me know when you're ready to leave," murmured at a party, invites inversion; perhaps she can imagine being bored with me. God knows I sometimes am. There wasn't time (and a good thing, too) to begin a round of championship insight, most fascinating and perilous of parlour games, so I merely kissed Carina, and told her the propose-only-when-bored prescription put horns on a dilemma very like *un toreau irlandais*, giving the classic illustration: "If people didn't need to eat, all the grocers would starve." She laughed, and sent us back to our starting place with, "*Ah, Mark, que je t'aime.*"

I have made myself be reasonably at peace with her saying nothing about the resurfacing of awful Léon; in my mating life I've more than once been baffled, outraged and dismayed when an otherwise fairly rational woman, after lengthily, bitterly reciting all the shortcomings of her own recent Léon-equivalent, the physical or emotional brutalities he had inflicted, has somnambulistically gone back for more of the same, but am as confident as ever about anything that Carina, though damaged by the Lyon episode, is whole and consistent when it comes to heart and mind, and is not going to expose herself to any grisly reruns.

Good, but at the very end she found, mainly unawares, a new way to pink my patched complacency; Ketil, she said (with a rolling glance to heaven), has been expressing an interest in her. Handsome, self-regarding Ketil, the Icelandic Frost, recipient of fan-mail, lovingly wrapped cakes, hopeful, revealing snapshots, and occasionally, yet more wistfully, the provocative undergarments of and from his admirers (gossamer trial balloons to test the northern breeze), many of which pre-trophies end up tacked boastfully to the cork message-board which forms one wall of his personal den at Babel.

"He has asked me to have dinner with him."

"Oh? Where?"

"Here, in Brussels — " with a grin; as well as I she knows that Ketil likes to combine assignments with assignations, whisking his newest fancy off with him to Washington, say, Tokyo, or (less dramatically) Berlin.

"Are you going?"

"Should I?"

"If you would enjoy it."

She kisses me and tells me I'm droll. That we can call these delicate creatures ours... I don't know whether anyone has ever suggested that with Othello's blackness, his supposedly near-savage origins, Shakespeare has found a dark dramatic metaphor, not for a race but a species, how absurdly easy, for all of us, is the reversion, what a friable, rice-paper thing our mask of correct attitudes and civil acceptance turns out to be. Over the feelings, not necessarily the actions; we smother only ourselves, and churn as my innards may — and the two-week absence I'm committed to adds impotence to all imaginings — they're not going to drive me to anything more extreme than a dull unhappiness, and all the while the eternal accountant, balancing the books, aridly reminds me that the unsound, if popular, notion, that the onset of jealousy is a displacement test (Eureka!) for true love is the cause of more miserable, doomed marriages than even alcohol. But my Carina couldn't possibly be charmed, disarmed, disrobed (unthink this) by Ketil's preening act. Could she? I'm far from certain that "my" Carina has, or should have, any existence, outside my own romantic idealising — and I am more than adequately aware of the pressures on a Carina, on a woman who, by no design but her inherent enchantment, becomes more than desired, becomes in male imaginings a prize to be striven for, symbolically as well as actually fabulous, the Rolex, the Ferrari, the villa near Fiesole — how men strangely turn their recognition of desirability into a claim, the property-rights of an inventor (a link here to Lise's analogy with wine-connoisseurship). Walking home last night I diagnosed my awestruck feelings; one of the treasurable aspects of Carina is her complete unawareness — or possibly dismissal — of any special magic, but I can easily turn that very quality into myth, just as recognition of our real and effortless friendship can evoke an atmosphere where ease can no longer breathe.

Words quite often invent what they purport merely to

identify, but this case is no such thing. There's no help for it; once recognised, consciousness of my umanageable feelings can't be wished back into its hole, to let me once more be the bloody fool Lise jocularly labels me, or the insensate oaf I suspect I've seriously been; I am in every kind of love with my well-liked friend; I can see her with my skin, and my fingertips possess the memory —

But I don't have or want any exclusive claim on Carina, not when I'm sane, and sanity is what rules my observable behaviour — this, no doubt, is what Lise perceives as my "fatalism." Not, repeat, when I'm sane, but who is, in the privacy of muddled reflection, given the time and solitude for brooding? There is no cure; romantic, carnal men are made in incompatible halves, and all I can hope for is not to bully Carina with the egoist arrogance of my selfless compassion. So resolved.

With the sun westering, I am climbing very gradually through an ashy grey landscape intersected occasionally by rows of bare poplars and alders, vast flat hectares where wheat and rye have been harvested and the stubble burnt. A sweeping turn, and I have reached Yekhalets.

Well short of the mountainous, but definitely and quite abruptly raised above the surrounding country as if pushed from below by an impatient fist, so that much of its southward hem hangs over low cliffs, and the few roads that climb there wind up, as I do, from eastward. Westward, some gentler gradients slope down to the shores of a long frontier lake, while a river-gorge, famous for its wild aspects, divides this dome from the northward mountains; the top, the scalp, as it might be, four or five hundred square kilometres, mostly of gravelly heathland, tough grass, bushes, scrub and small, wind-tilted trees — firs and furze, some shocks of slender birch.

It has never been enthusiastically inhabited, some herding, various livelihoods dependent on woodcutting, which, during one of the five-year plans, coalesced into a small factory, still dingily surviving, turning out fruit-crates, lath, and other low-tech wood products. This enterprise, together with grey barracks housing, inevitably followed by a skein of grocery, shedlike "workers' club" and other dubious amenities, expanded and, as I find, so spoilt Zmin, immemorially the entire region's nearest attempt at a city, where the main road, climbing from the southeast, is crossed by a lesser way, and the ancient, raftered inn is now boarded up and empty, except perhaps for the hoarse ghosts of smocked and cross-gartered revellers, still chanting their ribald *chastushki* (mocking songs).   Nearby, I stop to refuel and to confirm my directions with a stooped, sore-eyed rag-wielder, who, hearing my accent, peers closer, and pronounces that (rather than questions if) I am Czech, which I do not dispute, bequeathing him unbegrudged the complacent smirk of the infallible provincial oracle.

After Zmin, there are only scattered dwellings and tiny, ramshackle hamlets, till, crowning the crest, a moderate wrinkle somewhere near the middle of the region, I sight the old and uninhabited castle, sombrely functional in a massy, turreted, yet half-Asiatic style. Seen against a latening sky it is for any money that daunting place where, their horses having bolted, the touring newlyweds, obliged to seek shelter for oncoming night, are greeted by the silken and saturnine host in full evening rig, while augural bats flitter, and the *Nachtkinder* carol their yearning *Nachtmusik* at the unforthcoming moon. But no, the domain of bloodthirsting Vlad lies several frontiers and several hundred kilometres to the south and west, and this castle, much battered, sagged into disuse well before Bram Stoker was born, being replaced administratively by a modest, almost contiguous eighteenth-century château, which, whilst incorporating the standing walls of what had once been a dark Eastern monastery, was and is of a less murky era, where toylike pencil-pointed turrets and woodblock-print gardens with low hedges and gravelled walks hint instead at witty riposte and amorous intrigue in fashionable French; the flaying knout, no doubt, kept out of sight in the overseer's quarters: the Empire of the Tsars merely simulated a Renaissance under Peter, when in provincial fact it stayed mired in the Middle Ages for another two centuries.

The way, after skirting a wide tarmac space suggesting coachloads of sightseers clambering down to gawk and snap at the frowning mediaeval, sends out a spur to duck beneath a shaggy outthrust elbow of castle, ending abruptly in a lesser, oval court under the complicated symmetry of the château's portico — in fact, its rear; like all such structures of its time, its face is turned to its own and away from the world at large, though here a stone terrace with balustrade runs the entire width. I halt my staid car just behind a rakish if elderly Citroën, note a magnificent honey-furred larch, and between two pairs of gigantic granitic Ali Baba pots mount the steps and cross the flagged terrace to the entrance, illogically relieved to see that the enormous apparent double-doors are a whimsical illusion, a mere mat of panelled bronze to frame a practical human-sized door of burnished mahogany, with an anachronistic bell-push at its margin. Which I press.

Immediately, the door swings back, and I have, after all, blundered into the realm of the undead; an extraordinary gnome with a large head and a small body is looking up under ponderous eyebrows from about the level of my sternum. He (I am fairly certain *he*) is of no determinable age, except for the remarkable eyebrows virtually hairless, the deep creases next to the dark eyes and beside the fleshy, lopsided mouth contradicting the smoothness of an abnormally broad, bulged forehead, the amorphous, almost foetal cheeks and chin — if he can be said to have one, the face melting imperceptibly into a lard-white, sagging neck.

Recovering from shock (which I hope has gone unnoticed, though such reactions can hardly be new to him), reprimanding myself silently with the word, *unfortunate*, I state my name and purpose. In a fluting voice he agrees I am expected, and confident I'd follow, wheels and crouches away, hunching one shirted shoulder, dragging one plimsolled foot. *If his name is Igor* — We emerge from a short, dim vestibule into a high, well-lighted hall, a lacy stone stair sweeping down past a giant heraldic window still struck by the dying sun to orange, gentian and blood. Where this curve, the carved banister scrolling back like the head of some monstrous marble violin, debouches in a wide estuary to the flagged main floor, a tall man has paused in descent, soberly ornate in full evening regalia, the scarlet-and-gold sash of some order across his chest, and a fluffy white carnation for buttonhole. He beams.

"Good evening, Mr. Kearns — " in English, with all the vowels amply, chewily Slavonic. "I wish — no, I hope you had fewer than too much troubles to discover us."

This is Galek, the off-target expressions fully typical; at our only other meeting, for example, he told me that the English translation of his novel, whatever its inadequacies, had nevertheless made him "a hill of plunder" in the United States. Not correctable except by the Fowleresque rule of cast-iron idiom, and as a matter of fact such departures can shine an unexpected light into some dusty and unregarded corners; asking why they're wrong, we often find we've been parroting nonsense; *plunder* and *loot* are after all equal in inaccuracy for fair-gotten gains. So, too, with his ironic "inform me of it!" but not his pronouncement that certain English critics had "toasted" the book; he meant *roasted*.

His oddly-chosen gatekeeper hobbling away to vanish through an inner door, Galek, radiantly conscious of tailored resplendence, though the relatively sedentary years since his Olympic triumph have begun to make a cummerbund more than a mere gesture, comes down the last six stairs, extending a cordial hand, but the carefully staged tableau is at once fractured by loud and angry voices from above. Women's voices.

The stridency, in fact, is unilateral, a young female rancorous in Bulgarian, which I follow well enough to understand the annoyance is over some indispensable article or accessory of dress, the *blue* one, mislaid, or stupidly omitted from *the suitcase*. Older and thicker, the voice on the other side of the dispute is sullen rather than irascible; I can't make out the words, but the tone is deference pushed to the limit, a long-suffering servant, perhaps, at the brink of antipathetic mutiny.

Galek, smile struck stiff by sudden frost, fails to conceal the extent of his displeasure, uttering "Pardón," through clenched teeth, a pulse oscillating in his temple. He wheels, climbing in two strides to where the stairs turn, and calls, "Evgenia. *Evgenia!*" — more sharply against the continuing tirade — "Our guest is arrived — " in English, and attempting impossibly to make hostly affability compatible with the resurgence of accustomed, unquestioned authority.

He achieves a startled silence. While Galek beams on at me, eyes almost disappearing in fatty crinkles, there are quick mutterings above, suggesting the furtive darting of mice.

"My niece," he explains, not quitting his post in front of the window, its garish colours cooling now as the sun expires.

Evgenia's arrival provokes the wicked thought that she might well have been niece to a variety of Galek-aged men; very slender, anything but shapeless, just a petal too overblown to be beautiful, flowing seamlessly down the staircase in an undulating dark-green tube to perch a largish, garnet-tipped hand on Galek's forearm; she has a dusked, blue-lidded, languorous sensuality; nor is she as tall as in my first impression, reaching to brush his cheek with her self-indulgent lips.

Younger, too, than the boldly-drawn features at first conveyed; twenty-two, twenty-three, perhaps, when brought to confront me, but the brown eyes very shrewd as well as inviting — a purely congenital quality, with no reference to any of mine.

"I have watched you in television," (*vees'yahn*) she says. "Most informal."

"Informing," Galek amends, and they both mean *informative*; apparently we are going to remain approximately in English, which is a bit absurd. I am, too, prepared to resent the gamesmanship of their garb; on the phone he told me our meal would be a casual one, no need to fret about my clothes. I am wearing a tie, but my aging grey suit is way-rumpled, shoes comfortable but glossless.

Through a white double-door picked out in gold, we are in an ample, high-ceilinged but nondescript lounge — or perhaps *eclectic* is the in word, elements of Second Empire, (a mauve brocade ottoman, the pedestalled bust of a generic Roman) and Edwardiana (mushroom table-lamps with leaded-glass shades; at the unwindowed end, as backdrop to the quietly browsing piano, a colossal oil-painting by some Frith of the Steppes, remorselessly depicting an antedeluvian garden-party at this same château; parasols, cheroots), struggling for the stylistic mastery with some less-is-more furnishings from the Thirties (the starkly functional cadaver of a sideboard, a couple of gaunt high-backed chairs) and boxy upholstered stuff which might represent the era of Soviet Realism, all filled in with post-disintegration knick-knackery, a Porsche-like German clock for the porphyry mantel, some Scandinavian occasional tables, a couple of really good French art-glass vases, with shocks of dried flowers.

There rises from the rectangular sofa a Demetz, who has the middle-aged boyishness, long neck, round spectacles and preoccupied air of a scholar or specialist in something, also a vaguely pretty and prettily vague blonde wife named Anya. But when Galek, at last cornered into using his own language, explains that Demetz manages the château estate for him, I realize that the double-door I had passed through was the time-lock between Transylvania and Chekhovia — confirmed when, with glasses of wine poured and distributed — a patriotic bubbly, sugary miles from *brut* — there is one of those silences where all throats simultaneously seize up, and into the dead spot comes a small, fussily overdressed woman, who looks shyly round at the company and says, "Time can be so confusing, I always think."

Not the metaphysical utterance it momentarily seemed; she is Evgenia's mother, Ludmila, explaining why she had been late getting dressed.

Evgenia, unkindly, "You shouldn't have wasted so much time looking for a silk scarf you know you forgot to pack — " this in Bulgarian. Shocked, I recognise the mother was Evgenia's browbeaten servant in the offstage clash. Ludmila, I at length discover, now a widow, had married and survived a widower from Sofia, bringing with her Evgenia, child of an earlier marriage. Her second husband was the brother of Galek's early, long-discarded wife; thus Evgenia's only relationship to Galek is that she was for a time stepdaughter to his former brother-in-law, putting her supposed niecehood a fair piece (as they say in backwoods America) from the tables of consanguinity.

Though pitifully cowed by her flamboyant daughter, Ludmila is far from stupid. With promised dinner looming, talk is desultory, not to say vapid, mainly weather and problems of the estate, Chekhov indeed, without the underlying tension of the playwright's stealthy agenda, and when Ludmila leans to me to confide, "Up here, there isn't much of what you might call social life," it isn't — or not only — to maintain the Cherry Orchard atmosphere; she is slyly explaining why I have been afflicted with a pair of numbing bores like the Demetz couple.

She, by archaically formal standards and a process of elimination, has to be my pairing, and when food is proclaimed and the adjournment moved, I stand, offering my arm, thinking but not uttering polished Wildean epigrams — you'll excuse this procession of literary references, but at the time, perplexed and uneasy, I was hunting for a frame to contain sheer oddity, this banally innocuous meeting with a novelist and thug I wanted to outwit.

"Who knows?" Ludmila murmurs, with a conspiratorial smile, "There might be a pie — " and it is a pleasant shock to realise she is consciously allied with my whimsy; that was *Three Sisters* (I am to discover she played minor roles in provincial rep until Evgenia was born).

But we are an odd number for dinner after all. In the dark-panelled, relatively modest but still high-ceilinged room, already seated, is a small, slight-shouldered, serious girl, straight light-brown hair, thin, irresolute lips on a thin face made more so by large bifocals; she might be thirteen or so, but she has chosen, or had chosen for her, an absurdly grown-up costume, a brick-red, scoop-necked sheath whose slack fit only emphasizes her shapeless immaturity. She is announced rather than introduced by Galek as Celeste, without further definition, although everyone else seems to know and accept her as part of the decor. She smiles slightly and generally, exposing a mild overbite, and is unenthusiastic about being engaged in conversation by Evgenia;

despite the name, Celeste is evidently not French, and what I can overhear of their talk is certainly Russic.

She is enclosed between Evgenia and Galek, and the rest of us alternate ourselves at the massy oaken table, which has ample space for twenty. There is no lack of servants, four or five to keep the courses cleared and replenished; they seem mainly Polish and Belarus, though there is one slight and stunning Russian Oriental girl, the small face unjustly hinting at a sybaritic cruelty — most likely an ordinary post-adolescent who likes steam-hammer music, shoes, fast food and the ads in American magazines, but the flat, implacable cheekbones and smooth eyelids, the bright scarlet chevron of mouth, stir images of joss-sticks and jade, a steady succession of outworn young lovers put to lingering death with unspeakable tortures; it is perhaps as a competitor that Evgenia, who no doubt expects to monopolise any masochistic fantasies that are going, singles out that girl for special mistreatment, twice and brusquely sending her back to the kitchen to make good some imagined defect in food or cutlery ("What do you call this fork?" she demanded in Bulgaro-Russian, pointing to undetectable residue of scamped washing). But then, she is highhanded with all the help; while the socially unassailable almost always treat those who serve them with consideration, rudeness and unreasonable demands come reflexively to the ones who, but for the grace of a shrewdly-chosen bra and a well-placed uncle or two, might themselves have been waitresses or dishwashers — I pass this along by way of a hint to those who imagine they are showing their class by being unpleasant to shopgirls; they are, but in the opposite to the intended sense.

The meal, for me filled with unease, is memorable chiefly for its many courses — the bewildering number rather than their quality; there is a murky lemony-garlicky soup, a sliver of poached trout (possibly), which comes with an onion sauce and an apology from Galek about the difficulty of obtaining first-rate fish in these parts, there are terrines with tomatoes and breadcrumbs and a lot of dill, a rather insipid rose-petal sorbet, a ragout of lamb with turnips and mustard-greens, a rich ice-cream generally relished (and shovelled down with sombre dedication by the taciturn Celeste), which I decline so as to pass on to some bland cheese and a selection of fruit Demetz modestly ascribes to the château's own groves, apples, green pears and small, dusky, somewhat wizened peaches. And there are wines of every hue, none I find any reason to ask about; their balance-of-payments problem and sluggish international demand have made home-grown wines, only a few of any distinction, the rule in Galek's land. A lengthy, show-off state dinner, then, all the talk determinedly inconsequential, and Galek, who empties glasses at a gulp and easily outdrinks any two others, presides in monarchical geniality, with a special sidelong gleam for me, a kind of flirtatious promise that we will eventually discuss the translation he believes brought me here.

Or that I trust he believes. Shimmering in the distance always, somewhere behind the servants, or glimpsed through a half-open doorway to an adjoining room, is another presence my depth of field seems inadequate to focus, certainly to count, an indefinite number of young or youngish men, on the square-framed, beefy side, all dark-suited, certainly not household staff, nor guests to share our table; a simple surmise is that they are supported by the taxpayers, but under Galek's sole orders, and like the recruits Minghela offered me, not morally averse to using weapons or breaking things. Not for the first time when suddenly face-to-face with the fragility of the conventions that sustain an illusion of safety — with my own fragility — I experience a dark shudder, like the wrenching-open of a coffin-lid.

Not willingly, I am obviously stuck here for an overnight; I left the possibility open when Galek included it in his initial invitation, but now a surreptitious glance at my watch tells me ten is nearer than nine, and I saw nothing on the road that looked like lodgings after leaving Zmin; as little progress as I have made towards a meeting with Solyitnova, it would in any case be stupid to leave the area where I know she must be.

Galek puts down his wine-glass with ham-fisted finality, and proclaims that while he and I have matters to discuss, coffee and cordials will be served to the rest in the music room, where, for a special treat, perhaps Celeste would play for them. She is still unplaced for me, and I can't plausibly sustain the conjecture she might be the daughter of an unrecorded liaison of Galek's; his manner with her is proprietary but not at all paternal: he beams and beetles massively over her, and she, neither eager nor offensively reluctant, shrugs her assent. When she stands, her rusty red dress is mid-shin length, and the thin, straight legs terminate in ankle-socks and tennis shoes.

There is on the sideboard an unopened bottle of Massandra, the legendary Crimean dessert wine, which one of the discerning Waughs once said was everything Imperial Tokay was falsely reputed to be, but Galek, gleaming sidelong to proclaim a special treat, opens and pours instead — into mercifully small glasses — *Kontuszowska*, a Polish cordial, tasting horribly of lavender. I've witnessed Trev Hassett, the Aussie journalist, in one of his compulsive episodes, swig down mouthwash for its meagre alcoholic content, and had been told the permanent partial loss of vision in his right eye was the result of imbibing after-shave in desperation when other sources ran dry, but never expected to find myself drinking shaving-soap.

"You understand, Kearns — " we are back in Galek's idea of English — "I have contracts for publishing, paperback, movie rights, translation, bom, bom, bom, all signed off."

"But the translation must be subject to your approval; I'm certain that if you told your publisher you were dissatisfied — "

"Why am I to be dissatisfied?"

"If I could show you — " I have left my valise on a table by the foot of the stairs; Galek strikes a tiny gong which stands on the sideboard, and gives forth a clear and penetrating note. At once, the Sino-Russian appears, demure but dangerous, and is sent to fetch it.

She returns swiftly, hugging the valise to her two-armed, and gliding away as soon as it is deposited in front of me. Opening, I perceive instantly it has been riffled through; I have my habits, and my passport is too near the top, my ruled pad buried too deep. Call it a routine security check for weapons; I can call to mind nothing that might even hint at my real mission here.

I have with me the English (or actually American) paperback *Nevertheless*, and pass it over opened to the chapter I retranslated, together with my version. Dalek studies the book, making small grunts or staccato humming sounds, *mm, mm, mm*, then with a grandiose flourish folds back my cover sheet.

He knows enough French to roar with laughter at "Mayor Dalore," but I have to explain my changing the name of the mayor's nymphomaniac daughter from Masha to Sonya, so that when she runs off to be a singer in a flamenco troupe, I could refer to her "Dalore, S." — a sly allusion, besides, to the Nabokovian strain in her ancestry.

"Great, terrific — " without looking up, he reaches for the bottle of *Kontuszowska*, and instead of his empty thimble of a liqueur glass, fills up a wine-glass, ignoring the inch or so of chardonnay already there. "You know, Kearns, I write this book once only — I never write it — " a large gulp of lavender — "if I could know what aching it would be in my arse. For my service; I had to win horse-medal at Olympics, then I was okay to trust again; they were such countlessly stupid, the Communists, you never believe."

Galek's cravat is now well off-centre, a lollop of greying hair hanging near his melting eyes, cheeks blotched and mottled with raw colours.

"Vátilar Tcheytz," he announces from nowhere, "You consider him important?"

Some preternatural capacity lets me decipher a familiar and revered name, and agree that many, I among them, regard William Vátilar Tcheytz as the greatest poet of the past century.

"'Things fall apart, centre cannot hold — ' Moskva, don't you think, when the Union came undone?"

Through an open door I hear faintly the opening toccata from a Bach partita, a strange choice, either for the audience or its executant; Celeste (presumably) is note-accurate but rhythmically wayward, not in any attempt to interpret and romanticise, but with the unmeasured gait of one who has no innate sense of time, and whose teacher has failed to insist (as Mozart used to) on keeping it.

"Many genius lovely things that seem miracles to the multitude, gone," Galek horribly misquotes, and I recognise how drunk he is, genuinely drunk, disturbingly dangerous, all the more for remaining, when drunk, dangerous in his sober sense; no matter how he babbles he isn't going to blurt anything useful to me, and his cockeyed gaze is still alert for clues as to my hidden agenda —

"Man is in love," I can't resist capping him, "and loves what vanishes."

I have small doubt with my history and the otherwise godforsakenness of this region that he remains suspicious of my stated purpose; for many years he made a profession of being suspicious, and a mere two percent of alcohol in the blood-supply to his brain won't change those habits.

Which surface in a flash of clarity. "I demand myself," he says with deliberate discourtesy. "Is it factually for this you come this great, not convenient way? Two planes, yes? and long drive; I have wrote little book, good book, but not big book — but you, big journalism, journalista — "

"Not so big."

"Big enough, one assesses, so? So, if I have my committee meet and we chew this, someone wise-ass say, Kearns, this is guy who, when in Dusatia, was such a problem for Nationalists — maybe he think Kvitka is the same thing, maybe he collect for a strong television, ah, denouncement? If he butter over Galek, maybe Galek says things Kearns can use against Kvitka."

Going into his own language — he seems hardly to notice — I have no need to simulate offence (absurd enough, in the circumstances). "That is not how I work. It's true I don't like what I've seen of Kvitka, which is not very much. If I were planning a piece, I would interview him, face to face, and go to State Television for background; I don't sneak around trying to trip up ministers, and I never use unverifiable quotes. If you're not interested in a new translation of *Nevertheless* — "

He makes a big, circling, shrugging gesture, as if to invite me to comprehend his responsible position, but we are, however spasmodically back on track; his Western copyrights, he informs me, reside with his publisher in Berlin.

"You should talk to Walther there, Walther Schmiede, if he still works; I lose his trail. But I have not time, we have to renovate the country."

Preposterous, so much so that I very nearly let the whole thing drop, except that to do so would proclaim my fraudulence. Instead, as to a small child, I explain that I can hardly descend unheralded on Herr Schmiede and expect a sympathetic hearing; he must have some advance word, a hint that the author is unsatisfied with the existent translation.

"Oh, yes, I ring him up, say, I meet this Englishman, big author, yes. You drink rakija? I got a bottle here was from Marshall Tito's cellar — " reminding me that though they come in shapes and sizes as various as suave sons of Domesday privilege and this crude and dishevelled vulgarian (who once, inexplicably, wrote a decent novel), a spook is a spook, the world over, and inclined to boast: there's not so much to choose between Gossbrooke plying me with the Kaiser's cognac, and Galek offering me Tito's slivovitz.

My declining of which is barely taken note of, as Galek serves himself with a generous hand, and after allowing that we should, perhaps, join the other guests, declines into inarticulate mumbling, seated at the table, bowed low over his glass. The piano in the next room has ceased.

I stand, and catlike he rouses instantly, though an elderly cat, somewhat bewildered. Audibly, he tastes his tongue several times.

"You must be put down properly for the night." Once more he strikes the tiny treble gong, and soon the cruel Chinese princess reappears: *This, our newest candidate, will attempt to guess your name, and whether you use underwear. Having failed, he will of course be beheaded* — No, he doesn't say that, maintaining his precarious focus to issue instructions about a bedroom — rather, to confirm instructions given earlier; the girl nods impassive understanding.

"First," I venture, "may I make a phone-call to Brussels? I'll pay, of course."

"Pay? No — " backhand expansiveness. "I have very special communications, use them, blue phone, straight dial to anywhere, Kremlin, White House, Placido Domingo. Blue phone," he says, in his own language to Fire-and-Ice, a flicking index-finger telling her to lead me there. Following her pantherine pace, I decline to be ashamed that my eyes do not remain level, browsing neat but complex muscular dynamics. At our destination, she turns with, might it be, the remotest shadow of a knowing smile.

An oval table in the alcove formed by the scrolling-back of the broad stair; quite blue, handset wafer-thin, very special, no doubt, but for me, probably not secure. It doesn't matter; Carina was preinstructed against any reference to my real aims here.

Purr-purring, the off-white phone on the little book-shelf by Carina's bed (Dante, Larousse, *l'Écume des jours*, Toye's *Verdi*, in Italian, *A Room with a View*, in the original). Purr-purring, not loudly. In Brussels, a quarter to ten. Purring. She has no answering-machine, and is not entirely compulsive about picking up — that is to say, she has been able to ignore a distracting phone, once or twice, when she and I were — nonsense, nightmare nonsense. Purr-purring; disconnect, dial again to be sure I had it right, same result, purr-purring. Perhaps with Lise, perhaps they went out to dinner; with a palpable effort I dismiss the nasty notion of trying Lise's number. Besides, what would I say if she answered? That I wondered if Carina — oh, very sophisticated, Kearns, and wonderfully consistent with your proclaimed unpossessiveness, especially if Lise hasn't a clue where she is. Purr — oh, all right, damn her. I don't mean that, but here I am, trapped among backwoods imitations of characters from post-Wagnerian opera, Baron Ochs and his mistress, Marie (*Wozzeck*), her mother Ellen Orford, Turandot hovering behind me; a breathing-tube back to reality is what I need.

And fantasy, acknowledged or not, is made to cease; led docilely upstairs, lugging my small baggage, which I have firmly declined to have carried for me by a wisp of an enigmatic girl, I find more than sleeping-quarters.

A baronial bedroom, quite cool now, not to be imagined in grim January when the playful breezes swirl.   There are ponderous hangings, massive furnishings, a broad empty fireplace, a vast oak-framed bed in the middle distance.

Evgenia is there, standing by the bed; a faint depression in the brocade coverings suggest she has regained her feet on hearing the door about to open. She smiles with exactly the air of someone being met for afternoon tea, *am I late, or were you early?*

"You are an interesting man — " in her bad French, as I approach. "I wish to make a collection of interesting men — women, too, it may be."

"So do I," putting down my suitcase and sliding the attaché onto the gothic dressing-table. "I interview them." Note: I am on the defensive, genuinely disconcerted by this unpredicted apparition.

A chuckle; *pearly* is not the newest of dental adjectives, but Evgenia's small, even, slightly convex teeth have, undeniably, a nacreous lustre. *Und der Haifisch...* "Interview! One comes together, face to face, not so, with the other? My uncle says my breasts are a miracle of sculpture."

Galek, then, is recycling his lines; in his novel a woman is described in almost exactly those terms, though the original has a play on the words *sculpted* and *tinted* (in English, something might be done with *hued/hewed*). "Why do you call him your uncle?"

"It amuses him, the idea." A shrug. "Me, I'm an atheist, anyway, like the English."

Let that go; many in odd corners of the Continent, instructed by incontrovertible, barely-literate parish priests, devoutly believe that Henry VIII with his divorce wrenched England clean out of Christendom, and that the Channel, scooped out about then by the Almighty, makes the sceptred isle no fortress built by Nature for herself, but a quarantine, that streak of frequently-turbulent water guarding the mainland, rather, against infection and the curse of disbelief. But Evgenia's formative years were spent under a system for which atheism was a virtue; she is aligning herself, as well as letting me know she is unmoved by the contrived pretence of incest that evidently gives Galek his buzz.

Shoes shaken off, Evgenia half-sits, half-leans on the edge of the bed, and it would be extremely stupid to ask, as occurs to me, "What can I do for you?" What is perfectly clear, but *why?* is acquiring an unexpected importance: time, perhaps, for me to wear white flannel trousers and walk upon the beach, if I can no longer trust greed to lie to me; in reality I've never been able to treat mating with the nonchalance it ought sometimes to deserve, but could always rely on temporary insanity to keep me from the nightmare prudence of abstention.

But here there may be strategic questions, too; I am not so irresistibly attractive as to eliminate the possibility Evgenia has been loosed on me by Galek, and that I can't imagine with what purpose does not mean there isn't one. Or, if not, it might be she overestimates his complaisance or fecklessly shrugs off his possessiveness (he twice her age and then some, and I have observed that the desire for exclusive rights is often fiercened by decline of the capacity to make it a reasonable demand, while if he habitually gulps down strong waters at tonight's rate, he must make a repellent and mainly ineffectual bedful) in which case — well, make up your own ending; what is certain is that it would be folly to add personal vengeance to Galek's reasons for hostility. Evgenia demonstrates with one wristy gesture that her dress, surprisingly enough, unzips in front, all the way down.

Some follies are not to be avoided, though I'm not certain why; Galek could hardly arrest me if I tell him my plans have been modified, and it is not physically undoable for me to say goodnight and cede the bedroom to her gradual, determined disrobing (the forest-green sheath now gaping wide to reveal a gleaming, expensive-looking daffodil-coloured slip, nipple to thigh, making Evgenia a vivid reminder of maize freshly stripped — shucked, they say in America, suggesting rhymed improprieties — needing only to be buttered and bolted from the cob); I owe her nothing — where and as she is are not the result of anything I've said or done, nor of a generous gesture, but only of her own wayward appetite, yet chivalry and concupiscence, as ever, make common cause, and it is unnerving (as well as inciting) to hear my side of the dialogue click onto automatic pilot with delayed endorsement of Galek's admiration. The breasts are quite remarkable, not with the bulged rotundity of so-called (and miscalled) 'enhancement,' but pleasantly (for want of a word) sculpted.

"Harry likes to see me in gloves."

"Gloves?"

"Long black gloves — any gloves, really. Just my gloves and high-heeled shoes, all naked otherwise, that excites him. Sometimes I think he would be just as excited if I gave him my gloves and went away. Funny things get men going — lacy knickers, anybody likes that, but for some it is — anything, you can't imagine. There was a man who went wild when I put my little-finger up his nose — would you like that?"

"Not particularly."

"When I first saw you, I wished to kiss you. You have nice lips, kind but not weak." Gee, I bet you say that to all the guys. The vivid purplish grease, I note, has been scrubbed from her still-generous mouth.

From here should be a toboggan-run, but there is an annoying, baffling and in my memory unprecedented hitch in the proceedings, absurdly linked to my inability quite to convince myself that Carina, at this moment, is delighting Ketil (or, alternatively, sending Léon away not comprehensively disappointed); in reason there is nothing to say it should not be so, which would make my failure to enjoy so consumer-tested an experience as I'm offered laughable, as well as irrelevant; irrelevant it surely is, or always was before.

That I don't much like her is not necessarily germane; she is, by any accepted standard, desirable, and I would not have believed autonomous chemistry (often able to convert me to preposterous illusions) could fail so miserably to overcome my intellectual and temperamental disinclination. Which my overactive flair for analysis is turning into the feedback effect, whereby a tiny hesitant hum can be rapidly cycled into an intolerable screech of misgiving, and what was proposed as innocent recreation acquires the potential for scarring the soul. Soul, together with weapons and other loose valuables, must be left at the front desk.

On an entirely other plane, but equally demanding, there is my self-respect to be defended. We fear in advance the contempt of adepts — but there, there, luxurious Evgenia has not come this far without encountering and dealing with dysfunction; lovers fecklessly humiliate, whores are astutely empathetic. She says, "You're thinking about someone else — " nothing like an accusation, pure diagnosis, and I concede the point with an assenting noise.

"You are married? Is it your mistress?"

Not alternatives but bracing realism. "I'm not married."

"Oh. In love. Don't mind, everyone should be in love sometimes. Close your eyes — no, close your eyes — " do it, really, she means, and when I comply, tells me softly, "Think of a thing you would like to do with her — that you have not done, but have dreams about, to tie her up, to chastise her bottom, to be punished by her, to watch her love with another woman, then join in with both, to pretend she is a boy, to have her in the bath, in the public park at noon..."

Consciously, none of the above, but there is, I discover, if not moral, healing virtue in this ludicrous inventory (in which, for taste's sake, I have toned down or omitted some of the most graphic suggestions) — perhaps that very absurdity, its brisk dispassion, stealing in below the intellect — and on the mesh of reassembled gears her knowing hands advance. But, Christ, I'm lost to impossible sentimental cliché; all this is mere process, and I'm finding that frenzy itself can be vapid and ecstasy somewhat repellent, when the one I want to be with is absurd leagues away, perhaps alone. *When I'm not near the girl I love, I want, dammit, the girl I love.*

In late, filtered moonlight, Evgenia says, "I don't know why Harry has Demetz and that lapdog wife of his. Celeste's mother comes sometimes, very plain, but not as boring as Anya Demetza — some sort of science person at those labs, Lydia — Tsolitnova, or something."

"Celeste is her daughter?" A most unnatural response if I had been hearing of Solyitnova for the first time, but when Gossbrooke had spoken of a child, now fifteen, I had somehow assumed a son.

"Celeste is just a kid, but at least she's alive, or she could be. She only plays that cemetery music, you know, all that antique shit, her crazy mother thinks it's the last word. Christ, at her age I was making more money than my step-father — also, he made more money because of me keeping his bosses happy. Celeste doesn't even smoke dope."

Crazy? "I didn't know there were labs here. Here, at the château? — " with too much interest; Evgenia darts me a puzzled look, and I have to cover: "I thought it had some sort of protected status, as a national treasure."

"Well, the mother has a cottage on the grounds, right by the old back gate. To live. The labs are down the road, about another kilometre, they're under some ministry, but Harry gets involved."

That, unchivalrous to relate, was to remain by far the most prized of the night's gleanings. It is possible, I'm amazed and somewhat ashamed to report, to remain inattentive right through repetitions of what ought to be and physically is the most vigorous and intense of recreational experiences.

III

Waking for the second and definitive time, I'm hardly stricken to find Evgenia gone, leaving behind a few dark hairs, a linger of old-fashioned fragrance (patchouli?), a visible depression in the other side of the bed; later I am to find a mulch of other small legacies; an open packet of American chewing-gum and a couple of envelopes of diet sweetener on the dressing-table, a tiny, genial felt elephant felt underfoot, which might have covered the tag of a zip-fastener, but then again might not, the collection as a whole conducting me unwillingly towards some melancholy and even guilty reflections on her aggressive assertion of long-established maturity.

It is still very early, the house cold and silent; unwashed I put some clothes back on and, unsure of finding the lesser ascent up which I was led last night, make my way through a dim and draughty main corridor, pilastered and lined with a more-or-less random scattering of reproduction busts and beasts on slender marble or wrought-iron plinths under a grimy, once-painted arch of ceiling, to the majestic coil of the main stair. Hairless Igor is evidently not yet on duty, but by the front entrance, in a plain wooden chair tilted back, one of the suited young security-toughs rouses from shaveless, leaden-eyed contemplation at my approach. With a cheery, "Good morning," I boldly tackle the brass lever of door-handle; he opens his mouth as if to cite some house rule I'm violating, but before any words come I'm out into a damp, chilly, monochrome morning, shutting the door behind me. There is, inexplicably, always a feeling of temerity in solo early-morning sorties, to which a guard on the door adds very little.

Momentary clutch of panic at the absence of my rental Volvo, but I recall my keys being asked for (this was still during the *mauvais quart d'heure tchekhovien*) so it could be moved "round back." And the keys restored to me? I pat my trouser-pocket; yes, they were.

Round back is where I need to go if there is to be any attempt to find the cottage Evgenia spoke of. By the end of the château steps descend from the terrace, and a gravelled but badly-kempt way leads me to the broad bay where, nosing up to the house, my Volvo is stabled amongst a miscellany of others, Russian, German and an ancient, battered, still-monumental Packard, the entire fleet beaded with lavish dew.

And here are the grounds, while hardly Versailles, adequately extensive, somewhat sketchily maintained, the evergreen hedges losing their boxy outline in a haze of undisciplined newer growth, the gravel walks largely repaved in slippery brown and yellow leaves. I descend a short flight into a neglected rose-garden encased in low brick walls; leftward and indistinctly, the mouldering bulk of the old castle is less a thing than an absence, a featureless, irregular hole in the farther prospect. Nearer, on that side, the grounds are enclosed partly by tall wrought-iron fencing, and when that gives out, by an ancient high wall of crumbling tawny brick, tufted with moss and more substantial growth; at one point, I note, a fecklessly optimistic birch has taken root head-high above the ground. Nearer still, a flicker of peripheral motion makes me aware I am being followed, watched, both; whether by the same man I said good morning to is impossible to say in this light; he is progressing swiftly from tree to tree, and these bozos are in any case clonelike in their similarity, dark suits, square, muscular frames, cropped hair, no neck.

His evident mission is to keep me unobtrusively in sight, and clearly, I must lose him without seeming to try; the innocuousness of my visit can survive neither an observed attempt to contact Solyitnova, nor the plain desire to evade observation. Dropping my pace to a purposeless saunter, I make my way round the rose-garden with its largely bare sticks of plants and empty central pool, take three steps up to an iron gate. A divided wall of high, boxy hedges looms; it can only be a maze. Not a large one, but sufficiently diverting, apparently, to warrant somewhat more barbering than I've seen elsewhere.

Risking a quick look left, I see that my tail has kept level with me, and is lurking not-quite-behind a larger tree, possibly an oak, a position which in fact gives him a rather partial view, perhaps for a moment none, if I take two more steps, bringing me up to the opening between blocks of hedge. I do so, and then in a sidling scuttle, almost brushing the bushes, reach and turn the corner of the hedge-wall, where soft, wet grass, not recently trimmed, mutes and saturates my headlong dash along the side-wall. My watcher's assumption, I believe, will be that I have entered the maze, and if, as is usual, there is only one way in or out, he'll be content to keep that in view for some time before worrying about my failure to re-emerge; nor, necessarily, will his mistake convict me of intentional evasive action.

Still, I feel better when I can turn another corner, putting the entire block of hedgework — which can't be much more than forty metres square — between us. Beyond is a grassed slope down to a small and sluggish stream, crossed swiftly on stepping stones, to where a broader drive, snaking in from the right, bends among trees to the glimpse of an ornate rear gate of wrought iron between stone pillars. Probably guarded, but short of there, tucked in between drive and rear wall, what must be the cottage occupied by Lydia Solyitnova, an abrupt, startled-looking dark-and-light brick structure of nineteenth-century origin, with pseudo-gothic upper windows and the luckless look of railway architecture, suburban stations, early signal-boxes.

Keeping my head low, so far as I can tell unseen, I wind amongst what might be lilac-bushes to a crazy-paving path leading to the hooded back door of the cottage, too many years ago painted what must have been a bright green, now faded and peeled. Faint light within spills from a high lozenge of grimed glass; seeing neither knocker nor bell, I rap with my knuckles. I hear a stirring within, but not until I rap again, more firmly, does it take on any suggestion of purpose. A bolt slides back, and the door swings open.

"Oh," she says. A short woman, middle forties, so slender as to be almost gaunt, long in the neck, short unstyled hair, dark with greying tendencies, large, dark eyes under an ample forehead and prominent brows; the whole face is topheavy, with a remarkable amount of space between the sharp thrust of nose and a small, pursed mouth, the chin receding almost to non-existence. I have no idea who she might have expected to find on her doorstep, but have only surprised, not alarmed her.

"Lydia Solyitnova? I am Mark Kearns."

"American? English? Should I know you?" Nearly an attractive voice, musically modulated, but with a slight nasality that makes her sound permanently querulous.

"I have come from Brussels to see you."

Detecting, perhaps, my unease at remaining exposed here, and evidently assessing me as no threat (although unshaven, shivering in wayworn but inadequate clothes, trousers soaked to the knee, I would not fill me with confidence), she edges aside, swinging back the door to admit me. A kitchen lacking in charm or cheer, brown-walled, lighted by a reluctant circular fluorescent tube overhead; a profound, rust-streaked antique of a porcelained iron sink, a small, stark cooker of a pattern turned out in the millions by the Soviets for installation in the `kitchen areas' (often a space contiguous with that containing the convertible sofa-bed and all-purpose storage units) in the filing-cabinet flats of Moscow and what was then Leningrad.

"You will have coffee?" She makes a vague gesture at the tiny formica-topped table, evidently inviting me to take one of the two matching tubular chairs. Chromium peeling like a bad sunburn.

"Thank you. Madame Solyitnova — " Come, now; this is what I'm here for. I'm reminded of when I was eighteen and in despairing love with one of the acknowledged Oxford goddesses; I evolved a complex and ingenious strategy to be alone with her in my room (not unlike the Five-Year Plan cubicle just cited, though immensely more expensive), and, having succeeded in masterly style, made an agonisingly polite idiot of myself with my hot-faced ineloquence. *Viens*! the audacity, again the audacity.

"Madame Solyitnova, I am a television journalist; I work out of Brussels — "

"I cannot give — " change of directions — "I have nothing for an interview."

"No, no; that's not what I am here for." In simplest terms, I explain how I was approached by what I believe to be British Intelligence, and why.

She stares at me as if at some unclassified species (of mould, perhaps), and gives voice to a loud, long, unconvincing laugh. "The Protein Bomb! British Intelligence believes in the Protein Bomb! How about pregnancies from alien implants — what a convenience for playful wives. `Yes, dear, I know it can't be yours, but you see, I was teleported aboard this space-craft — ' Who told you about the Protein Bomb?"

"No one. I have no idea what British Intelligence believes; I'm only a conduit — " this is met by a small, doubting noise, somewhere between grunt and cough; I must be about as plausible as Ian Gossbrooke making a similar disclaimer. "I agreed only to deliver their message, to which you can respond or not, as you decide. But at a glance it seems to me someone besides British Intelligence believes in something important enough to take a lot of trouble over. Harry Galek is a drunk, but no fool. Solyitnov didn't die for a fairy-story."

This, wanting in tact, is like throwing a toggle-switch to change the entire basis of our dialogue. "Andrei Vladimirovitch — " the old-fashioned patronymic threatens to nudge us into the world of Turgenev — "had too much imagination for a scientist."

"For a mediocre scientist," I gently correct. "All the great originators had vision as well as logic."

With a sharp reassessing take, she nods vigorously. "Just so. Not for me, but with those like Solyitnov, there is the dream, out there in the ocean, and once they guess where it is, they commence with slow logic, bit by bit, to build the bridge to reach it. But if they decline to begin the bridge, then the dream is nothing."

"Until someone else dreams it."

"Never, not when the vision is a mistake, not a mistake, but nothing more than the dream. He was pigheaded, Andrei — a much better scientist than I, I can't tell you how many times better; I am only infantry, he was a marshall with strategies and war-maps — not for the practical world, you understand; dealing with the *apparatchiki* he was quite like a child, but in the lab, more in his study puffing his foul cigars, he was Zhukov, Frederick, Marlborough."

"They gave him a Nobel."

"But — " she pauses mightily on this. "There isn't any super-weapon, can never be. Andrei saw something, a conception, but in his heart he did not imagine it could ever become a practicable device. There is an insuperable problem of control, containment; without that it would be the Doomsday Machine — oh, this is absurd, it could never be made, but even if it could be triggered, it would most likely be the end of all protein-based life on earth. How can this be a weapon to blackmail the world? If by chance you discovered a way to extinguish the sun, you couldn't hold the world to ransom; nobody would believe you unless you did it, and then — " she gestures universal nothingness.

"Then there isn't any problem." The obvious conclusion.

"Only Galek. He would not believe Andrei, he drove Andrei to his death over this. You see, Andrei — he was very serious, except that he loved to tease, non-scientists especially, about the theoretical possibilities, turning time backwards, alternative realities — science fiction stuff, really, though the theory may be valid enough. With a lever long enough, one could shift the earth; true, if you could make a lever of virtually infinite strength and negligible weight — and then, where would the fulcrum be? You see?"

"Indeed."

"When Andrei first told Galek about fissionable RNA —
"

"At a celebration, was it?"

"Ah, you know about this. A stupid celebration, Andrei thought; he had been made scientific director where they would have done better with a design engineer — these things happen with state projects. He had drunk down three or four vodkas, far more than he could ever take, though he didn't show it — he never seemed drunk, only that he would talk nonsense with the face of a priest." I note her almost predictable alternation, in recalling her husband, between admiration and exasperation, as if desire for, even the possibility of, affectionate memories, is swamped out by rancor over an unnecessary departure, for which, however illogically, she blames him.

"With other scientists," she concedes, "This was quite good fun, but for a man like Galek — I have said this to Galek, a hundred times, but he's also stubborn — Andrei was vain, too, and had contempt for Galek's intellect, and Galek is too vain to allow he could ever be on a wild-goose chase." All this is in what I perceive as her declamatory manner, as if addressing a meeting, but now, very quietly, she leaps to, "Besides, he has my daughter."

"I saw Celeste last night. She played for us."

Lydia wrinkles her nose. "You are staying at the château?"

"Galek," I try to reassure, "knows nothing about this; I found an excuse to visit him."

"Celeste does not really play well, would you say?"

"What do you mean, Galek has her? He can't keep her from you."

"I have to be at the labs," she murmurs, with a glance at the large, numberless wall-clock. "Oh, no; I see Celeste every day, or nearly every day; she sleeps here quite often, has some meals here, and I can go to the big house at any time — but she is his guest. Also his *protegée*." A two handed gesture of limp resignation suggests she herself doesn't know what she means; the charge she laid against her late husband may also do for her; cogent and penetrating with philosophic ideas, she is, I deduce, fatally flustered by reality.

Which irritates me. We are both for our separate reasons becoming edgy about the time, and the promised coffee has come no nearer than a kettle filled at the antiquated tap.

"This is not 1970; you have courts, you have newspapers, you have law."

"And Kvitka."

"Kvitka doesn't control the police, not yet, at least."

"In Yekhalets, Galek does."

"And what could they do if you packed a suitcase — today, and one for Celeste, picked her up at the château, and drove — anywhere, into Poland, into — " (I omit the other alternatives cited, to avoid identifying where we were.)   "You could fly to London tomorrow."

"And be brought back, extradited. The government will say I stole something, or committed some crime."

"No, no. The British government — this is the message I've been given, that they're offering asylum, without conditions."

"Why?"

"To be satisfied that what you call the Protein Bomb can never be built. I'm certain the man who made the offer is in a position to guarantee it." Not quite the whole of my feelings about Gossbrooke and what he represents, but true as far as it goes, and my gesture of faith to the commission I did not refuse.

Lydia's dark eyes are hard to read, but there seems to be a momentary gleam of — not hope, exactly, but a reconsideration of hopelessness. Then she shakes her head. "They would stop me, here, or at the border, at the airport if I went there."

"For how long? Kvitka has not yet managed to intimidate the media; if you were detained I would give the story to State Television, and nothing would stop them."

"Oh, no — " her alarm echoes Gossbrooke's. "If this stupid business about the Protein Bomb becomes known, my position will be much worse — the Americans will condemn it, and try to bully me into making it for them, the Arabs, Israel, the I.R.A., everyone will want it for themselves, and none of them will believe it can never exist. As it is, it's bad, but Galek, in the end, has to see I'm telling the truth, that there is no conceivable device, and then — " another vague, circling gesture.

"There's no reason for it to be known; we say Galek is using your daughter to bring pressure on you, because for reasons of conscience you refuse to work on biological weapons — Galek is certainly not going to make that any more specific; he wants to keep the secret. In any event, he may not have much to say about it. New Nation needs to win the parliamentary elections in — February, is it? The minute it is known that one of his inner circle has more-or-less abducted a girl of fifteen, Kvitka will throw him to the wolves; he's not counting on the paederast vote."

Again, tactless, but if Lydia has ever worried over any darker personal intentions in Galek's annexation of Celeste, she hardly reflects that now; "That's not what it is, there's none of that."

"The question is, how it will appear. Kvitka campaigns on decency and family integrity. He was willing to put Galek in limbo over the Ancestral Estates scandal; he won't hesitate to dump him overboard over a schoolgirl hostage."

The proposal, it should be said, is entirely mine, and would, I'm sure, not please Sir Ian. But I feel no loyalty towards his suspect scheme — or rather, am more than willing to work for Gossbrooke's stated aims — saving Lydia, losing the doomsday weapon — by means that leave no slack for hidden agendas. Saving Lydia, it really is, *from* the chimerical super-weapon; she and Celeste appear to be its only conceivable victims.

"Not many foreigners," Lydia says, frowning. "Speak our language as well as you do."

Subtext: How do I know you're what you say you are? — and if she knows nothing of my work I have no resource to fall back on except that blue-eyed innocence cited by Christa Rasch. But this is no disaster; for Lydia to query my credentials means that she wants to give serious consideration to what I say.

I say something inadequate about my Slavonic mother, and she's not really listening. "You Anglo-Saxons," she reflects, a cultural, not an ethnic term, "Are always so certain about what governments can and can't do; the *Kahn-sti-too-shun*, Magna Carta — but I think you would find there are people, scientists, others perhaps, in America, even in England, who believe they are free, but who cannot leave the country, not without a great deal of trouble, and who are never unwatched if ever they do. There is an Aladdin's lamp called national security, which any country can rub to make freedom vanish. If you speak with State Television, you will interest them, and in the end they'll tell you they have decided, *decided* not to pursue the story. They will have been warned not to — not by Kvitka, by some perpetual grey department of the bureaucracy, who will tell them it is a question of national security."

In the early activist days Gossbrooke mentioned as a permanent scar on Lydia's official reliability, I would bet Lydia was as ready to pamphlet and protest U.S. involvement in Vietnam (a bit young for that, perhaps) or Somalia as the Soviets in Afghanistan, the Chinese erasing Tibet — and yet the very undoctrine of her idealism strikes me as sophisticated enough to make me question my dismissal of her practicality. Yet when, rather than debate these points, I say, "Obviously, then, the thing to do is just leave, without asking," she begins to flutter once more.

"Just leave — Andrei wanted to do that — to vanish, all three of us, but then he saw, he said, these things, threats, cannot be solved by running away from them."

"But he did run away, didn't he, and left you to deal with the threat." Having got out this near-taunt, I feel an instant urge to apologise for its shrivelling effect; it is worse than tactless to identify and loudly label someone's most assiduously repressed, most unthinkable thought.

"I must be at the labs — " agitatedly loading herself with looseleaf binders, a pregnant brocaded handbag, an ancient attaché with her husband's initials (Cyrillic). "I cannot think why you would trouble yourself in this matter, Mr Kearns." Her eyes are like a wall of obsidian. I can't imagine for what reason she goes to work so early at an institute she nominally directs.

No doubt you have many calls of a similar character to make in the neighbourhood. She's quite right; it is none of my business; I've delivered my message, and can report back to Gossbrooke with no twinge of guilt; whether or not I can convince him, I am satisfied there is and will be no Protein Bomb (it's clear, by the way, from how Lydia first spoke it, that the label was a derisory one adopted privately between the Solyitnovs). My mission here is finished; Lydia has given me no personal reason for taking up her cause, and as for freedom, human rights in the abstract, my reflexes are callused from over-exposure to causes; there are young contributors at Babel — Ada Boyle is one — who, reporting the hundredth or thousandth flagrant abuse, can still fill their voices with real-seeming (and insidiously lovable) tears and anger, but my reaction by now is mainly boredom, a coded term for resentment at the unending demands on whatever empathy is left in my tank; the world is not a fair place, nor any approximation attainable.

Carina; Carina would say with arresting simplicity, "*Mais, Mark, la pauvre,*" meaning first the daughter, and living up to the certainty of that compassion may be why I hear myself say, "My interest is not career-based; coercion, intimidation, annoy me. I can probably prolong my stay here another day or so, and you can reach me via Celeste, if you make up your mind you've had enough of this."

Less forbidding eyes locked to mine, she struggles with a range of feelings, and eventually decides on, "Thank you." Not heartwhole or definitively convinced of my good intentions, it is, in effect, a hedged bet, in case I am what I claim to be — but nonetheless, a small, welcome warmth is kindled between us, and I can suggest without giving offense, "Celeste deserves better than Harry Galek. I can get you out."

"At my age," she begins, and visibly rejects continued debate. "I must go. I will think about what you tell me."

"Not too long," lightly. "I have to leave here without being seen to."

"I'll go first, the front way; Sergei, the security man, walks with me to the labs. Go the way you came; if you stay this side of the drive there is plenty of cover — " Is it movies, or the corrupted world we're forced to live in, or is it just the memory of childhood games, that lets ordinary people glide so effortlessly into the language and manner of conspiracy?

Morning is growing lighter, but no warmer, if anything the opposite; what seemed a chilly dawn is turning into a raw day, ragged clouds sliding swiftly out of a bleak northeast, and I think affectionately of the lined anorak prudently brought, hanging in the back of the Volvo; it is not only for surreptitious purposes that my going is swift and huddled.

And seemingly unobserved; I have no way of knowing whether my watcher was the same Sergei who (I trust) carries, like an enamoured schoolboy, Lydia's clobber to the labs, or some other Sergei who concluded he had missed me, and returned to base, but I regain the corner of the château without sighting anyone, retrieve the anorak and put it on, deciding that to appear warmly dressed will give plausibility to an innocent stroll in the grounds, if anyone asks where I've been.

At my age, and I could follow her thought; Lydia has, so far as I know, never left her homeland, unless you count Moscow (then held to be the capital of her homeland); from indications in her talk I gather she knows some English, and as a scientist may well have a working knowledge of German, but she comes at the end of a generation, the last, probably, for whom (especially in this part of the world) foreign countries were far more *foreign* and forbidding than ever they could be for mine. Conceived in Dusatia, born in Washington, speaking my first word in Paris, I'm scarcely typical, but everyone my age and younger grew up in a blanding world; if we travel without fear, it's also without much excitement, knowing that at the end of almost any flight will be enough tawdry imitation America to make us feel right at home, folks, fast foods, formica, fast highways besieging the anciently typical in self-conscious ghettos, where the tourists tour, so as to make once-proud countries into collections of theme-parks, Windsorland, Shakespearland-on-Avon, Montmartreland, Mozart-and-Trappland, tee-shirts for all.

I was saying; for Lydia the prospect of beginning again, in a new place and a new language, is understandably daunting — but surely anything would be better than the present intolerable impasse. Perhaps I should have hammered harder at her duty to the daughter. Perhaps, in rebuttal, I should tend my own potato-patch.

It is still too early for Galek to be stirring; by myself I pad about till I find a place to shave and then to bathe, though the effect, with a strangely-designed shower head which, instead of a spray, produces a stream of varying intensity, doggedly tepid no matter how the twin controls are manipulated, is more like hosing down. Not until all memory of Evgenia has been soaped, scoured and towelled away do I judge myself fit to return unintercepted to the magical blue phone and tap out Carina's number. Moment of apprehension, and she picks up, and conveys delight.

"I rang last night, but there was no answer."

She snuffles a small laugh. "Ah, yes. I went to dinner with Ketil (plangent internal chord of the augmented eleventh). So that's done. Poor Ketil, he's even more fragile than I thought. When I told him I wasn't going home with him, he gave me a list of all the celebrities he's slept with, like a C.V. I think it was meant to make me grateful he had lowered himself to my humble level. Oh, the men — not you, my love."

Mais si, me too. "`I see that nose of his, but not the dog I shall throw it to — '" in English.

"Quoi?" She follows the words, but lacks a context.

I explain, and her response is to half-sing, half-hum a few measures from Verdi's setting of the Willow Song. Then, "We should read the big Shakespeares together, in English, no? In Italian, in French, they are wonderful, but poetry — so much is lost. Where are you?"

Relieved that my acknowledged and unnecessary and, in the expression, unprecedented descent into moorish hell has left her unfazed, I tell her, and cautiously answer her cautious question as to progress (how could any bugger know that, between us, `the translation' refers to the hoped-for change in Lydia's state?), while with infantile sensualism I urgently wonder whether and how she's clothed, and am both gratified and perturbed to hear my throaty self enquiring. Carina, if startled, loses no time on that; there is a small laugh, and she drops instantly into a matched voluptuousness, breathing me exact, caressing details, here omitted, Charlie. "If you were here — " she teases, and I respond with a tender aggressiveness made the more elegantly sensuous by our language (French). Despite last night's protracted and now damned exercise, more than my morale is raised when we reluctantly disconnect. It verges on the occult, that purely aural signals, electrically and electronically encoded, transmitted over great intervening space and retranslated into sound, can bring about, or trigger, the most observable of transient physical changes; no wonder there has been, through all recorded human experience, an awed, ribald virtual cult of tumescence.

IV

Hoping not to encounter Evgenia, who would instantly diagnose my condition (or, for that matter, the porcelain princess, who might not), I shuffle off, directing my thoughts to the Plantagenet succession, to Carlyle, to the policy-speeches of Lady Thatcher, the intriguingly-spaced sums of consecutive prime integers. It may be that at the same time, eavesdroppers are doing their best to perplex a conspirators' code out of what is, in their sense anyway, perfectly innocent.

By still very slanted daylight, the monstrous painting in the lounge is even worse, all the stiffness of Seurat mated to the painstaking technique of Holman Hunt, but I do note that one of the sober revellers, a wasp-waisted, blazered bloke in a boater, strongly resembles Galek, and wonder whether he introduced the picture in evidence during the 'ancestral lands' scandal. The conjecture leads to closer examination, and I become fairly sure that some of the paint there is newer, and that Harry has had the face altered to emphasize the resemblance. No doubt he has been guilty of more lethal lies, but none, surely, more pathetic than forging an ancestor.

The nearby piano, a three-quarter grand of an obscure Russian make, has a very deceptive action, oddly counterweighted, so that while the initial attack must be resolute, after inertia is overcome the key seems to drop away from the finger; this evasion of anything called touch is partly responsible for the hard, percussive sound it produces, though I can't help suspecting that the actual cabinetry must be a wafery veneer of glossy cherry-wood over something like galvanised steel, or possibly high-impact poly-something. My arpeggiated chord, more obtrusive than intended, dies away to silence, and underneath Bach on the music-stand I discover an old Mozartian friend.

"Don't stop." Celeste, her hair merely brushed, looking, in jeans and smock shirt (white cotton with highly traditional appliqué strips of bright embroidery), much more like a conventional teener — if that; the absence of any lipstick or introduced allure makes her younger than most Anglo-American fifteen-year-olds as they have now become. She must, I suppose, resemble her late father; I can catch no echo of Lydia, unless in the vague aura of perpetual resentment.

She crowds in to breathe on my neck. "Would you show me that?"

"What?"

"*Di-um*, that, is it a grace-note? I hear them, but I don't know how to do it so it sounds right."

Understandable, I suppose, with her woefully neglected rhythmic discipline; it's hardly possible to talk of anticipating the beat when the pulse itself is so wayward. Fortunately, I instruct better than I execute; by contrast with Wilde's Algernon, I don't play with wonderful expression, but I do play accurately, or mostly so, as is expectable with someone whose mother always considered piano teacher to be her reserve occupation, fallable back on in any unforeseen emergency. Having Celeste replace me on the bench, I turn to the *rondo alla turca*, and with a forefinger beat out on the piano top a rhythm for her — well below customary performance tempo (which surely exceeds Mozart's suggestion of *allegretto*), but still not slow enough for her to maintain.

"I have seen your mother — " a murmur whose bare audibility itself enjoins discretion.

"When?"

"This morning, at her cottage. Galek mustn't know."

From her stooped, peering attitude she swivels to look me in the face, her own bright with mysteriously-triggered hope. "Are you going to get us away from here?"

"Sssh." The girl's extraordinary leap of perception must mean, I'm afraid, that I appear for her as the coming-true of a well-worn dream. Forefinger business again, lowering the tempo further; Celeste with a last flicking look in my eyes obediently turns back to the keyboard. "If possible, yes. If I can — if your mother — "

"Ah! — " the exasperated interjection might equally be over once more smudging the notes. "I'll see her later, for lunch, perhaps." A suggestion almost of menace, like `leave her to me.'

"Who are you from?" she mutters.

"No one — " which is true now; Gossbrooke's programme has gone out the window. "No, no, don't lock your wrist — " hearing noises off that suggest we are to be interrupted.

Now at about half-speed and encouraged to drop notes rather than mess up the tempo, she can get it fairly right, and I can demonstrate the quick turn of the wrist that gives the grace-notes their negligible duration; her delight at learning the trick, coloured as it is with larger hope, makes her sober face shine with authentic youth, a pleasure to witness, and a sad caution, now that I am rashly committed to what may not be possible.

"Ah, you play — " Galek is with us, and morning has also worked magic with him; he is groomed, sober, reasonable, hair and eyes in place, canvas shoes, casual fawnish trousers, light-blue shirt over a cream turtleneck all irreproachable; he is, therefore, more to be feared. Only a head made of titanium could withstand last night's nightmare melange of congeners to wake unpunished.

"Not well — " the new day has also ushered in linguistic sanity; as with Celeste it is Galek's own tongue we are in.

"Oh!" Celeste reproaches, inaccurately convicting me of false modesty. I wish she could stop looking at me like a happy spaniel anticipating walkies; if Galek weren't so absorbed in some preoccupation of his own he would surely guess something is up.

"What are your plans?" he demands. "You can stay for another day, two days, perhaps?"

"I'd have to clear it with Brussels," I lie. With no other base for maintaining contact with and pressure on Lydia, this is, of course, exactly what I want, but it would be a mistake to appear too eager.

"We have another piano," Galek adds, at first mysteriously, but how this connects to his desire to prolong my visit is soon to be made plain.

"I have an opera," he proclaims, going to a cabinet and producing, after a brief rummage, a bulky sheaf of pages. "Short opera, *Popula* one-act, never performed. I wrote it for full orchestra, but it is fine in a two-piano version; Celeste and I have played it — " (could this be the reason I seemed to detect a slight wince from the girl when the work was mentioned?) — "But for a full performance, my voice is needed, basso, small part, but I can't perform it at the piano; if you play, we can have a full run-through, tomorrow, tonight."

He is an eruption of enthusiasm, riffling pages, and it's only prudent to point out to him that my playing, especially of unfamiliar music, will be lucky to rise to the level of mediocrity.

"Nonsense, English nonsense. At the European shooting, nineteen eighty-something, I met this man, Goosebrook — "

"Gossbrooke?" I'm startled, but the reference appears, or is passed off as, innocent.

"Gossbrooke, Lord Ivan, yes, and he tells me that with a pistol he is `not so bad.' English not so bad, he took the medal by a mile. You and Celeste can play very well, it is not difficult.

Popula, the title part, is mezzo, perfect for my niece," and Celeste mentions that Evgenia, astonishingly, had some training at the Akademiya in Sofia — all the more improbable considering her dismissal of Bach as `cemetery music.' At my purely telepathic request, Celeste now is doing what she can to mask excitement, with the smug, overly poker-faced look of an especially bad player picking up four of a kind with nothing wild.

As an astonishing instance of self-absorption, Galek, quite obviously, ascribes her ill-suppressed radiance to enthusiasm for his opus, putting a large, seigneurial hand on her head, as if to murmur, `there, there, my child, I know.'

He does say, "Evgenia's mother can do the spoken role. She was an actress, and I can coach her."

Poring over his text, he also mutters something about a tenor on the security staff and an ad hoc chorus — oh, this has all the components of an epic disaster, and could not be less related to my reasons for being here; nothing would make me miss it.

The score Galek unfolds is, thank heavens, an actual two-piano reduction, with relevant patches of text pencilled in; I hadn't been fancying an attempt at running transcription from a full score (at Oxford, I knew a girl, Czech, who could apparently do that brilliantly, even with Mahler and Strauss, but maturer and more sceptical consideration convinced me she stuck the scores on the piano simply for effect, and knew the transcriptions by heart).

And all the time I'm considering how this project can be made to serve my reckless resolve. Clearly, and for no more valid reason than her own desire for freedom, Celeste has bought me on sight, a trust that might be touching, but strikes me, before that, as demanding; children (and in this she is very much a child) draw on frightening energies to turn conjecture into a binding promise. One obvious point; with her daughter taking part, Lydia will undoubtedly be invited to the performance, and to have the two of them in one place may be a beginning.

Evgenia sails in, a voluminous, huge-sleeved surcoat of violet satin worn over blouse and jeans, endorses Galek's project and her part in it with somewhat dutiful enthusiasm, and with an induced shudder complains about the chill; Galek, turning pages, only pays attention when she threatens she may be unable to sing unless kept comfortably warm.   When, with a house-proud reference to `central heating, all new,' he goes off impatiently to see to its ignition, Evgenia throws me a conspiratorial look of triumph; I smile slightly but am not convinced, as her expression brags, that she has Harry in the classic signet-ring (or cigar-band)

conformation of the aging sensualist and the poppet with a whim
of iron; probably, without his opera to bring off he would have
brusquely told her to put on a sweater.

   With the wind moaning outside, and the new installation
rumbling, hissing, and occasionally banging into life, we are
launched, after bread, stewed fruit and coffee, on the oddest of
days, centred on what Galek calls, and may actually have been
built as, the theatre, high, narrow, lavishly rococo, although it
might as readily pass for the chapel in some Styrian Benedictine
monastery, discounting the secularism of some of the gilt-and-
plaster ornamentation, the well-fed, jocose *amorini* and a few
wanton but never ambling nymphs, thrusting knees, breasts, and
caressable flanks from flanking pillars; overhead is a moulded riot
of restless (and grimy) decoration. approximating coiling ribbons,
stylized foliage, seashells, armorial bearings, eruptions of fruit and
vegetables, ineffectual weaponry...   There is no stage, only low
wooden platform in the open area at one end, under a blind cupola
painted with various foreshortened and unimportant half-dressed
persons ascending to where a cluster of bright lights has been
hung, all faced by several rows of pew-like seating.

   Here, the piano is manhandled; the other one, also lugged
in by a squad of spooks, is an upright, aptly called, being a
century-old instrument in mahogany sobriety, fully twenty hands
high, with a dour-faced aspect of unassailable moral rectitude, fit
for metrical settings of the psalms and salon songs of sensually but
never sexually longing lo-ho-hove, next to which the newer
instrument, with its shamelessly displayed legs, looks positively
indecent. At first, the placement, absurdly, is back-to-back, as if
in the classic yin-yang interlock of paired grands, but I
successfully protest that the upright turns the two players, who
must be able to communicate, into Pyramus and Thisbe, divided
by a wall; a saner side-by-side formation, angled next to the stage-
left edge of the platform, is adopted.   Another problem is
anticipated when Galek arrives with both his holograph and a new-
minted copy for Celeste and me; I am unreasonably jarred by the
idea that somewhere aside from all the archaism the château
includes an office with a photo-copier — no doubt, with
computer-terminals as well, and if I have been sifted through its
memory, my part in the rescue, if that's what it was, of Christa
Rasch, already twice alluded-to, can never be far from Galek's
mind, and the analogy with Lydia's detention, or Celeste's, hard to
ignore. Yet if he has suspicions — and I don't know what reports
he's had of my early-morning wanderings — he's concealing them

effectively under blazing obsession with the opera, and he stands by the two pianos, humming darkly and privately conducting with a pencil, as the girl and I tackle the music for the first time.

The piano part, reduced from at least the conception of an orchestral score, would not be particularly difficult if it weren't so wretchedly laid out — allotted may be the juster term; the *primo*, which, deferentially, is assigned to me, at the grand, has to play low left-hand octaves (trombone and basses?) while simultaneously lunging for a (flute?) trill with the right, whilst the *secondo* part uncomfortably crowds in the middle; sight-reading, never a leading skill of mine, I drop bundles of notes, and poor Celeste with her defective rhythmic discipline, is often obliged to skip whole bars just to keep up. I ought to mention that while both pianos have been kept in relative tune, the two middle Cs are an excruciating quarter-tone or perhaps fractionally less apart.

Galek, oblivious to these technical and executant shortcomings, nods proudly when something comes off according to plan, and utters directions to supplement those written in the score: "Gradual, gradual *crescendo* — now, *sforzando*," or, "Here is merely support for the voices, quite subdued," and, "These are trumpets and other brass, with the drum, *brrr-mm*; now comes the chorus, D-flat, orchestra *mezzo-forte*, so, yes, excellent!" He never stops us, and the only halts come when Celeste or I or both of us get into an impossible tangle; using a red pencil I mark those passages for further attention, but any hope of really working at the music is doomed by the needs of the vocal performers, for whom we have to supply the needed accompaniment for parts Galek particularly desires to try over.

Noon comes, and Celeste, with a meaning sidelong look for me, informs Galek that her mother expects her for lunch today.

"No, no. We will have a working lunch here, sandwiches and beer — well, not beer for you, sandwiches and milk."

"But my mother will be cooking. I can be back in an hour — less, if there's need."

Galek's reluctance seems innocent of any motive except the compulsion to have us all devote every breathing moment to the production; on the other hand, if he wishes to mask Lydia's forced sequestration from the influential international media (*i.e.*, me) he can't be seen denying a girl lunch with her mother.

To me, he explains, "Celeste's mother is an important scientist, biologist — "

"Bio-chemist," Celeste emends.

"She is doing very important research, nutritional research

for the government. Solyitnova's husband, Celeste's father, was a very great physicist, he did important original work."

"Andrei Solyitnov," I supply rather than query, supposing that of alternatives, bland ignorance would be the more suspicious. "He won a Nobel, back in the eighties."

"Ah, you follow science — " still affable, but with appraisal now in his narrowed eyes.

"I'm a scientific illiterate, but some time ago I was thinking of doing a television series interviewing Nobel laureates — " Gossbrooke's original cover-story given posthumous half-life. "Solyitnov — "

"Yes, he died — " extending an arm to hug Celeste's shoulders. "Very tragic — I knew him quite well, we were friends."

The girl's face is altogether expressionless, but Galek sees his sentiment has painted him into a corner. "Yes, you must not disappoint your mother. Go, go."

"You should wear a warm coat — " Evgenia has sauntered into the discussion. "I think we'll have snow."

"Be back in one hour," Galek warns.

"If you're going to rehearse Ludmila in the long speech — " my entry — "I can manage that accompaniment by myself." It consists of simple chordal and arpeggiated punctuation, reminiscent of *continuo*, but with no indicated opportunities for improvisation.

"Lydia will wish to see the performance — she must come — " Galek, once more setting my teeth on edge with his larded solicitude towards the impassive Celeste.

"When?"

"Seven, yes — seven this evening, and after, there will be wine and small food, *refreshments* — " the English word, with a grin. "I can send a car."

"She can walk, just as easily."

"We'll see how the weather goes. Now, go, go, have your lunch."

At school and after, I've been peripherally part of some amateur productions — which this ostentatiously is — and often observed that at some point the instigators or leading participants are always tempted away from their rapt devotion to the actual show by the wanton Thaïs of Audience, a lust for filling seats often diverting energy and scarce time away from making sure there'll be something worth seeing and hearing. The command directed at Lydia has given Galek, as it were, a glimpse of that inviting thigh, and after our sandwiches he abandons us, to `Make some calls to people,' willing, it seems, to arrange transportation for the far-flung or reluctant. The alleged tenor, a short-legged, blue-jowled young tough in an olive-green shirt, poring over his part, asks me to give him a note, which he hums but does not sing, and after pacing for a while, mouthing a silent performance, puts his jacket back on, pats at the bulge in his side pocket, and wanders uneasily away.

Evgenia, who, apart from her habitual rapid, candid inventory of possibilities, has scarcely acknowledged her fellow-performer, seated in a front pew, score lain aside, yawns catlike over a Russian paperback *Great Gatsby*. Her mother, Ludmila, looking far less fussy and a great deal more actorly in ribbed sweater and loose slacks, half-glasses perched on her nose, comes and seats herself at the upright. With a sidelong glance for me, she picks out a one-finger *Frère Jacques*, which I dutifully echo in canon, adding the harmony, but the assurance with which she modulates to the black keys, then, two-handed, tacking on the spectral bugle-call of a tail-piece to take us into Mahler's grotesque version, suggest that she might have made a better orchestra for Galek's opera than either of the nominated pianists.

When I say so, she shakes her head. "I have no understanding of these new forms." So today it's Arkadina.

"Then won't you tell me all about your triumph in Kharkov?"

"You must allow, I've always known how to dress." She laughs attractively, and without using a hand, lifts her chin to waft me a small kiss.

"Mother," Evgenia complains, having somehow observed it without leaving her novel. "Nobody thinks anything of your flirting. It's so *yesterday*."

Never conclude that you have completely catalogued anyone; who would have supposed that Evgenia is a somewhat haphazardly trained but authentic mezzo-soprano, not the breathy seductress her offstage persona would suggest, but with an ample and even matronly quality to her voice. She is not shy about a whooping portamento, and generally arrives well sharp going down, flat going up, sliding blandly onto the note like a cat disguising a misjudged leap, and her acting is light years over the top, what Wagner (speaking of Meyerbeer) called uncaused effect, consistently impassioned, and even up another notch from rehearsal when the dragooned audience (about thirty, including staff) is in place, and the opera launched.

Galek's remark about coaching Ludmila in the spoken role was not, as it seemed, the pure arrogance of authorship; though an experienced actress, she speaks no English but has managed so soon to learn the part phonetically — meaning, of course, Galek's idea of English phonetics (after lunch he did check with me on the pronunciation of *throughout*; true, the perverse English addiction to the *ough* combination, which has at least six pronunciations, not counting regional variants, sets a booby-trap for learners). To my eye less than happy with a half-understood part, she covers unease with well-schooled rep-theatre routine (the `how can I put this?' gesture with a circling finger, the quick turn on a heel to convey impatience), and I doubt the content really matters; there's probably no one in the audience who can follow it completely, or could, even if the English was idiomatic and the pronunciation native.

The piece, heavy-handedly, is intended as a satire against the inherent romantic hypocrisy of corrupted western democracy — it is hard to dispute Galek's diagnosis, impossible to endorse his cure — very likely conceived in the Cold War era, but effortlessly adaptable, like Galek himself, to the authoritarian nationalism of Kvitka and his party. Evgenia's part, Popula, is a `virgin wishing her happiness,' a quest set forth in the overlong opening monologue, part spoken, part sung, which, insofar as it emerges from the tangles of misusage and the red-herrings of Evgenia's overacting, is a rejection of `old manners,' as represented by Ludmila's wordy character, Mater, pronounced, in dated British style, to rhyme with *later*, thus unconsciously reminiscent of Victorian-Edwardian school stories pitting jolly good chaps against frightful rotters; among many moments of unintended humour, the best comes when Popula, rejecting the charge of (political) immaturity, wishing to assert, on the contrary, that the elder is, in her opinion, criminally impervious to any new ideas, chants, *Some say old ways are best to stand firm, but I say, Mater, what an utter brick you are!*

Rigid adherence to received wisdom, she reflects, is `worse sin by much than follies by commitment,' but Galek's high purpose does not allow him to complete the retro-Freudian metaphor with some robust unvirgining.

Instead, after odd, wordless warblings, half-liberated Popula is blandished by a sinister but `superficiously attractive' (so designated in the text) libertine, Balloton or Pollon (why the divided personality is at first obscure; the characters are indistinguishably repellent), who wishes to purchase her passive compliance with the false jewel of Choice, later glossed (for those who don't get it) as `so-called Free Vote.'

While the thug tenor has evidently had some voice training, belonging to the Semi-Strangulated Slav school (he might be unwittingly effective as the Idiot in Mussorgsky's masterpiece), he has none for the stage, stiff with the self-consciousness of the feeblest village amateur, who thinks everything, standing, moving, shaking hands, asking a question, must be acted and seen to be acted; *this is me, crossing the stage.* Something he does to excess; at length I recognise the intent behind his character's double-naming is to portray more-or-less identical twins or tanists, approaching their prey, Popula, now from right, now from the left, so to satirize the illusory nature of electoral alternatives, where `all is for commerce, all profit-making mega-corporation' (and here the accompaniment baldly raids *Butterfly*, with its echoes from *Oh, Say Can You See?*).

Chivvied, confused, brave but nonplussed, Popula is rescued from dilemma by the entry of the basso, Novy — Galek himself, with the widest vibrato I have ever heard — whose arrival routs Balloton-Pollon, not quite with `*O, Freunde, nicht diese Töne,*' but a distorted reminiscence, in my left hand, of the Big Tune helps me identify a weird version of Schiller's Ode:

> *Fresh system! nice present from the Heaven,*
> *Elisium's feminine offspring,*
> *Here we come with drunk god-given,*
> *Into where is terrific everything —*

which has the minimal (and lone) merit of avoiding the obvious.

As with Beethoven, however, this ushers in the chorus, and the chorus, also more-or-less sight-reading after a very brief and partial run-through, is a revelation. The actual music is cheap and nasty, too reminiscent of Prokofiev's scores for Eisenstein, with some jarring interjections borrowed from Britten and an underwash of that spurious, ubiquitous Triumph of the Masses style found (for example) in rhinestone adaptations from Victor Hugo, but Galek has raided the Church, a contingent trucked in from the Zmin congregation (whether Roman or Orthodox rite is unclear and immaterial), cunningly costumed, anyone would say, but these fitless trousers, stiff-necked shirts and shadowed chins, the ample scarlet and royal blue skirts, the hooding head-scarves, are, I recognise, merely their normal Sunday get-ups; characteristic by nature, they live their archaic peasant parts.

There are only seventeen of them, but the three deep basses lay down a dark, cast-iron foundation for the plummy baritones and altos, while the tenors and sopranos clamber belatedly onto high notes with the unanimity of long practice, and provide that edge, that hint of hysteria, that eternally haunts (and makes haunting) Eastern liturgical music.

What they are singing, in the weirdest-yet approximation to English, is both incomprehensible and immaterial; happily, the instrumental parts are limited here to some low pedal points (probably trombones and tubas) and an inoffensive mid-range shimmer (muted violas with cellos?), little scope for error, and for five extraordinary minutes it is very nearly convincing; if Galek had been satisfied to end with the grateful proletariat hymning the advantages of a prescribed but benevolent nationalist oligarchy (some obvious erasures in the text suggest it was once the all-knowing politburo), his opera would leave an impression well beyond its overall merits. But, no, his anxious determination to have his message understood by any nine-year-old (one, that is, able to understand wild dialects of English) causes him to bring back didactic Novy and transmuted Popula, even to reintroduce verbose Mater as a repentant, prosaic convert telling her daughter she now 'lengthily sees the light,' before, too late, the chorus throws in a very abbreviated, attenuated snippet of terraced Mahlerian transcendance, both pianos thundering away below middle C. It is over.

Now, while the applause swells and Evgenia's damned snow, an unneeded potential complication, is beginning to powder down, I must fill in the detached but cumulatively headlong events of the day, a newly competent Celeste and I contriving opportunities for swift conferrings, while Galek endlessly clarified his already over-explained intentions, and Evgenia, during a technical conference involving poor Igor (his real name is Mykola), who had to manipulate various light-switches, found a moment to tell me not to waste my time with a child, or alternatively an old hag (her mother, presumably), and ask if I would not like to see her again late tonight, after Harry, who would predictably be drunk, was asleep. With undisguised aphrodisiac intent she reminded me, if that's the word, of last night's recreational tanglings, and my preoccupied failure to make disinclination final adds one more superfluous anxiety to muddy my scheming.

It's all wrong, the jerry-built substitute for a plan, but idiot simplicity may turn out to be a virtue, and there might not be another chance — given the opportunity for more reflection, Lydia's nerve might fail. I don't know and can't imagine what persuasions Celeste used, but at our first chance for private communication when she came back from lunch — we had our heads together at the upright, copying various markings (and a two-bar edit) from my score to hers — Celeste muttered, "My mother says, when?"

"She's agreed to leave?" The sudden squeeze at my heart, Oh, God, told me my wimpier or more staid component had been treacherously hoping she would remain indecisive, and I could go safe home and tell Gossbrooke, no dice.

Celeste made a sour face. "Just about. She says, when?"

I wanted to say, tonight, right after the performance, but that was obviously impractical; how could she be told? No doubt she had returned to the labs, and Galek was not going to tolerate another absence by Celeste. Besides, the roads hereabouts are not generously signposted, and darkness, while comforting, would also be confusing. My intent is simply to drive into — into an adjacent country — and either put the Solyitnovim on a plane for — not for London — and drive back by myself, or to fly with them if it seems more prudent, in which case Gossbrooke's untouched advance can pay for repatriation of the rented car.

"First light in the morning," I said.

"What about the guards?" — meaning, I supposed, on the door, but possibly others.

"We'll work that out. Your mother can bring her stuff through the grounds — one suitcase — and wait in the car, the dark-blue Volvo."

Here, we had to switch to music-talk. Galek having finished instructing a driver who was helping to assemble the audience, bore down on us, beaming. "What do you think, Kearns — should we have a drum? One of the guys used to play drum in a military band — perhaps when the chorus comes in, and again at the end; I have tympani there in the full score."

I judged that unless his guy had access to such a rarely-owned instrument, anything less or less tunable would only be intrusive. Galek quickly conceded the point, and had me mark down a couple of dramatic pauses he had decided on.

About teatime, though no tea came (we were promised a light early dinnerlet to carry us through to the post-performance buffet), there was a break more formal than the frequent spells of inactivity distributed by the haphazard cobbling of this rehearsal, and Celeste and I found another private moment in a corridor, waiting for the loo to be free.

"Do you have enough of your clothes here? And a bag?"

"Most of the things I like are at home. My mother knows. We're going to have to leave most of our stuff behind, aren't we."

"You'll get new stuff."

"I've got books," gloomily.

So, I would bet, had her mother, and not merely recreational reading, but there have been scientists, scholars, writers before who've had to abandon their libraries to escape oppression. In English, I quoted, "*Who cannot cast away a treasure at need is in fetters.*"

"What?"

Assuming she knew enough standard Russian, I managed a suitably archaisized translation in that language, and, astonishingly, she recognised it. "Oh, Tolkien. I love Tolkien."

When the audience began to assemble, I was duly introduced, amongst others, to Lydia Solyitnova, still spare and anxious, but not unattractive in a dark-blue calf-length cocktail-dress; her decisive nod meant more than the brisk acknowledgement (of my name, my function, my presence here) that it simulated, the dark eyes resolutely meeting mine.

Enraptured audience (Harry must have rounded up every sycophant in his fiefdom) and performers now mingle — not the chorus from Zmin, who remain in sober formation amidst the swirl, looking prepared, like the Old Guard at Waterloo, to die but not surrender; such earned compliments as come their way are received with corporate smiles, corporate modesty. Galek, of course, is the central attraction and has an arm round Evgenia's waist, pulling her against him like a security-blanket. Much of the praise for the tenor is coming from four of his litter-mates on the security staff, who seem obscurely puzzled by his hitherto-unrevealed talent; there is a glowering reserve in their felicitations, but since his part required him more than once to embrace the unwilling heroine (which he did with stiff and posturing determination), I foresee some private ribaldry to come; the licenced opportunity to molest the boss's mistress (who is doubtless the subject of frequent guy-talk) has, surely, universal appeal.

I nod politely to undiscerning praise for my pianism, while Celeste wanders away on the trail of her mother, who is complimenting Ludmila, only slightly the shorter — I'm assuming the topic; their animated nose-to-nose intimacy looks just like swapping recipes, or remedies for the rheumatics.

Galek, glowing — in part because his chosen costume for the oracular role is a dark red turtleneck with a sort of subdued luminosity — holds up his free hand to move an adjournment to the `big hall,' where food and wine are waiting, and in the resultant tidal movement for the door it is natural enough for Lydia and Celeste to linger for mother-and-daughter talk, which I ignore, letting myself be captured temporarily by blonde Anya, the wife of Demetz, who once, as a girl (she says), was introduced to Sviatoslav Richter, he having just played the *Appassionata*. I can't think why anything that happened tonight should remind her of that occasion, but resist the ludicrous temptation to airily explain how my approach to *Pictures at an Exhibition* differs from Richter's.

By the look of it, Hartmann, the wretchedly inept artist-architect whose abysmal paintings, posthumously displayed, somehow inspired that work, might well have had a hand in revising the decor of the Big Hall, hitherto unvisited. Whatever its original style, someone, about the time ill-starred Nicki and Sasha ascended to their doomed throne, overlaid it, with either an eastern variant on pre-Raphaelite baronial, or a borrowed Kirov set for the palace scene in *Swan Lake*; the result is neither grand nor even grandiose, but merely cluttered. Under a ceiling given unfunctional carved and gilded beams, there is at one end a faux minstrels' gallery (no access, and with no more than 20cm of space behind), massively made and supported on massive, complicated brackets, given writhing red-eyed dolphins, pregnant gold-striped pumpkins and fat-petalled flowers (for example; my eye cannot take in all that is carved) while the centre of the gallery sprouts a shock of romantic and fanciful banners, their brilliant colours dimmed by age and dust. The long side-walls are decorated with helms, crossed halberds, broadswords (all reproduction), chrysanthemums of fanned arrows, and brazier-like wrought-iron sconces now given over to grape-clusters of small, low-wattage electric lights. Across the head of the hall is a ponderous high table on ornate trestles echoing the style of the gallery, and behind that, intricate panelling to represent a row of archways that lead nowhere, the central one, flanked by curving pillars of knights and ladies in low relief and a Byzantine excess of overwrought decoration, frames giant-sized armorial bearings, a complicated shield, quartered and requartered, surmounted by a ferocious, golden-eyed, carved gryphon, regardant en couchant.

Not a great hall by mediaeval standards — and therefore overwhelmed by the scale of its ornamentation — this must be where large and formal dinners, various celebrations occur — likely enough, the place where Andrei Solyitnov, after gulping down some unwise vodkas, blabbed to Galek about his notional Protein Bomb, and so bespoke his own grave.

At present, a pair of long tables have sandwiches and other portable foods, and plentiful wine, red and white in large bottles, phalanxes of plastic glasses; the Zmin choir, I note, is not slow to slake its corporate thirst.

Neither is Galek, but he is enough the feudal host to hand out more than he swallows. I have just been overtaken by mask-faced Celeste, now slightly and casually separated from her mother, and am extending congratulations for her bravely sustained part in the music-making, when Harry bears down upon us precariously managing two-and-a-half glasses of white wine, and initiating a miniature comedy. Retaining one, he hands me the other filled glass, and extends the half-filled to Celeste, calling out to nearby Lydia, "A special occasion, she must be allowed some wine." The mother enters no objection, and now Galek has one hand free, to allow a large gesture, calling general attention to "tonight's fine orchestra, our two pianists." There is applause from all sides, and both fine pianists evince shy gratification, Celeste linking hands at the stem of her glass, waist-high, and dropping her chin as if in smiling prayer, while I nod diffidently in all directions, like a mechanical mandarin on a music-box. But obtaining maternal sanction for Celeste's minor debauch has made Galek acutely conscious of Lydia's winelessness, and he abruptly thrusts the third glass at her. His right hand now being unexpectedly — and no doubt poignantly — empty, he uses it to seize mine in a determined handshake, effusing to the effect that without my contribution tonight's performance could not have come off so happily.

"It was a success, do you think? Not perfect everywhere, but — "

"The choir is excellent." He still has my hand, or my wrist, now with his left, and is without seeming to persistently manoeuvring to get us side by side and sauntering to where he can replace his lost wine, like so many human enterprises, made difficult only by a meaningless desire for subterfuge.

The only windows here are well above head-high in one long wall, but word from the greater world is that the snow is barely accumulating, and appears to be tapering off. Still, the threat to driving is already starting to abridge this celebration, with those with farther to go than the small contingent from Lydia's labs (near where, I understand, is a new-built hamlet of small, efficient houses) re-emphasising their delight in Galek's opera as cue for taking their leave. A few, however, intimates and those who have come farthest, are being accommodated for the night, and this includes the Zmin choir, though I cannot imagine how; perhaps the security people have spare dormitory space.

I am captured next by one of the stayers, a tall, stylish, not pretty but pleasant woman near my own age, who is both wife to Galek's lawyer, and a sculptor; she knows my work, and tells me Harry is 'so proud' that I have come so far to discuss a new English version of his novel; she is even aware of my mother's Shakespeare translations, and the civilised tone of our chat is very seductive, almost persuading me to disbelieve the dark universe of the Protein Bomb, Solyitnov's suicide, the detention of Lydia and Celeste.

Who, peripherally, have their heads together near the sandwich table, near enough, when Lydia puts her wine-glass down with a clearly final air, to hear her announce departure.

Galek also overhears, and breaks off his own conversation. "No, going, why?" he booms, approaching her. "The weather is poor; stay the night, go home in the morning."

This is awkward for her; she wants to adhere to the plan as outlined for Celeste, and I am unable to tell her, yes, no problem, we'll all sneak out together at dawn, and drive round to her cottage to collect her luggage — but, of course, there would then be the manned back gate to negotiate.

In any event, though visibly flustered, it is an act, and quite a skilled one, the brainy academic who, outside her own field, does daft things; Lydia cites (invents, I'm sure it is) a casserole requiring long cooking which she has left in a slow oven. Galek, perhaps with no ulterior purpose, says, very well, but why walk; he'll have someone drive her, and dead on cue there arrives a very junior colleague from the labs, sharp-faced, yellow-haired, destined for early baldness, who tells Lydia he and his girlfriend are about to leave, if she would like a ride. Her relief is visible to me, and Galek merely smiles.

She comes to shake my hand. "How long will you be here?"

"I'll be leaving quite soon."

"Oh. I hope to see you again before you go."

"That would please me, too."

Brief, banal, bourgeois, and now I have no doubt; we're on go.

At the rate he is emptying glasses, the prediction by Evgenia (she is, by the way, very subdued, demure in Popula's plain virginal robe of dark blue) of Harry's drunken slumbers seems a safe bet, though I would feel easier if I could rely on at least twelve hours of untroubled sleep for him (enough time for me to be over the border, well on the way to Warsaw), spiking his drink with one of those `common soporifics' so readily available to characters in crime novels, so rarely found in life: the only common soporifics I ever encounter are pretentious films and leaden books, and I can hardly force Galek to sit through Kubrick's *2001*, or attempt Mann's *Buddenbrooks*. Perhaps, after all, I should have let Minghela in the capital supply me with a thug or two; I am now completely alone, embarked on a course which separates me — I hope — from Galek, but certainly from Gossbrooke. As when journeying to meet with dangerous Ariosto, I have left some rather puny safeguards in Brussels, alarm-bells to sound in the event of my detention or overlong silence, but there is no defence against contrived accidents, and the embassy can be counted on to ask no questions; oh, Carina, Carina *pourquoi ai-je quitté tes douces caresses?* And Evgenia, solicitously bringing me fresh wine under Galek's already-blurring eye, is conspiratorially glittering unsought promises.

V

     Not amongst my prouder memories, it is unchivalrous as well as less than robustly masculine to admit that my means of dealing with Evgenia simply followed the line of least resistance; to let her have her way with me seemed the easiest way to be rid of her. Not to say my part in the actual transaction was passively supine (nor without its strictly physical rewards), but to tell her, quite truthfully, I was disinclined was too risky; who knew how long it might be before she would take no for an answer? — and I had arranged with Celeste to rendezvous with me here, prepared for our departure, near dawn. Alternatively, departing unserviced, Evgenia might have attempted, at about that same time, to rouse (in all senses) the slumbering Harry, clearly undesirable.

     There's a lot less nail-biting in fiction, where laying the arch-villain's beautiful mistress is all in a night's breezy recreation — but that's a post-pubescent extension of juvenile fantasy, a world where there is (for example) no thought of disease, impregnation, substandard performance, regret — no after-odour — how does our suave spy keep himself socially acceptable, going, as often, direct from beddings to briefings, badinage with malign and boastful megalomaniacs, dinner-jacketed chemin de fer, without time or opportunity for bathing? Short of sleep as I am, some cunning internal mechanism allowed me to limit to mere minutes the quite genuine doze during which Evgenia (placated, to be sure, but never satisfied) performed her wraithlike disappearance. Whereupon, yawning and dull, I padded to the nearest bathroom.

     Evgenia has taken up more time than I budgeted for (and let that be my apology, now, across the intervening terrain, and the tenderest farewell I can, in conscience, waft: Evgenia, you made me go on longer than was wise); only another brief, controlled three-quarter doze has intervened, and I am up and quietly dressed, feeling the imminence of dawn rather than reading it on my watch. The snow, a slight but universal dusting, has made it difficult to judge how soon the light will come; at the window, where, in keeping with the generally slipshod maintenance here, most of a broom-handle has been used to prop up the broken slatted wooden shutter, I see a few lazy flakes — or clumps of flakes, larger than last night — sauntering down. My suitcase, never very heavy, is perceptibly lighter now; I'm wearing most of what I brought; having no idea whether the rental car has a working heater, I hope Celeste and her mother will also dress warm — but Lydia surely will, if only for her trek through the grounds.

For the first time, this being that despairing hour, when day, this time, may never come, I am wondering uneasily about night-time security for the château grounds, whether it might enlist, for nasty example, dogs. But Lydia, surely, must know, and some objection to my plan would have come back to me via the daughter — as perhaps it still may; I haven't exchanged any words with Celeste since the last of her earnest, undertone conferences with Lydia. If necessary, we could pick her up, driving to the back gate and finding some way to penetrate the defences there — perhaps I could convince the sentinel that I'm doing Galek a favour, driving Lydia to some eccentrically early conference.

With very slight noise, Celeste arrives, fleece-jacketed, half-carrying, half-dragging a substantial duffel-bag, where angular protrusions suggest she has included some favourite books. No, no dogs, she tells me; her mother is by now or should soon be waiting in the Volvo. In the dim light (I have restricted myself to the small bedside lamp, whose bulb is almost off the low end of the wattage scale) the girl's face is beyond alert, listening, watchful, anticipatory, gravid.

Very briefly, one eye watching for any sign of dawn, I outline how we are to proceed, glossing over the weak part about distracting the guard at the front door. Trusting Celeste only nods understanding; I get into my anorak and we heft our baggage.

"Ah, Kearns, you are going out so soon?" Galek is in the doorway. He means, *early*, and in fact quickly abandons his near-English. "And Celeste, also. You should not be here in a man's bedroom at night, even if dressed for winter." His smile is not a pleasant one.

In a sort of flare-skirted black-and-red Cossack dressing-gown (minus the pectoral cartridges) over baggy blue pyjamas, he comes fully into the room, pushing the door to behind him. His confidence he has the situation well in hand may not be misplaced; one of his non-metaphorical hands is in a pocket, and I don't doubt he's armed.

"I heard a soft noise," he explains, "And as I come out to see, there is little Celeste, going quietly into the bedroom of our guest. This I cannot permit; the girl is in my care."

The girl makes a face. I suspect Galek is lying; the soft noise of someone using a bathroom must be commonplace. Probably that's what he was doing when he by chance spotted Celeste; waking sour-mouthed he might equally have been in quest of the hair of the dog. Belatedly, I see feckless optimism in the supposition a couple of hours of immoderate wine-gulping would indefintely immobilize a Galek; the night before last his somnolence was brought about with the help, not only of much wine, but large helpings of lavender cordial and plum-brandy, man-sized proof, not mere ten or eleven percent of alcohol by volume; I have relied too much on Evgenia's experience, without allowing for either her wishful thinking, nor for the difference in our interests. For her, that Harry would certainly be snoring between, say, midnight and four, was all that mattered.

"What did you think, Kearns, that we were another bunch of simple-minded Dusatians, to let you walk in here and repeat your famous knight-errant act?" He wheels on frozen Celeste. "Your mother, I imagine, must be waiting. She will be so disappointed."

Every vestige of the hearty, appalling feudal host has vanished, leaving us with a highly plausible, coolly calculating counter-intelligence officer. All the same, he doesn't know what to do with a captive western journalist in this newer era, where the appearance of legality matters, and is still interested in keeping a lid on his reason for detaining Lydia; that's why he hasn't summoned reinforcements. But the unfamiliar new persona makes me reconsider all my explanations for his presence here; suspicious from the first, taking note of the earnest conferences between mother and daughter, he may simply have been keeping vigil.

He goes to look out at the dawn; Celeste, in doubt about his intent, shrinks back beside the window, but he hardly sees her.

Thinking it through, a deal perhaps in the making, he turns to confront me again. "Plainly," he says, "you have been told some nonsense about Galyitnova, who, with her daughter, has been under my protection since the untimely death of the husband. Perhaps you have been misled by British or American intelligence, for whom, perhaps, you are working — or you may be simply a Don Quixote — "

It is possible to be the direct agency of someone's death — driving an express train when someone strays on the tracks, locking the airtight truck-door on an undetected stowaway — and suffer no legal consequences, if neither intent nor negligence are there; cause, not effect rules. Fair enough, but our comparative leniency towards attempted murder, when all the elements of the accomplishment — malice, intent, effort, everything but final execution — are present, is surely inconsistent; we reward inefficiency, or let pure chance or a victim's abnormal robustness whittle the penalty down from life (in places, execution) to a fleeting four or five years in chokey; effect and not cause has sudden primacy. I bring this up because, although any judge, any jury in the world, taking into account the whole history of her annexation by Galek, would be inclined to go easy on Celeste, there is no question that her failure to kill him has nothing to do with her intentions, which were clearly murderous; she hits him with all the force of stored frustration, hatred and fear, and he is left alive — moreover, conscious — only because all told there is no more than five-and-a-half stone (say, 35 kilos) of Celeste, and because broom-handles here are made from fir, not ash. As the defective window-shutter comes down with a rattling bang, this one snaps, hitting Galek high on the shoulder, neck and lower skull, and he goes to his knees with a grunt.

Dismayed (so am I) Celeste drops what's left of her weapon. Galek is dazed, and there is no choice; if he collects himself and rises, we're sunk; driven outside the protective pale of friendly outrage, I'll be arrested and convicted (of something provable), the Solyitnovas trapped. Extreme distaste for physical violence is too much of a luxury at that price; from behind, I press Galek down by his shoulders, getting a forearm in front, equally to stop his mouth and save his face — from injury, not embarrassment. Knees on his back — he is still unresisting — I tell a paralysed Celeste to get the hand-towel from the rack next to the bed, then tell her again, more sharply; at last she understands, and moves.

Galek is starting to come alive, but it is not until I pull the gag fiercely tight that he becomes hard to handle; by now Celeste is fully participant, and together we lash struggling arms behind his back, using my necktie, which she brings from the bedside chair. Unable to turn himself over, grunting, Galek kicks out randomly with his feet, and when I capture them it takes all my effort to hold on, while the girl, making a deft noose, loops and secures his ankles with an airy but rope-strong binding conveniently found on the bedside floor. Now I can go into his pocket, and take away the nastily effective-looking 9mm automatic, which is loaded. Galek continues to writhe, making noises like a peeved sea-lion in a sack, but is for the moment neutralized. For the moment.

Celeste says thinly, "I didn't mean to hurt him. I didn't *mean* to," like a very small child blandly, desperately denying the self-evident.

"Yes you did," not curtly, but incontrovertibly. There is no time for guilt, or denial, or anything but action.

"There won't be any shooting, will there?" — as I slip the pistol into my own side-pocket.

"I just don't want to leave it for Galek. He won't stay tied up." The knots aren't bad, but he's going to work free in time.

We emerge cautiously, lugging our bags. Behind the closed door, Galek's muffled bellows are barely audible, and it all has a *déja vu* feeling of familiarity, except that last time my companion was an exasperating if physically flawless international celebrity, and the only person she assaulted was me.

Celeste of course knows the way to the minor, merely functional stair by which I was first brought here. At its foot, a corridor leading to depths of the château inhabited by staff not yet stirring, I take off my anorak, and leave it with Celeste and the baggage, out of sight but within easy earshot of the front entrance. Climbing back upstairs, I take a deep breath to prime myself, and come rattling down the broad main stair, getting the immediate attention of today's doorwarden, who comes up out of his chair.

"Something has happened to Galek, I believe. I heard him cry out, but I'm not sure which is his room." All precisely, if selectively, true. This Sergei, who is in fact Leonid, last night's tenor, has a walkie-talkie clipped on his belt, but except with the fanatically trained, emergency procedures often get lost in an emergency, and without sounding any more general alarm, or even, as the phrase goes, calling for backup, he quits his chair with a barked expletive, and goes bounding up the main stair with all the alacrity of Douglas Fairbanks (senior, need I specify) to rescue or ravish Merle Oberon (I believe it was).

Hastening back to collect Celeste, I very nearly collide with fragile Turandot, making her yawning way in the direction, I guess, of early duty in the kitchen. In breathless Russian, rather than launching into a rousingly appropriate *Nessun' dorma*, I say good morning, and her unperturbed, inexplicably knowing smile, as Celeste emerges, humping her duffel, seems at the brink of a giggle. *On our side, or simply leaping to lubricious conclusions?* Doesn't matter, no affair of hers; she passes on, presumably towards vast samovars for redoubled numbers of wakers.

"You had better put your jacket on," Celeste reproaches, but I won't spare the time; laden, I lead our dash for the door.

On the whole, however, she's quite right; the cold comes like a sudden punch to the diaphragm, and there's blindingly more snow, almost negating what little daylight has struggled to arrive: impossible as it seems I am momentarily confused about our proper direction, then unsure we have found it, though we have only to traverse the terrace, keeping the windowed facade at our left hand.

The descending steps at the corner are a precarious ordeal. but as we round what is the southeast corner of the château, the wind, at least, is abruptly lessened. We grope our way to where the cars are parked; someone, yes, Lydia, emerges from the Volvo to hug her daughter; she has made it so far. Great, except that immediately behind, and walling in the car — not to say, two others — is a vanlike vehicle, into which, I suppose, with some shoving and wedging, the entire Zmin choir might be crammed. Close harmony. The driver's side door there is unlocked, but the key not in the ignition.

Grasping the dilemma, Celeste, scraping snow from her face, says, "We can take the American car." Because of its length, the big old Packard is clear behind, just beyond the van, and Celeste, taking it as settled, has wrenched open a giant slab of back door, and is bundling in her duffel.

"I don't have the key."

"No need. The key was lost, or broken or something. Harry had a switch put in, under the dashboard."

Can I drive the bloody antique? In a blizzard? With hot pursuit surely only moments away, and no confidence whatever in my ability to hot-wire the van, I'm going to have to try.

Lydia has several questions, but sensibly defers them, getting herself out of the Volvo, and then bags, a bulky one over the authorized limit, I note; her snowlashed stumble through the gloomy grounds must have been an epic in itself.

There is an instant sensation of having shrunk; the Packard's interior is like a plushy, by now rather shabby cathedral, where everything is oversized, more than ample room in front of the broad back seat for all the luggage, no need to even consider tackling the great cupola of the boot — *trunk*, I should probably say, considering the car's provenance. Where Celeste shows me, under the elderly mahogany dashboard to the right of a vast, upright steering-wheel on which a fatigued driver would have to stretch upwards to rest his chin, there is indeed a small toggle; I push it, and some of the large dials react with a reflexive jerk of needles — the one for `Gas' settles reassuringly on F, and I see that the large round speedometer gives up keeping track at a nostalgic 120 — that's m, not kph — like a senile athlete displaying the cups and medals of his triumphant springtime. The odometer, by the way, displays a youthful 136-odd miles; counting noughts and calulating years, not likely to be less than 400,136.

This machine, of course, predates key-starting; the ignition merely takes us to On, the starter a plunger by the wheel. The gear-lever is on the steering-column; I give it a waggle to make sure we're in neutral, and tug at the starter. There is the cough of a bored leopard, and then a joggling roar, eight or perhaps even twelve cylinders, not often missing.

Everything makes me feel like a hobbit in a house of the Big People; we are all three ridiculously high up on a fraying, prairielike, continuous front seat; the accelerator the size of a snowshoe, the stroke of the clutch like pedalling a bicycle; if Galek were not, for his size, short-legged, I would have to use up non-existent time discovering how to adjust the seat, but as is, I can manage, just.

Reverse must be up in *there*, and the clutch goes in without much of a jerk; we travel back a few feet, and stall.

Celeste, in a taut near-whisper, "They must have found Harry by *now* — " annoying me; she's saying in effect, hurry up, as if I weren't trying.

But puzzled Lydia says, "Found Harry?" It can wait; even if not preoccupied I would see no need to increase anxiety with merry details of how I and her daughter — also unforthcoming — battered, silenced and tied up Galek, thus adding a fresh urgency, not to say necessity, to this escape.

Having found and slightly tugged out the manual choke beside the starter, I try again; once more we shudder into life, and I back hard right, wrench the heavy wheel over, and with a brief whizz of slipping snow, avoid the van and turn down the front of the château, coming instantly into the full effect of the wind, me groping hastily for a control, somewhere, to start the wipers.

"People by the front door," Celeste reports as we trundle by. "One of them could be Harry."

No matter, I'm into second, and the wipers, though worked (with an audible sigh) by compression and annoyingly intermittent, have given me the ghost of a view. Enough, in a moment, to discern that some sort of alarm must have been sounded; across where the drive ducks under an unnecessary outwork of the old castle, a barrier pole has been dropped. The frontier, so soon?

Matchwood, I should say, for the juggernaut I am driving; all this stuff familiar from countless films, I lean on the pitted chrome horn-ring and (what else?) give her some gas; wipers halt in their tracks, the arm-waving figure in the archway leaps for nick-of-time safety. The barrier does not, as in the movies, shatter; to judge from the feel of the impact, we tear away one or more of its brackets, and the trailing pole snaps as we run over it with our big white sidewalls. Ration of pressure restored, the wipers flick back into their jerky oscillation.

"Oh my God," from Lydia (= `this is not the safe, orderly jaunt to an airport you promised by way of an escape.').

We fishtail, though only slightly, as I turn right on what I trust is the road, the rapidly accumulating snow obliterating most (normally subconscious) visual cues. Like, I imagine, a former celebrated visitor starting a run for home, though from well to the north and east of here, I ask why I wasn't told that winter came so soon: Napoleon quit charred Moscow on a damp late-October day in 1812, and was too late; today is, I believe, November 16, and I'm poking on, doing well to achieve the pace of a steady (human) trot, the excessively large clock on the dashboard frozen at some long-forgotten twenty-five past eleven, which the time certainly is not. Yet my agonized desire for more speed, impossible in this blizzard, is not necessarily rational; pursuit may already be hopeless for Galek's lot; they have to sort out the mess with the parked van, and at the rate conditions are worsening, a ten-minute lead will soon be insuperable, so long as I can keep on the invisible road, keep this monument nosing forward. More to be feared are alerts going out ahead of us; the assault, followed by theft of a car, have irretrievably altered the nature of this flight, bringing ordinary, apolitical crime-fighting in on Galek's side.

Those actions have also irretrievably shattered my screen of journalistic immunity; I planned nothing illegal, with the threat of international embarrassment for Galek and his party as my ace in the hole, and have in a moment become a mere fugitive.

It comes to my attention that I am chilled to the bone, my soaked shirt settling on shoulders and chest, so that belatedly to put on my anorak, even if I could spare the vigilance, would only make me colder. I poke and twist at various enigmatic controls, hoping for the heater; the cigar-lighter goes scraping in, and stays there.

Celeste says, "Harry mentioned the fuel thing, gauge doesn't work, by the way."

By the way? By the way is where we may all die, if that fixed, reassuring F conceals a catastrophic descent near E; that the inaccessible boot, the *trunk*, may be crammed with jerricans of petrol is irrelevant; all at once I wish I had turned the other way, towards Zmin, where there are service stations.

Lydia offers, "If you take the lower road at the fork, quite soon, you can strike the way that leads down to the main road east."

If, that is, I can detect the fork — and here, or not much after, I lose the way; the front wheels drop abruptly, and I stop just short of a snow-shagged mound that may be a bush, and is certainly no part of any road.

Calm; this is nuisance, not catastrophe (I hope neither Celeste nor her mother commands enough low-life English to recognize the curse that escaped me; the tone could hardly be clearer); into reverse, clutch in gently, the wheels grab. then begin just the start of an ice-making spin before I can get my foot from the accelerator.

`Rock it out,' I was instructed once, in a similar situation in Switzerland, which means, nudging forward till the front wheels climb, then quickly back, using the momentum of the short descent to take the rear wheels up and out.

And it works; there is a brief, daunting whine of rubber on new ice, then a blessedly welcome lurch, and I have regained the road. Out of the murk ahead, swarms of crazed albino bees swirling in bright headlamps, comes shouldering and hooting a big, square lorry, fitted as a snow-plough but with the scraper-blade raised, very nearly clipping my hastily-illuminated front wing.

"Going down to clear the main road," Lydia explains. "They don't waste time on these minor routes."

Perhaps not, but the knurled swathe made by wide snow-tyres defines my way ahead; perhaps, too, the light is getting better, and the next couple of miles are relatively easy, if hardly carefree; I am worried (in no particular order of priority) about pursuit, interception, the condition of any even more minor side-road I have to use, the dumb unreliabity of the fuel gauge. This is not a game, and mechanical or navigational failure could be, quite solemnly, fatal; there may come a time, quite soon, when arrest, imprisonment, disgrace, the loss of my career may be the price of survival, and not only for myself.

A choice I should perhaps grasp while still available. Turning round is hardly an option, but if I halted, over to the extremest perceivable right, and waited to be caught, using whatever fuel remains to keep the engine driving the heater (now emitting waves of rather sooty warmth), the chance of anyone actually dying would be significantly lessened — dying in the next couple of days, I mean; lives can never be 'saved,' only prolonged to whatever extent, though the difference, in Celeste's case, could be as much as seventy years or more, of which I haven't any right to deprive her.

Has my foot, at this thought, eased on the accelerator? The girl, in the middle, knees hugged up to her chest, gives me a sharp, mind-reading look, and she extraordinarily declares, "I would rather be dead than go back there."

Her mother has small time for astonishment, or any other reaction. We have been descending somewhat, now among dark conifers, and Lydia says, "Here, here!" as we come to the parting of ways.

The branch left, less gradually downhill, is narrow, but the even ranks of man-set spruces plainly define it, and have also halved the amount of accumulated snow.

"How far to the main road?" I ask, having come to a halt at the fork.

Lydia says eight or ten and her daughter twelve kilometres. I hesitate, on the brink of giving the mother a chance to echo (or not) Celeste's 1776-ish choice, but while my tongue is moistening much-gnawed lips, she says, "If the highway is being kept clear, we can be across the border before nine."

Oh, can we? — but obediently turning, with only a moment of spinning wheels — in a borrowed car which could not be more recognisable if it was painted bright orange and given a large neon sign to say Fugitives? Well, we're committed, now, to madness; there is, I know, a railway, for long miles paralleling the main road, and there must be stations; near one we can perhaps ditch the car (a figure-of-speech only), and get a train to Warsaw.

Up till now ruler straight, the way, still a tunnel through the trees, begins a steady leftward curve, and Celeste, releasing her knees and straightening up, says, "This is that other road. Mother, this is not the right road."

Lydia, stricken, moans agreement, but quickly recovers, saying, well, but this one leads to 'that other way, round by the power station,' and then mutters, as a kind of apology to me, that everything looks different in the snow. So will we, when they find us, I don't say but grimly think.

Quite soon, we are lost enough to admit it. The falling snow has, for the moment, diminished, though dark and yellowy clouds promise plenty still to come, but the going is awful, with seldom the tracks of any other cars to help me. I have made two more tentatively suggested turns, wound through what was either a tiny hamlet or a large, many-structured farm headquarters, past what turned out to be not the power station but a lonely and wholly abandoned brick building of unknown former function, down a sudden slope so sharp that had there been, as was briefly the illusion, an answering gradient to climb, we would have been helplessly stuck in the declivity, but the road ahead slid down, in our descent, into a mere level continuation.

The topography is significant; we are coming off the Yekhalets upland, and any slopes must be its western to northwestern flanks, the general direction we want, so that downhill, as well as more feasible, must be more or less correct, or so I repeat to myself, like a mantra. Rummaging in her sacklike handbag, Lydia finds and passes out rolls filled with mysterious near-meat; I am at once ravenous, but driving this behemoth is (at minimum) a two-handed occupation. At the start of another helpful downhill, I slip into neutral, and the car swishes shortly to a halt, held by untried snow.

We, Lydia and I, are calm to the point of banality; "I made some tea," she says, fishing out the Thermos and unscrewing its nest of red, yellow and blue cups. It is milkless, lemony, sugared, not as hot as might be, but very welcome.

"So much snow is not usual this early."

"In England the kids would love it. In the south, anyway, there is seldom a deep fall; they consider it a treat."

Shrug. "A woman I met from Sudan told me that if there is ever heavy rain, their children all run out to play in it."

Now Celeste, studying her second roll, embarks on a flat, sober account of our dawn encounter with Galek, managing to make `and so I hit him with this stick' sound the normal, natural and even boring outcome of what went before.

Her mother's small, isolated mouth squeezes into a tiny sphincter, and the arched eyebrows under the high, now puckered forehead descend into a continuous double downcurve; she shakes her head. "But he is alive?"

"He'll have a sore neck," I predict. "Some concussion, perhaps," (the missing hangover, at last).

Lydia, I must say, the story complete, displays an admirable equanimity in accepting what she must perceive, also, as her own altered status as fugitive. "Then we have no choice," she says, engaging my eyes as if settling a contract. "We have to get across the border."

The horde of impediments to this laudable resolve defy enumeration; leaving out the more immediate ones — doubt as to our whereabouts, worsening roads, the fuel gauge — I leap ahead to my idea for getting rid of the car and continuing by rail.

"The police — " Lydia begins, and opts to retain the rosier view. "This weather — it may be a blessing after all. There would have been patrols — the police would have stopped us on the highway."

"If we ever get to the highway," Celeste says, brushing crumbs from her knees. Our picnic is over.

Our lostness only deepens. The road desired (I have it in my mind's map) swoops in from a more northerly course, before adopting its definitive north-westward direction; we are headed too far west, and I need to turn more to the right, but there are only miserable, snow-choked ways that might as easily be mere farm-roads, coming to a defeated end among barns and henhouses. Then, when there is a better road in a more promising direction, the uplands have put out a long ridge only gradually tapering down, and I have no belief whatever in our ability to conquer any sustained climb, and none in the possibility of reversing back down when we fail. These compass-directions and even the idea of 'rightward' must be understood as relative references; the way we do take is winding with frequent selections to make, unsignposted, the signs obscured by snow, or coyly revealing three- or four-kilometre distances to unheard-of places; only the lie of the terrain is any rough guide, monotonous landscape or a series of identical landscapes, almost without feature, nearby white, unidentifiable mounds often obscuring the view to farther white, unidentifiable mounds; the stands of trees, white above, black below, pressing in on the road, or marching down the spine of the endless rightward ridge. Like the wind the falling snow is diminished to a half-hearted gesture, sullen flakes tumbling down, but the yellowed slate of the sky has all the patient menace of a quiescent but ferocious dog, held for now by a chain it can break at will. Throughout (*threw-out*, Harry, not *thruffot*), there is the murmur of Lydia and the silence of Celeste, one finding, or pallidly expressing, new hope at every turn, the girl grimly fatalistic.

Other travellers, now, when the day has reached mid-morning, remain rare; for half an hour I am behind a slow-creeping but trail-breaking tractor, dogging the chunked chevrons of its spoor, before it abruptly slews into a gateway; more than once for a time I am in helpful tyre-tracks made by no observed agency, and let these lull me away from the gathering feeling of being doomed to endless, futile exercise on a snowclad treadmill, the bitter unresolved debate between *this is insanity* and *what else can I do*? If going on increasingly seems hopeless, there is most certainly no way back.

Yet another set of those tracks, in fact, has seduced me into a road I should never have taken, narrowing, deteriorating, dangerous with piled snow once the tracks, emerging from, I believe, rather than entering an even-more constricted alleyway, have abandoned us. Approaching a rightward turn at the crest of a steep fall, we have, over treetops strangely obese with snow, a view to an improbable, extensive flatness hemmed with trees; it can only be a large lake, stretching away into doubt and dimness.

Lydia, naming it, finds joy in knowing where we are — the lake, in fact, bears related but distinct names for its eastern and western halves; on a map it has, not exactly an hourglass shape, more a Victorian dress-maker's dummy reclining at an angle, ample at both ends, pinched at the middle, and as Lydia says, the international border cuts across that waist. More germanely, the road that crosses that border runs near, the railway for a long stretch right along, its northern shore; we have only to find a way north — north-easterly, it really is — not twenty kilometres, fifteen as the crow flies.

Perhaps there'll be a road of some kind that follows the near shore. Towards which the way now bends, beginning a descent I dislike for its steepness and its windings; once more among trees, having no other choice, I edge down painfully in low gear, afraid of running off the badly-defined surface, bland with untouched snow. A sharp and tilted wrap back to the left, jockeying the cumbersome car, wheels spinning in quick bursts, then taking hold again as I manipulate (wrong word, but *pediculate* cannot be said to exist) accelerator and clutch; Celeste, upright like a sentinel meerkat, is audibly breathing hard in her nostrils, and Lydia's taut mouth almost vanishes entirely. Back again hard right, and I have too much length; taking a chance I deliberately nudge a couple of feet off the road, up a low bank, almost butting a sombre tree, to give myself some chance of reversing, as I must. And do, wrenching the heavy wheel over, perilously milling snow into black ice, but achieving the three-quarter car-length back that lets me complete the curve. The slope is still steep enough to make traction the least of my challenges, so long as we're going forward.

Here, as we come down near the level and perhaps a thinning of the forest, I once more lose the road, am just about the full length of the car off its hidden surface before I can check my mistake. Breathing long, declining panic, I change into reverse, and very gently ease in the clutch. The rear wheels begin a furious spin, and the car dies in a knocking rattle and a sneeze. Yes, I am going to try the starter, anyone would, but have no doubt; somewhere in an ideal existence, the Platonic perfection of a fuel-gauge, of which the fuel-gauge before me is merely a deficient earthly imitation, is correctly registering E.

One of my passengers emits a high-pitched little cry, as if she has slightly cut herself while chopping onions. "This is not good," I comment, fatuously, but with an intuitive purpose. It is, a half-wit could see, far worse than not good, but while we are surely in one way or another doomed — either to sit here and die, which is absurd, or to kill ourselves going out on foot to find shelter and assistance, or, finding it, to make our capture practically inevitable — nothing can be gained and what slight chance we have quickly lost by any surrender to wailing and gnashing of teeth.

As to anger; having, as promised, tried the starter too many times, achieving no more than an impotent grinding, I close my eyes and carefully reregulate my breathing when Celeste asks if I'm *sure* it's not just stalled or something? My mind is running again on the possibility of emergency fuel stowed behind, and Celeste agrees that Harry usually does have some with him, but when (having at last got into my anorak) I climb out and awkwardly plough there, the handle to the great boot, trunk, apparently a lift-latch, like an old-fashioned refrigerator, is securely locked — on, amongst other things, probably the tools I would need to pry open the lid. Its metal, like the entire car, is of unheard-of gauge, and I idly wonder on which side of 2 tonnes the Packard would weigh in at; its mpg rating, to our misfortune, must be scandalously low.

To emphasize what journalists would call our plight

(honestly, now, how often lately have you heard *plight* in ordinary conversation?), as I crouch there, wishing for a crowbar, the reawakened wind comes rushing, and with it not merely snow dislodged but fresh snow, lots of it, stinging and blinding. Leaning forward, hands on the car, I sidle back to the driver's door, and dive in, shuddering. Yes, but the warmth here will soon dissipate; this is very temporary safety.

"I saw some houses," Lydia offers, as if apologetically.

"Where?"

"At the turn, where you almost ran into the tree. Not there, I don't mean the houses were there — there — " indicating forward. "A row of roofs, they might be dachas, by the lake. I could not see the lake. They must be quite close, now."

"Wait for a lull," I advise (myself), the resumed blizzard having reduced visibility to the length of our bonnet, *hood* — only the skimming wind, with the wipers felled, has slowed the closing of the two aureoles (three-eighths of a circle, twice) through which we peer; soon we'll be altogether blind. "I'll go and have a look."

"Aren't we better off here?" Celeste questions. Again, Lydia's eyes catch mine, and she comes close to a wintry smile.

"For the moment," she explains, putting out a hand to cover one of her daughter's. "We can't stay here; the storm may go on for days." Celeste grunts grudged understanding; she is too kiddishly invulnerable to see that real death lurks in all choices. And I am an irresponsible idiot to have brought her, brought all of us, to this. I have with me, so far kept discreetly out of sight, my mobile phone, and can, in the last extremity, ring Galek's number; though I can't say where we are, no doubt he commands the technology to home on my signal, and dispatch a helicopter; *I'd sooner die* is easily said, but death from creeping hypothermia is not in that bargain, and I could not admire a Mark Kearns who could watch others, a young girl, die, rather than face the imprisonment that would come on the heels of rescue.

As when sheltering from teeming rain in a really boring place, wishful seeing goes into my detection of any fragment of *lull*. Hood up, as never before, on my anorak, wearing the serviceable fake-rawhide gloves I tossed, last thing, with a derisive laugh, into my bag in still-mild Brussels, I brace against the wind and its cargo, and struggle forward to where the dark, close-set firs cede to scattered sprays of birches, bare and shivering. Almost bare; here and there a snow-coated, shrivelled leaf clings on without hope, waggling stiffly in the wind.

The visibility is intermittently awful — alternating, I mean, with non-existent. Ducking my head in a particularly fierce gust, I straighten, and very nearly bump my nose against heavy-gauge wire. A high, very high, chain-link wall, four, four-and-a-half metres, the top strung with razor-wire, and even with a miraculously refilled tank the Packard would have been stymied here; the road, the guessed-at road, meets with a gate of the same materials, chain-link with iron framing, bolted and heavily chained.

It is, I perceive and part-deduce, a compound, and within it is Lydia's row of dwellings, close-set, substantial lakeside dachas for the affluent or the influential. My mind runs on the idea of a resident caretaker; I can see no glimmer of light, and no one would be indoors on this gloomed day without illumination, but such windows as I can discern, nearest to me, are heavily and opaquely shuttered. Likely enough, the whole place simply shuts up in September and waits for another May, although I can imagine a midwinter, perhaps Yuletide arrival, for skating, ice-boating, and that most dismal of diversions, crammed in a temporary hutlet dangling a baited hook through a hole hacked in the ice.

Not, I would think, a typical pursuit for members of the board, upper-tier bureaucrats, power people at large, whose chosen discomforts require a more heroic, more expensive stance; traversing an icy rock-face, waders and a trout-rod in a bone-soaking Scotch mist — it's likely this shore has segments where the *lumpenproletariat* can come to swim and sunbathe (hard to imagine just now), but this compound is a defended enclave of privilege; the high fence, of which the near corner is only a few steps to my left, appears to run right down to and perhaps out into the lake — out into the ice, as it surely must be now.

To stand still for, what, ninety seconds, in these conditions is to recognize how soon it would be impossible to move, feel the proximity of death, not necessarily fear, but a grim acknowledgement of limitations, the smallness of the engine that struggles to keep pace with escaping heat, the fragile will that puts one foot in front of the other, and again.

Back at the car, I report my news, and permit myself to speculate on how big an advance over our present situation is (if we can penetrate its defences) an unheated summer dwelling.

"Not quite unheated," Lydia corrects, claiming that any well-off person owning or even sharing such a dacha, which would have proper plumbing, normally installs and keeps on through winter a small electrical heating unit, just enough to keep pipes from freezing, and prevent other frost damage.

Well, I thought there was a glimpse, through veils of falling snow, of a large, dropsical water-tower looming on the far side of the compound, but nothing can make me believe in this climate that it would not be emptied for the winter; full and freezing it would burst apart. But the individual dwellings may well have undrained cisterns of their own, and Lydia's offering does explain an anomaly till now only marginally noted; some at least of the steep-pitched roofs showed a narrow, uneven, dark stripe at the peak, as if the snow arriving there has melted.

More or less agreed on our course, we wrap and gather for departure. Getting out, I tell the others to slide across and use this same door. It's true that their side the road is closer, but on the driver's side I have clumped out, coming and going, the rudiments of a track, and on the passenger — and windward — side, a forming drift is already piled against the door.

"No, bring everything," hauling open the back door, as Celeste suggests what might well become undoable, that we come back for the baggage after finding a dacha we can invade. Near knee-high the snow is heavy going, in another hour, thigh-high (and with the car mostly buried) it will be impassable. I with my valise on its auxiliary shoulder-strap, my small case, and one of Lydia's soft, well-stuffed bags, leaving the other to her, Celeste wrestling with her duffel, we plod and stumble forward, heads mainly bowed, breath labouring.

It is not my intent to try forcing the gate, which I doubt would be possible (that massive case-hardened chain, the heavy slab of lock) even using the phantom crowbar locked inside the expired Packard together with the useless petrol. Instead, we are going to outflank the defences, following the side-fence down to the lake. Though the freezing weather has not been with us long, the lake, relative to its extent, is not deep; the ice may not yet be solid out in the middle, but should be safe enough for the short distance from shore we need to go. All the summer cottages must surely have access to the lake, and once past the barrier there is a reasonable chance we can force a door or window and break in.

All this I outlined before we left the car; Lydia gave terse approval based, obviously, less on conviction than a review of our limited reserve of options, and Celeste sank deeper into her mood of silent, sullenly sceptical compliance; perhaps she feels the fuel-gauge is her fault, or merely resents that most of her recent suggestions (being ill-conceived) have met instant dismissal; who can guess the mind of a teenaged girl?

Though cold, especially face and ears, but cold in general, and the colder for being fatigued, neck and shoulders, from wrestling the big car and the strain of pathfinding, I would have thought myself a long way from delirium, but in my head is running, beginning again, a less-than-apposite patch of Shakespeare: *The torrent roar'd, and we did buffet it with lusty sinews, throwing it aside and stemming it with hearts of controversy* — Caesar and Cassius swimming the troubled Tiber, according to the latter, whose corrosive envy is showing — but I would not object if somebody were to pick me up and carry me to safety, as *Aeneas...did from the flames of Troy...the old Anchises bear*. But except for the Greeks at sea, when they annoyed some god, the heroes on both sides at Troy, for all their difficulties and dangers, could count on consistently splendid weather; neither Hector nor Achilles ever had to slog on, burdened with baggage, snow piling on shoulders and backs, crusting faces and blinding eyes, snow underfoot growing heavier with each looping step.

Once, when I was walking a long-distance path in England or Wales, I overtook, resting on a stile, a weathered-looking Midlander, who had foolishly worn mountain-boots, and was now nursing his blisters, regretting that he would not, in the day-and-a-half left to him, reach his original goal. Suddenly, as if angrily disputing a suggestion never made, he spat out, "Well, it in't a bloody race, is it?" Here, too, it in't; if not too fast I am setting too unrelenting a pace; Celeste tries to drag her duffel behind her, turns to haul it two-handed, and falls backwards, then angrily shakes free of my help once back on her feet. We are beside the high fence, where the going is uneven, many hidden holes and camouflaged hummocks, but the lake is quite near. There are limits to how much exposure any of us can withstand, but nothing is falser than that pet slogan of derring-do, 'You've got to keep going.' It won't kill us (probably) if we take half an hour over the next two hundred yards. I call a short halt, and we draw in close together, searching faces, restoring breath and a measure of equanimity.

"It's hard," Celeste states; I can't call it a complaint.

"Give me that — " Lydia swaps her heavy bag for the heavier duffel, and at an exchange of nods we shamble on, allowing a pause to restore breath after each twenty-five clogged paces.

The lake's frozen surface, except for shoals and arrowheads of snow, a few clumps, perhaps where actual sandbanks or islets are, is swept virtually clean by the wind, which here at its edge hits us with new and devastating force; doubled over we creep forward into it between gusts that halt us, Celeste grabbing at the fence with a gloved hand so as not to be blown back, or over. The ice is gritty but solid underfoot, and the fence is descending sharply, but in the few steps still to cover before we can be within the confines of the compound my cocky calculations are being shredded by the painful wind and whipping waves of hard white missiles; it is going to kill us, and soon, unimagined awfulness, negating all reason. *For, once, upon a raw... For once... For once, upon a raw and gusty day...* The entire fence does not actually plunge beneath the surface, but still more than a metre above, ends abruptly at a stout iron stanchion. One by one, we round it.

My laboured breath starting on its own to make small, rhythmic noises the uncharitable might label as whimpers, I cause myself to make a survey; *pick your favourite in a row of rears —* where are we, Las Vegas? the *Folies bergère*? Only sketchy detail is intermittently visible, but I decide on the second from this end, substantial, and with an attached probable boathouse looking, please, accessible. Not *in extremis* am I silly enough to strike out on the shortest, straightest route to this objective; on the open ice our legs will be scythed out from under us by the wind. Without the resources to do more than ignore the start, from Celeste, of a bitter objection, putting her, indeed, in front, I patiently plod back along the inside of the fence, and Lydia plods behind. Once there, I mean to keep to the extreme edge of the ice, roughest, and lightly covered with the tapered fringe of snow, but to do so means turning full face into the blizzard, which for a deluded instant seemed to be lessening. A long, agonized ten seconds, doubled over, I can at best hold my ground, lurching forward again at some momentary flaw in the pressure, ruthlessly prodding on the tired and straining girl.

To say I am tempted, after all, to attempt the first house is at the same time true and idiotic; the chance of any respite is fiercely attractive, but the cottage, timber-built, squarish, steep-roofed, seems both unpromising and dauntingly invulnerable, windows back and near side under stout shutters, back door behind a stout gate of iron bars.

It's just next door — the cosy phrase occurs, and causes a spasm of blind anger; just that, I can see nothing but my own blood, and am choked by the rise of self-pitying fury and infantile defiance; I'll collapse here, and someone must carry me. *So from the waves of Tiber did I the tired Caesar: and this man...*

There is a pause, a brief miraculous gap in wind and snow, and Celeste, I following, achieves a precarious, stumbling run aimed at partial shelter; the presumed boathouse, projecting from the upper level of the house, stands on stilts, flat concrete pillars, and it is under there that Celeste dives, collapsing in a heap with her burden. But it is mostly the idea of shelter; blown snow is piling against the inside of the pillars, and a fresh gust brings more, the cold untempered.

To the shore side is an apparent slip, though an unusual one, for launching a boat, a pair of widely separated sloping ramps, shallow channels of heavy, pressed metal (as used for getting new cars on and off those double-decked transporter-trucks), running out to disappear into the frozen surface of the lake next to a short, low jetty (at present no more than deduced), the near ends, I discover, vanishing under a massive hatch door, like a garage; I can conjecture a fair-sized boat kept on some sort of wheeled contrivance, which trundles it down to the water, releases it, then waits patiently for its return.

From the jetty, steps rise beside the ramp, then more steeply mounting to a side-entrance to the bunker-like boathouse. Celeste and Lydia, huddled together, the baggage piled beside them, are all the way back against the square-timbered wall of the house proper, at this level and on this side windowless. Unencumbered, using the pipelike handrail, I haul myself up the snowclogged concrete steps; everything now is absurdly difficult, and as expected this door, a solid slab, is locked fast.

The unjustifiable sensation of achievement at reaching this goal, dangerous at best, is quickly evaporating, misery and exhaustion coming uppermost; that the full force of the wind stays in abeyance is no comfort, and I feel a pressing, guilty urge to go and exhort Lydia and her daughter not to yield, as they evidently have begun to, to a false notion of available safety.

No need; Celeste has followed me out from under the boathouse, and as I start back down is doubled over using hands and feet to mount (like a sloth inverted) the farther of the two sloped ramps. Reaching the top, level with me, she lunges for one of the two handles on the giant, ribbed boathouse door, or flap. Her glasses were of course impossible in these conditions, but without them she peers uncertainly.

It is most likely to be bolted from the inside, but the slender chance it is not deserves a more considered attempt than the girl's furious, even petulant tugging at the handle. Ducking under my handrail, I make a risky giant step to reach the nearer ramp. The handle is horizontal, the shape of a stubby-stemmed capital T, and swivels a quarter-turn to the vertical with a hard anti-clockwise wrench.

"Turn it," I say — or very nearly shout — to nearby Celeste. Frozen lips and rigid face-muscles make the words come out ill-formed, but she understands and does it; I tell her we are going to heave up together on the count of three. We both very nearly take a dive from our ramps, as, to my astonishment, the lid-like door starts, and, counterweighted, rolls up out of reach.

We are looking at the rakish bow of a sleek, expensive sailboat settled comfortably on a low, fat-tyred — what? trolley, dolly? it reminds me most of those tractors you see scooting around airports hauling trains of luggage. On either side there is ample room to go into the dim interior, experiencing instant respite from the wind and blinding snow, although this place, stark, illuminated only from a slender line of windows up near the roof, inhabited by a gnawing chill, is no part of the actual house.

There must, however, be a connecting door. That over to my left is obviously the one I have already tried from the other side, at the top of the steps. At the upper end of the boathouse (the concrete floor, carpeted with treads of stout rope matting, has a slope, partnering the slip for the boat) we find another, just past a set of light metal steps for boarding the boat, a slab of blue-painted metal, rattling a little in its frame when tried, but forbiddingly firm.

"Let's fetch your mother — " get her under this much cover, I mean, and almost add, `and the baggage,' which is stupid. Though the bags, like Lydia if she permits it, will soon be buried where they are, this place is a very temporary shelter; if we can't break into the house; we'll have to try one of the others, possibly when conditions ease a little (but before we're too frozen to move).

Celeste grunts agreement, but having fumbled for and replaced her bifocals, has an eye down near the lock. "You have credit cards, a phone-card, perhaps?" — with an air almost of contempt. The vulnerability of locks to the Ali Baba omnipotence of plastic is something I have heard of, but would scarcely expect this particular teenager to know about.

She is waiting impatiently; it takes some blunt-fingered prospecting beneath the anorak, but I do find my wallet, extract a card, and hand it over; she has stripped off and let fall one of her heavy gloves. Her hands can scarcely be less lifeless than mine.

"Go on." I urge, as she seems struck by sudden misgivings; clearly the place is uninhabited, and I doubt that the technology of silent alarms to cause noisy responses in ever-vigilant police-stations has penetrated this far into the hinterlands. Unless they drive snow-ploughs with the monomaniac persistence of a Javert, or have instant access to an improbable helicopter, the police are not, in any event, going to get here today.

Grasping the doorknob with her gloved left hand, with her frail-looking bared right she shoves the credit-card in next to the lock, simultaneously kneeing the door inward. A quick rattle, out and in, the card slips in; she pulls the door open without difficulty, and hands me back my bank-card.

A short, dark vestibule, and there are four steps up to another door, one less formidable, knurled glass for the top panel. The nearer door is on a hydraulic check, and I use for door-stop a heavy plastic tub of what says (in German) that it is Marine, um, Caulking (nothing to do with veal).

Celeste is already at the upper door. It is not locked.

A blessed warmth. More rope matting underfoot, we are in a dark and narrow corridor. I perceive paired switches on the wall by my shoulder; if chinks of light can penetrate the shuttering, there is no one out there to see them; I flick both down and lights of the skinflint wattage that prevails in these parts come on in the stairwell behind us, and overhead.

Now Celeste is ready to return for Lydia, but I stop her; if we now have the run of the dacha, there must be a door giving easier access than the way we have come; I have never fancied, in the horrible conditions (ours and the weather), the job of getting our clobber up those windswept metal ramps.

VI

A phenomenon of our present era (a fine, pretentious opening flourish) is how those who can afford otherwise choose ugliness; in the long ages when the comfortably-off were a slow-growing minority, they demanded and obtained beauty for their money, which supported Handel and Rembrandt, Molière and Pushkin, as well as Meissen and Aubusson, Cellini and Chippendale, Inigo Jones and Capability Brown. Escoffier. No doubt there were vulgarians who didn't know where to stop, and many for whom the outward flourishes of taste were no more than *noblesse oblige*, but I don't believe there was anyone, given the means, who would have chosen slum noise over music, infantile patterns over pictures, fast alleged food.

Cannon against sand-castles, this thought began with my first sight of this unattractively appointed space for lounging and casual dining, with the *casual*, as well as indestructible, fanatically emphasised; a big couch-thing that might furnish but not grace a dentist's waiting-room, a couple of chaise-longues that would do as well for garden-furniture, bright-striped wipe-cleanable coverings over durable rather than pleasing frames, chairs a match, except for the half-dozen fake-carven ones round the big fake-wood table, that could withstand unmarked the determined attentions of all the cats (7^3, isn't it?) encountered on the way to St Ives, exercising their claws in ferocious unison. On the walls, mass-market reproductions from what I believe is the Florida Motel Modern school, a couple of which, rendered in fabric, would make better upholstery than the upholstery we have.

But the big stone fireplace, though, alas, with no fuel to be seen, is pleasant enough. Immediately over the entrance, mounted by broad wooden stairs, there is a very partial upper level, no more than a sort of shelf, but behind heavy floor-length curtains, walled completely in glass, two sets of sliding doors. These are guarded, instead of shutters, by massive, must-be removable sets of jutting iron bars (rather like vertical bicycle-racks), so permitting the bleak, blurred hint of what might on a better day be a brave prospect of the lake, across a broad, railed terrace, obviously the lid of the boathouse, two iron tables each with a small section of bared rim still showing to windward, and there are what can only be stacks of folding metal chairs, now curious, puffy, tiered shapes, as if someone has tried to design an inflatable white pagoda. The wind, but for intermittent tearing gusts, has eased, but the snow is coming down as thick as ever.

The corridor by which Celeste and I entered from the boathouse connects to a neat, even stark, up-to-date kitchen (dishwasher, twinned fridge and freezer, microwave), and ends in a steep, narrow stair down to the side-door, fortunately opening inwards, where a way had to be scrabbled and forced through a waist-high drift, before an alarmingly half-sleeping Lydia mumbling inexplicable apologies, our excavated luggage, and a large quantity of additional snow were all admitted (much of the last two still piled there, on more of the coarse rope-matting).

That lower level is a single vast tiled floor, partitioned into what doorlessness and only head-high, temporary-looking hardboard walls turn into *areas* rather than rooms; there is a games area (table-tennis, darts, very miniature billiards), a gymlet, with rowing-machine, punching-bag, medicine-ball, weights, a (quite large-screen) television area with couch and scattered soft, indestructible cushions, a laundry area with washing-machine, spin-dryer, and in a gesture to tradition, a pair of deep sinks with a skiffle washboard. Smallest of all, except for cupboards and various cubicles for loos, showers, a hand-basin, is the area where the heater broods with a baleful, HAL-like red eye, emitting an eternal fifty-cycle hum; its controls include a column of little square buttons, labelled in three-degree increments ascending from an optimistic 12 (the one in effect) to a reckless 24. I pressed in 21.

Not yet to much noticeable effect. That first impression of warmth was seduction by contrast; as my hands painfully, and my face less so, but with leave-it-alone itching (I patted gently), began to thaw, my objective internal thermometer told me it could not be much above 10°C, and I doubt that 21 is achievable; we may have found temporary safety, but not comfort.

Yet within twenty seconds of finding refuge from wind and snow all my thoughts of actual and imminent death were retrospectively transformed into frantic hyperbole — true, I can see, for renascent Lydia, too, and systemically for Celeste; we're all very ready if not to laugh then certainly to grin or shrug it off, so evanescent are the promptings of an undesired reality, once evaded. Those whose adventures have taken them within nodding distance of nasty death fall into two categories, the bloody bores who tell their tales, over and again, with the glittering eye of Coleridgian insistence, *on se fout du basson bruyant*, all points underscored, italicised, emphasised in an undimming suggestion of endured unfairness (that this should happen to *me!*), and the far larger number that 'never mention it,' preferring to be taken for grey souls, never exposed to anything more exciting than a distant glimpse of Her Majesty, or winning a nugatory sum on the pools, or perhaps the time our Edie was very nearly on that train that derailed. Both modes, histrionic and obliterative, may well have the same origin, the difficulty of getting beyond feeble verbal recall, to make real (as once it may have been, and of a certainty will be again) the pressing insistence of mortality.

We are all aware, or so I assume, that disaster is most likely only delayed, safety of the frontier beyond our crippled reach, but with more proximate, more terminal doom averted, no one is yet ready to ask, *What now?* Celeste, having steadily massaged her legs, stands, and still in her soaked socks, announces her intention to look over sleeping facilities, while Lydia, coming from the kitchen, says that water can be obtained from either tap, the lukewarm cold hardly cooler than the tepid hot. Both equally brackish, I suspect, having matured in the dacha's own cistern, and with no replenishment available, we shall have to use it sparingly for our washing, though as Lydia says, for hot beverages, we can always boil snow. She has a kettle on now for coffee.

"What about *food*?" Celeste demands, and her mother reports that there is quite a lot of meat in the freezer, some tinned and durable packet stuff in the cupboard. She has apologised that the coffee may be only instant, but when she vanishes again, after a minute, the high, hysterical whizz of what can only be a small grinder suggests that actual beans have come to light.

I go down to extract more of the bags from their nest of half-melted snow, and when I return, poke my head in the kitchen and find Lydia leaning wearily against the freezer; not seeing why her sex necessarily turns a distinguished bio-chemist into designated coffee-maker, I persuade her to seek what comfort can be wrung from the lurid furnishings in the main room, then am left wondering by what process a Harrods coffee-jug ever found its way here (picture blunt-faced tourists with their olive-green carriers, matching impassive gazes at Buckingham Palace, asking who, then, was this Nelson, that he should stand so manly, stiff and tall?). I wonder also, as always, why no drink can ever be made that tastes anything like the resplendent fragrance of new-ground coffee.

Before the kettle boils, Celeste joins me, back from her exploration, to report there is a children's room, with bunk-beds and a single, a small guest-bedroom with twin beds, stripped naked, and the main one with a big double-bed. She clears her throat, and glances cautiously in the general direction of the other room. "You should try to do sex with my mother," low-voiced. "She would enjoy that. You are a man — " in dismissal of any idea I might not be pleased. "She has been completely without that since Daddy died. She is young, really, only forty-four. It's important, I believe, once you've been accustomed to it — " all this with a strange and touching blend of forthright and shy. "I plan to keep that out of my life till I am twenty, at the least. Unless you mean to take advantage of me. If Galek had made me do sex with him," judiciously, "I would have let him, I think, all the time thinking of other things. But you — "

"Don't worry." The initial suggestion is scarcely less bizarre.

"But many men, without doubt, are excited by immature girls. Galek — "

"Some men," I forestall her faux-scholarly assessment, "think hip-hop is music and Mozart boring."

"I adore Mozart. To play, it is not always interesting, but I love his voice, so — ah, affectionate, you agree? I saw *Figaro's Wedding* on television. It seems to me the Count, you know? is very unhappy. Like Galek," she adds, just when I thought she'd been successfully sidetracked, "Evgenia was only seventeen when Galek first had her, but I think she was quite experienced before that, not like her age; she is always instructing me about how to make a man happy — with special sex-things, I mean. Or to make him unhappy, really, because she said these little tricks could make a man your slave, but I do not believe that. She has not done so with Galek — he is bored with her, I think, but she keeps watch over him. Did you have her? She is completely available when Galek gets too drunk, and I know she hopes some man can rescue her — she is very old-fashioned in some ways." A tentatively lascivious grin. "Those must have been her tights I used to tie Galek's legs, so I suppose she was with you."

I give no answer, baptising the coffee, unreasonably troubled on more than one front; by the evident confirmation Galek was feeding up (like poultry for the table, I mean) this serious, gawkily vulnerable child as Evgenia's successor. It's a relative term, vulnerable; she takes in stride the calculating notion of Evgenia keeping possession of a bored Galek while shopping for his replacement. But I don't want to care, would like to avoid the burden of any more individual traits, which tend to make demands; I'm willing to do all I can to help to improbable safety human units A (female, mature) and B (female, adolescent), my programming does not require intimate detail.

"Don Giovanni," Celeste meanders on, between rummages in the various small cupboards, "Can never be a woman — I mean, a woman, unless it is other women she wants, has no need to *strive*, like Don Juan."

"Boasting, you mean?"

"No — yes, boasting too, it's the same thing. A woman, a woman like Evgenia, if she wants to have a thousand and three lovers in Spain, I think she has only to flaunt — " (snag, half-blush) " — her behind, you know, so to say, *here I am, take me*, but Don Juan, even if he is a *real hunk* — " unexpectedly using, in audible inverted commas, the English, or American, words — "He still has to sing the serenade, yes? Or *la cì darem la mano* — he cannot just show off his chest or his thigh, and wait to be claimed, like Evgenia. You have a special friend? a lover, I mean to say."

Till now I have kept Celeste filed under *taciturn*, and *unconfiding*. Free from immediate threat, notwithstanding the endless unpleasant tingle, punctuated with jabs of pain, in my still-reviving feet, I detect seeping in that smug sensation of successful defiance, of hard-won security in a hostile universe, which, while of pure animal origin, has for self-aware humans a strong component of the sentimental, the sheltering maternal arms, the childhood tea-time, the womb with a view. Alarmingly, I let myself be warmly floated into a confiding mood, into an actual, heartfelt response to this wide-eyed question, but using the business of rinsing and setting out thick blue cups and their saucers as a line of defence, a safer place for my eyes. Special friend, I say, is for once exact; Carina is my friend — not, in hasty emendation, that there is any lack of passion; "As I now see, it can happen that — "

"Yes? Go on."

And I do, but getting the voice out of the depths of my throat, adopting a didactic tone more appropriate to our respective ages. "You see, it often seems that they are mutually exclusive, liking, and that kind of, well, love — " *How much I want to telephone Carina, hear her voice — and reassure her; soon she'll be wondering what has become of me. I don't know what resources Galek can command, am not fully up on the technology — GSP, is it? — of locating the source of signals from mobile phones, and in my ignorance would be insane to take the chance.*

"Erotic monomania, you mean? There was an article in a Russian journal discussing this, *Endocrine Basis for Erotic Monomania in Humans.* It seems that certain universal glandular responses may become abnormally attached to specific stimuli when — "

"It should make a lovely sonnet — " but what comes to mind isn't one: *I wonder by my troth what thou and I/ Did till our endocrine activity became so freakishly specific?*

"What were you going to say?"

"That it's rare, I think, for that kind of intensity to be compatible with a genuine friendship — not impossible, but rare." A judgement, maybe, that, like newly-purchased state-of-the-art electronics, becomes obsolescent while being delivered; now that children begin their matings far more casually than learning to drive, so that the most transient twitch of attraction (and even random autonomous endocrine arousals) may result in consummation, there's no reason why genuine if replaceable friendship and evanescent passion can't co-exist quite comfortably, though at a far lower temperature, rid of all the mess, torment and tears, everything of romantic love but the quaint, unmeaning terminology, still mouthed in our tranced addiction to heirloom verbal formulas, the white elephants of language.

"Won't she marry you, this Carina? You should make her your wife, even if it is only for some years."

The codicil is new, but the sentiment seems to be unanimous; the Fair Youth had only one voice, if a strikingly eloquent one, urging him on to matrimony, but every girl or woman I run into has me booked for hired Daimlers and squalls of confetti.

"Is she faithful? Do you find that important?"

I hesitate, fumble, and my complicated, shaded reply comes out as, "Yes."

"Why?" She struggles with a bigger blush, with a fleet succession of overlapping blushes, like raindrop-rings in a pool, but is not to be deflected. "If you love someone, you want her to be happy, yes? And if it pleases her to do sex with others, one, a hundred? Shouldn't you want her pleasure?"

"Probably."

"You mustn't tease me. I'm only asking, I have no experience. Why is that funny?"

"I'm not teasing — " but am recalling that state of developmental anxiety — the bewildered self-absorption of adolescent change makes a paranoid phase unavoidable; everyone will notice and scorn our disfiguring pimples, the unintended duets produced by the skittish voice, our spontaneous tumescences; all ambiguities may be slights, and all slights are intended; the world is peopled by self-possessed observers whose lives are devoted to censure of uncertain me. But, back in focus, no one ever learns from the experience of others; we listen and agree, but when we come to it ourselves we're always an exception; this I try to explain for Celeste, but don't dispel her conviction I am being evasive.

"Perhaps it becomes different," she decides, "When you feel those feelings. I will be very passionate, eventually, don't you think?"

"When the time comes — " a calculated response she identifies with a small laugh; there is no woman too young or too inexperienced to recognise precautionary fending.

With a trayload of coffee (there is even a cardboard container of time-defying milkoid fluid found in the fridge) and some newly-opened packets of rye-tiles and gentile matzoh unearthed by Celeste, we go to where Lydia is seated at the table, head propped on a fist; she looks up, takes in the new aura of (albeit firmly innocent) intimacy that encloses her daughter with me, and faintly but benignly smiles. Outside, the wind from time to time still comes in rattling surges, and the snow may fall for ever, but there does seem to be a slight improvement in the heating; only a clutch of blazing logs in the fireplace is needed to make our situation incongruously cosy.

Almost all the food packets, Celeste says, including the freezer, have a name written on the outside, three different names in all.

"These places are often shared — you remember, we had a share in a dacha, when your father was alive."

"Not with a lake."

"No, but that was pretty country in summer, the birch-woods." Lydia seems obscurely troubled, and not by nostalgia; perhaps by the thought of our intrusion on people all at once made actual, people with names.

"We haven't broken anything," I assure her, if that is her concern, "When we go I'll leave some money." When we go! hard to imagine; we have no transport, no fuel (check the boathouse; the boat there has an auxiliary engine), but even if, when the weather relents, the Packard can be started again, I don't know that it can be turned in the space available — or moved in any direction from where, off the road, it must by now be three-quarters buried. Besides, by then, every policeman between here and the frontier will be on the watch for the spectacularly distinctive monster.

Celeste, like a cat who has stepped in wet, flicks her left forepaw three quick times, and glowers again at the chunky Red Army watch on that wrist. "It must have stopped," she complains. No, it is right, our internal clocks wrong; after what might be days of fumbling along snow-choked byways, and a weeklong campaign to reach and break in here, it is still short of one in the afternoon. Our start, don't forget, was early in the extreme; superfluously, I observe that whatever our next move, we are going nowhere today, and equally, are unlikely to be disturbed; the suggestion of a nap to compensate for missed sleep is adopted without dissent. After the others have made their exits, I go to the kitchen, and from the freezer extract three swathed mummies that might well be large trout (property of the Kosenko tribe), leaving them to thaw on an ample work-surface. Like Lydia's, the kitchen has an annoying clock with no numerals on the dial, and I wonder tiredly whether the manufacturer likes to brag, 'we made numberless clocks this week.' When I investigate sleeping arrangements, Celeste, pointedly, has taken the narrow bed in the children's room, leaving her mother (enticingly, as the pragmatic daughter would hope) alone and profoundly unconscious on the broad *matrimoniale* in the master-bedroom. Securing a light, synthetic blanket, I return to the main space, and stretch out on a chaise-longue.

Not to sleep, apparently, but in useless self-reproach to go over the unalterable bad choices that brought us here — I should, of course, have called off the escape when the weather turned on us, but by the time I saw how bad it was, Celeste's felling of Galek had taken us beyond possible postponement, yet the same weather, after almost killing us, is preserving the mere illusion of partial success, while preventing any real continuation; we are free like prisoners in the exercise-yard — all this runs by itself through my mind, while underneath, ever since the girl's interrogation, I have been gnawing away once more at *Fall* Carina.

Putting a bet on a horse, mulling whether to open a book-shop, even planting a temperamental exotic, attention must be paid to the odds — which comes down to the experience of others in a similar enterprise. Marriage; I review those I have known, and begin, of course, with my parents, not mutually enthralling after all these years, but civilised enough to present the veneer of *ce qu'on appelle* suitability, each nurturing a saving patch of contempt for the other, my mother for Dad's undeniable occasional pomposity, my father for her supposed spasms of dithering unworldliness (wholly mythic). With which exceptions, they have managed mostly to maintain a statistically improbable mutual regard — my mind plays over the sharpshooter marriages, each using lengthening experience to snipe at the other with ever-more-wounding accuracy, the unequal ones, loud, patronising men with damp, defeated wives, sourly strident women and their whipped-spaniel husbands. Bored marriages, death made deader by the absence of oblivion, doomed marriages, protracted and farcical, like Lise's, brutal and, thank the Lord, brief, like Carina's — but the numbers say that failure, acknowledged, legally ratified, is everywhere becoming the norm, one short pace behind affluence (loveless pairs no longer chained loathily to each other by sour economic necessity), whilst couples who stay together because of religion, or `for the children' express their exasperation in inadequately-concealed affairs, or contrive meaner, more patiently erosive daily (and nocturnal) humiliations. Living happily ever after is an outsider so improbable that the odds can't be computed, yet such is our addiction to formative fantasy, so powerful the illusion of eternity induced by present euphoria, that most, most first marriages, certainly, begin I'm sure as a besottedly confident bet on that — lamed but unseen unicorn (rotten forced image).

I am unwrapping fish, wondering what to have with it (no potatoes, no bread, but there may be broccoli or something in the freezer) when Lydia, bringing our coffee-cups for rinsing, says, "Mr Kearns — Mark; I am sorry you have been brought into our troubles."

"And made them worse." She has broached her luggage, changed into lighter trousers and a loose top, an old-fashioned fringed affair decorated with coiling leaves and daisies outlined in tiny coloured beads.

"No, no. Not for us. For yourself, I'm afraid. Can we get to the frontier, do you think?"

Well, yes, for you, too; Galek can use the attack on him to have Celeste put away in some sort of juvenile non-prison, where she'll be as much a captive as I, if less uncomfortable. Answer the question. "There is a chance — if Galek thinks we have already. But they're not going to stop looking for that car."

At present, tucked under laden trees, it must be just about invisible, even for helicopter-borne search.

"I would like to get to Strasbourg," Lydia announces. "I know, we cannot go anywhere at present, but if, later, we can get to an airport — "

"Friends there?"

"No — yes, Andrei's friend. But there is money for me there. No — " grinning. "Not a secret bank account; it is money, dollars I think, being held for me. Andrei went there for some conference on disposal of nuclear wastes. Two years before he died, and he had said, many times, that he might have to leave the country, to get away from Galek and his hounding, and he wanted to have money waiting, in case we had to get out without, before we could — "

"Like this," I help her. Rice! there is a large bag of brown rice in one of the cupboards. With our fish.

"Exactly. Like this, suddenly. He flew to Strasbourg via Oslo, where he still had money from his Nobel, which he took as cash, and left with his French friend — well, he's Polish German, really, grandson of a *kashub*, you know? but he lives now and works in Strasbourg."

"A scientist?"

"He used to be quite a good physicist; he is a scientific adviser now, to the European parliament. Andrei respected him, and trusted him absolutely; it's a good bit of money."

Then why — ?" too late I bite off the question; *would Solyitnov kill himself*, the continuation could not be more obvious, or less forgivable. Nor more logical (but logic out of season can wound): the story is that he felt hopelessly trapped, but why? having provided so well for an escape. He had often gone abroad, and Galek had no power to prevent so eminent a figure from doing so again, nor from taking his wife and child with him this time; he would surely believe what Solyitnov left behind — property, work in progress, posts, standing — was adequate hostage to ensure his return.

"Andrei," Lydia states simply, "rather easily let things overwhelm him — intermittently for many years, he was under treatment for depression. I remember, not long after we married, he was in misery for a week, not speaking, sitting in the dark, not telling me what was wrong. At last I told him, if he did not talk to me, I was leaving him; I was no good to him like this, and he was making me as miserable as he was." A rueful smile. "He had a toothache. Yes. That was Andrei; if it rained he could not remember the sun, or in August — he suffered in the heat, his skin was sensitive, et cetera, and when August came, there was no hope, it was going to go on being too hot for ever. He was an idiot — oh, brilliant, yes, but if that is the price of genius, I am glad to be no more than competent."

Another instance for my catalogue of less-than-perfect marriages. Some key element in Andrei's decision to kill himself is still absent — it may be that any suicide includes the desire to escape explaining it — but I decline to let myself speculate, or even care; I am getting much more than I need or desire of that personal detail I have deemed irrelevant to my efforts. But it does seem that the pessimist sketched by Lydia might well have seen that getting out of the country, claiming the funds left in Strasbourg, would not be the end of his ordeal. As remains true for Lydia, in the unlikely event of our achieving that goal.

"And after Strasbourg?" I prompt.

"You said, the British will give me asylum." Her bewilderment is understandable; she has not been privy to my second, and third, and unending supplementary reflections on the wisdom of that course.

I supply a hint; "That would have to be your choice."

"Yes, yes, I understand — " and she really does, reading my face with a long, judicious look. "What about this man, this Grossbook?"

"Gossbrooke. Galek with good manners."

"Not truly?"

"I don't know. His pedigree is safer; any litter he sires will be unimpeachably documented back to the Norman Conquest; such men have the habit of being taken at their word — perhaps they earn the confidence they elicit. But only a small part of his government work is in the open, which means he tells lies for a living — maybe more lies than the ones we elect, though not to so many people."

She listens, considers, and visibly decides to circle the question. "Harry Galek," she says, "Is a dangerous man, not as clever as he believes, but very stubborn, very dogged."

Vindictive, to go with those qualities, I don't doubt. Lydia knows more about him than I would expect, or dislikes him enough to repeat gossip, back at the dining table, over fresh coffee, beginning with his baronial pretensions.

"Galek: his father was born at the château, but not as its heir; I was told his grandmother was housekeeper there, before the revolution, and his grandfather — well, it might have been the

Count, as Galek later insisted, but could as easily have been a gardener. The last count — not baron — fought with the Whites, was promised generous treatment when they finally surrendered, and died in a Siberian labour camp; there were no legitimate children, and he had sent the countess off to Paris. Galek's father was brought up in Kiev, and became, I think, a civil servant and a party member.

"The party had appropriated the château for its own use, but when the invasion came in 1941, the Germans used it — eventually, the *Einsatzgruppe*, but before that, for a short time, it was the headquarters of General Paulus — " here, Lydia gives me a look to see whether the name registers.

"Before he went on to the debacle at Stalingrad."

"Volgograd, they call it now, but, yes — " an epic stupidity, tragic in human terms, though it made certain the Germans could never win the war, and a sour, exasperating view into the military mind: as a Russian captive Paulus made broadcasts from Moscow, ineffectually exhorting the German army to turn on the Nazis. Yet he himself, with control over a quarter of a million troops, given the choice of doing that, or obeying orders he knew were impossible, lunatic, had obediently gone forward, like so many of those aristocratic satraps of the old order, hypnotised by the idea of loyalty to a leader their whole heritage rightly despised.

"I don't think Galek's claim to a made-up barony," Lydia resumes, "was ever heard of before his marriage — by then he was rising in the KGB. Natalja, his wife, you know, was an historian — she published several books, well-written, politically sanctioned, though she was specialising in a risky period, the late Tsarist decades."

"Oh, Natalja Kehrmann? I had no idea she was married to Galek." I have read one of her books, shortish, lively, loaded with irony, so that I was a little surprised she got it past the party watchdogs, in that era — but, as Galek says, they were such countlessly stupid, never seeing that her ridicule of the Romanovs (laudable) was founded in a witty, impermissible contempt for all autocracy.

"She also did a little outline history of the Yekhalets region; it is still sold in the shop at the castle, in a number of languages, French, English, German, Japanese, I think."

"So it was Natalja who primed her husband for his manufactured claim to the succession there."

A doubting face. "She may have, but I don't believe she was aware of doing so; she was dead well before he first called himself the long-lost baron."

"When did she die? She must have still been young."

"Oh, it would have been early in the eighties; yes, she was hardly thirty. They were estranged by then, living apart, and it was said she killed herself, with poison." Lydia repeats her resigned, shrugging expression. "A KGB divorce. Once you had been married to someone high up in Soviet intelligence, you knew too much ever to be allowed to break free; Natalja probably had many western contacts, emigré families, in her work, so — But later, with the Soviets in retreat, and Natalja gone, Galek could use her history to construct his own."

I say with sudden absolute conviction, "She wrote a novel — she wrote *Nevertheless*." The only possible explanation; I am willing to accept that Galek could have been a KGB colonel and a Olympic equestrian, could be a leading nationalist politician and the boorish alcoholic I witnessed, but I can no longer convince myself that the sledgehammer didacticism of the opera — every allowance made for Galek's rotten English — and the mercurial allusiveness and word-play of the novel, its sharply if not affectionately drawn main characters, came from the same mind.

I am not the first to think so. "So was asserted by one of her colleagues, her friend — her lover, it was said. This was only a few years ago; his letter was printed, I think in *Argumenti i Fakti*, but it came to nothing. It was in Russia, anyway, and no one in our country seemed to care. Or they said, they were trying once more to take away our indigenous achievements. Galek's novel. Because she was, you know, Russian."

I do know; Russian *and* Jewish, by extraction if not faith, doubly alien. Galek must have had her manuscript tucked away. He told me the book caused him career-problems when published, and that was in the loosening years; what was more likely than that he had persuaded his young wife her novel, half-a-dozen years earlier, could do them both irreparable harm? The bastard.

If I survive this, I'm really going to do my new translation, and get it published as *Nevertheless*, by Natalja Behrmann, with an introduction explaining my confident conjectures — perhaps find that friend in Russia who evidently knew it was Natalja's work. My publisher will do it, I think, if I sign a release assuming all responsibility. I would like to see if either Galek or his Walther Schmied in Berlin has enough nerve to bring an action, risk giving more publicity to a fraud I'm certain of. Well, not necessarily fraud for the publisher, who might have accepted the book in good faith, but for Galek, plain theft.

"As you say of your Gossbrooke, most of what Galek did for the Soviets before the breakup of the Union is not known. Many shameful things, I don't doubt."

"To do him justice — Gossbrooke, not Galek — he may be sincere when he tells me the only British interest in any new super-weapon is to make certain it can never be developed. Not that it's necessarily true, of course, only that that's what he's been told, and believes." The picture of a naïve and unquestioning trust in the virtue of his government fits about as well with Gossbrooke's known history as authorship of *Nevertheless* with Galek's.

"Yet you came to me with his story — " detecting and responding to my sceptical tone, and with a hint of rancour. I quickly resolve not to defend myself — assure myself, that is, that my actions require no defence: Lydia is an adult, and from the first minute of our meeting I made clear I was the bearer of a message, not its guarantor. "And now — "

"Now, we're here."

"But if we succeed in getting out of the country? How will it be better for Celeste and me? We need the protection of the British government, or some government. Wherever we go, Galek will find out, and there will be a very reasonable, perfectly legal demand for extradition, with a well-documented dossier of my crimes — and now you seem to think British intelligence will be no different from Galek, except more polite."

"What if you were to disappear completely — from Galek, from Gossbrooke, from everyone? If you could vanish from the world?"

Celeste, yawning in the doorway, says, "Without dying?"

VII

In the night, dying down of the wind makes profound silence palpable, a lurking thing, and I wake to the consciousness of restless, bitter cold pressing at our envelope of safety, probing for flaws, just as the brilliant morning light finds and sharply penetrates every small chink or gap in or between the shutters.

"You can see into Poland," Celeste says.

"Into Germany," I outbid her, with a grin. The world, seen from the upper platform between the long curtains, has expanded and despite prevailing monochrome acquired detail beyond recognition, the dully-gleaming lake, lumped with low islands, skimming into a distance undulled in the flawless air, hills, trees, houses, the smudge of a town mounting from the far shore, very distant, still hard-edged mountains away to the south and west. The calm is not total, a speculative breeze lifting, at intervals, a spurt of bright, dry snow from exposed points, the loaded tables, a corner of the terrace railing, like the shower of sparks from a grinding-wheel.

Comes a rapidly-mounting noise, resolving into the distinctive slapping roar of a helicopter, low and near, very near. It passes, so it seems, right over our heads, relents a little, then surges back; the craft comes into view, making a low pass along the margin of the lake — or the lakeside backs of the row of houses. Celeste starts to duck away, but I stop her; where we are nothing but sudden movement could be observed, though the helicopter, mainly black but with some sort of badge or logo on the door, is so close that I can easily see the features of the uniformed man, army or police, nearest us.

"They'll notice the boathouse door," Celeste whispers.

"No. I went back and closed it." It more or less closed itself, a lever just inside releasing it from the counterweights, so that gravity brought it down; I cannot explain what process raises and re-engages the weights ready for another opening.

Having made its pass, the chopper spirals up and snarls farther off, loudening again and then fading as it continues to circle.

We are all three shaken from complacency by the intruder, whatever its mission may be. Lydia who, having risked our water-reserves on a quick shower, is towelling her hair, offers the least threatening explanation, an ordinary scan for any who might have been cut off, trapped by the weather. Yes, or an equally routine off-season once-over of these particular dwellings, by police or privately-hired security. Or, finally, Galek-instructed forces, looking specifically for us.

On a small radio in the kitchen, after I wheel by snatches of varied music, Krakow comes in very clearly, a voice-of-doom bloke alternating with a soothing, motherly-but-sexy gal in emergency items mixed with merely meteorological notes; November records, it seems, have been set for depth of both snow and temperature, while many agencies are working to open roads and restore other vital services throughout southern and eastern Poland.

On a close and often overlapping frequency is the far weaker signal of local radio, with more of the same, including some sage advice about avoiding exposure, and if that comes too late, treating frostbite; the temperature in Zmin (amongst a list of other places) is -12^0C, with easterly winds from 11 to 16 kph; forecast, mostly clear and cold with light snow-showers possible, and a warming further outlook.

Waiting in the wings, we are repeatedly threatened, is a full hour of dance music (which might mean anything from disco to traditional *vesnyanky*), but before that can be launched comes a special police message, asking everyone to be on the alert for a large, black, antique *Peckerd* American car, plate numbers given. If seen it should be reported immediately, special phone number appended. There is no indication why the authorities are concerning themselves over this particular machine.

As the dance music surges in (it is in fact a dreary, recent local replication of Dorsey-Miller-Goodman swing), Lydia, belatedly losing faith in the Packard as a means to our salvation, observes that at these temperatures the lake must surely be frozen solid, and wonders with no particular conviction whether we might reach the safety of the frontier on foot.

It is not less than ten to twelve kilometres, loaded, a two-hour trek, perhaps, in good conditions on a friendly surface, and that's merely to the notional line dividing the two countries. Leaving aside that in the clothes we have we could not survive two hours in the open at -12^0, or that on ice we would be lucky to cover the distance in double that time, even omitting the unknown additional stretch to actual safety, the border is surely watched, and we would certainly be intercepted before we got there.

"Couldn't we *skate*?" Celeste improves, telling us there is an assortment of skates (together with fishing rods, scuba gear and tennis racquets, but not golf clubs) in a downstairs cupboard. The suggestion is too bizarre for more than a slight smile, but Lydia makes an angry sputter, like someone detecting a strayed hair in her mouth, and launches a withering catalogue of defects.

"Skate? And carry our bags? You don't skate that well, either. How do you think, even if we leave our baggage, we are going to skate twelve kilometres? What is this, the Winter Olympics?"

"I would be lucky to skate twelve metres before I was on my ankles — " but my attempt at light relief fails, as Celeste's look accuses me of endorsing her mother's scorn.

"Someone as stupid and useless as I am should have been left behind with Galek. I keep getting in the way of all the brilliant, grown-up plans."

"Don't be foolish — "

"But that's just what I am. How could such clever parents have such an idiot for their daughter?"

"I didn't call you an idiot — " an incipient mollifier Lydia cancels with, "But you're behaving like one now."

"Then, obviously, you should walk to Poland and leave me here."

"No one said anything — " but Lydia's tone is all wrong, didactic and self-justifying rather than tender.

This blaze must be left to burn itself out; any intervention of mine will be seen, by one or both, as aligning myself, one way or the other, and might, after much vitriol, illogically end with mother and daughter in hostile alliance (perceived as defensive) against me.

While the talk of skating which precipitated the quarrel is pure fantasy, I'm reminded that when I conjectured about the use of this place as a base for winter diversions, ice-boating was another that came to mind. Leaving mother and daughter at the glare, I slip out, down steps and the short corridor to the boathouse.

The trolley, or whatever we are going to call it, on which the boat rests has no self-contained power-plant, but is hooked to a fat steel cable wound on a motorized drum; since the slope of the ramp, becoming steeper outside the door, is continuous, I gather pure gravity takes the boat down to the jetty; under the surface, at a depth where the hull of the boat is in the water, must be some sort of stop — a simple ski-like upturn in the two metal channels would do. By some means, perhaps automatically, the boat would then be released to float free, and the wheeled conveyance remain where it is; I have not sufficient information or curiosity to work out how the boat is recaptured when docking, but the crew would disembark on the jetty, and the vessel be wound back into the boathouse — not necessarily after every outing; its wheeled undercarriage, while weathered, looks as if it could withstand indefinite submersion. Again, it could of course be hauled up out of the water once the craft is launched, and let down again only at the end of the sailing-season, or when there is need to get the boat under cover.

All these conclusions are for an imagined time when the lake is filled entirely with a liquid; at present the two metal channels vanish into the ice, and I presume releasing the toothed ratchet-wheel on the cable drum would allow the dolly, with its load, to roll down not only to but onto the surface. The question I have is whether, the cable once unhooked, enough canvas would give us a usable wind-powered vehicle, an improvised ice-boat.

Think it through (mounting the set of metal steps and going aboard); `canvas' is metonymy; the sails are actually of some unpleasant-textured but doubtless light, water-shedding and weatherproof synthetic, durable enough to be left in place (though all but the grommeted edges rolled inside fat cocoons) through winter; rigging the vessel will present few problems. Once, that is, the main and aftermasts are erected; too tall for the boathouse they are folded flat in the classic ship-in-a-bottle arrangement, so that winding the mainmast into place will at the same time erect the mizzenmast — a lesser foremast, just short enough to remain vertical, is independently rigged.

If the craft can be put under way, the rudder, naturally, will be perfectly useless (the boat has a wheel, not a tiller, in the forward curve of the cabin, to make the entire afterdeck available as a lounging, sunbathing and carousing space for perhaps three or four), and I'll have to get what steering I can manipulating sail; one or more of the small foresails, which the owner, I would bet, likes to think of spinnakers (not a word I know in his language), but to my eye are no more than old-fashioned flying jibs, might help, though for the most part I would just have to hope nothing, jetties, protruding rocks, skaters, islands, will get in our way; our speed would not exactly be headlong; even if the present wind held steady we would be lucky to achieve the pace of a jog-trot — I'm uncertain whether marine nomenclature is applicable when wheels are rolling rather than a keel slicing; 8 kph might be more appropriate than `about five knots'. That would still mean enduring up to two hours of the killing cold, but our baggage stowed, perhaps with some blankets borrowed from the beds here, it might not be so bad.

As escapes go (or don't go), that sedate imagined trundle down the middle of an empty lake would be, of all things, *visible*, hence easily intercepted — for my cowardly self, while escape would be best, if we are to fail I would far rather be arrested out in the open with quantities of independent observers available; Galek obviously wants to recapture Lydia and her supposed knowledge intact, and Celeste's physical safety is part of that concern, but a foreign newsman, even one compromised by car-theft and participation in a criminal assault (more, and more ingenious, indictments are possible), brings a potential for international embarrassment which it would be tempting for him to sidestep, or instruct some of his thugs to forestall, if it could be accomplished discreetly, as if we were to be found sloping through woods in the snow (with miles to go before we sleep). My disappearance, too, might bring him some awkward moments, but for him that must be weighed against the chance of my exposing his whole history with the Galyitnovs, and that balance-sheet doesn't look good for me. Bleak thoughts, but my burgeoning contempt for Galek completely changed its character in the few confrontational moments before Celeste coshed him, and might now be diagnosed as contemptuous respect, the one for his chosen calling and gangster instincts, the other for his probable effectiveness, with not much left of the booze-blurred buffoon.

At the last, the only valid test of feasibility is to try. Before returning to unveil (as the world of commerce phrases it) my plan, I make some minor but crucial checks; yes, the cable, with some effort, should be detachable, being held by a more massive version of those snap-hooks that connect, for example, shoulder-straps to camera-cases, a heavy leaf-spring closing the gap. No, the hull will not automatically (and disastrously) be released from its carrier after descending the ramp; it is clamped firmly in place by a pair of long, padded bars not unlike a vast trouser-press; the long lever to open and close them sticks up gunwale-high next to the cockpit, and was initially, muddleheadedly, assumed to be what is an unneeded, hence non-existent, brake for the dolly.

Lydia's hesitancy is met by Celeste's challenge; what alternative can she offer? The two are in a state of edgy truce, which may in fact augur better than if they had ended the earlier quarrel (as plainly they did not) in the teary hugs of sentimental reconciliation; Celeste would still have been vigilant, as she is now, for further slights, and any she inevitably detected come as bitter betrayals of trust newly bestowed; as is we may have no more than grumpiness to deal with — I say, we, but Lydia, in a singularly unparental manner, seems to provoke rather than avoid friction, as if she sees Celeste as an obscurely threatening rival — all this may well have origins in how Andrei apportioned — was perceived to apportion — his affection, and is certainly no business of mine, until it compromises our chances for survival.

Perhaps not even then. Accepting that my loony plan must be tried, unless I am going to ring Galek and tell him where we are, Lydia suggests we might wait till early afternoon, when the temperature is predicted to soar as high as -6^{0}C. I mention my thought of taking blankets, but when Lydia holds her ground almost agree to the delay, compromising on noon, rather than begin another round of bickering (Celeste primed to give me ardent support), a cowardice I am going to regret if the breeze, chilly but just about right as is, changes direction or drops altogether while we tarry for a marginal moderation in temperature.

A kind of deadpan pseudo-normality with the world slipping out of control, these hours are a quiet nightmare, with the often distant, sometimes nearer noise of the prowling helicopter, the restlessness of Celeste, who, between coiled sessions with a paperback excavated from her duffel, prowls to the kitchen for sustaining biscuits, to the upper shelf for a cautious view of unchange, the somehow prim inactivity and desultory conversation of Lydia, which, as it must, arrives at questions about whether I am married, have ever been married, have any constitutional aversion to marriage. Just like Evgenia rebuking her mother's alleged flirting, Celeste barely glances up from her absorbing book to say, "He's in love, and she's very pretty" (I don't remember saying that), which Lydia, beaming, says is nice, and then lightly on message chides me for not making her my wife.

Aside from which it is grotesquely like a rainy Sunday *en famille*, as drably depicted by some limpid but limp Bloomsbury novelist with a constitutional objection to event (but the growing roster, on the radio, of things that have reopened, places now accessible, means that roads are being ploughed, police and army trickling out into the web of capillaries, searchers searching, this dead time haunted for me by nameless threat, the shattering knock on the door from *The Monkey's Paw*), until at last I can suggest we begin loading the boat.

It was my initial idea to risk only my own skin on the descent from the boathouse, having Lydia and Celeste board from the jetty, but it occurs to me that with so much that would normally be submerged — the lower part of the boat itself, as well as its vehicle — sitting above the frozen surface, the gunwale would be, as it is here (where, however, there are steps), somewhere about the level of Lydia's head; nor is there any guarantee that its momentum won't overshoot the end of the jetty; backing up would entail a return to the winch.

And so, baggage and blankets stowed, together with some portable supplies and a freshly-filled thermos, we are to ride down together — no we're not; I shan't be aboard. First the boathouse door, and then I don't see how I can start the winch and board the moving boat before it is out of reach. I tell the others I'll catch up with them at the bottom and find some way of clambering aboard — that was necessary from the first, since I have to detach the cable.

Celeste, who has been busily exploring, tells me there is a rope-ladder piled in the stern, long enough, she thinks.

"Good. You had better sit down and hold on."

With an abrupt change to a mischievous mode, she gives the childish parody of a naval salute, grinning.

I go down and, hoping the vigilant helicopter is far away, heave up the boathouse door. Bright sun, still from a practically cloudless sky, and though less intense, the cold will soon be a new ordeal.

Back up at the top, I shout a warning, and pull the lever. With a loud clacking from the winch, the boat begins a slow descent, with which I remain content, although another notch on the control would entirely disengage the ratchet and let the drum run free. A hand still on the lever, ducking down I can watch the boat, whose pace quickens on the steeper slope outside; disregarding precaution, both mother and daughter are at the rail, watching their progress. To provide some momentum just before they reach the point where the ramps vanish into snow and ice, I release the winch, and there is a decided jounce as the trolley comes down and levels, quickly checked by full extension of the taut cable. Think it through; I'm going to need some slack there for disengaging the hook; I push the lever in the opposite direction; the motor hums alive, and with a softer clicking I haul the boat back a half-turn of the drum, then throw the lever over into the disengaged position. So far.

On the work-table to the far side is a lidless wooden tool-box, actually a drawer borrowed or salvaged from a desk or chest, and there I find a big (slotted) screwdriver to help in dealing with the hook.

Close the big door from the inside — no, not yet, leave it, I have to come back. I go out using the side-door at the head of the outside steps, and it strikes me as marvellous that in a half-frozen state, lashed and buffeted, I ever negotiated this snow-choked and treacherous stair.

"Is it going to work?" Lydia calls as I come down to the lake, where Celeste has already thrown out my lifeline, a rope-ladder with bamboo rungs dangled over the stern. There is no answer.

The cable is lying slack on the ice. At the third or fourth try I press in the tough leaf-spring enough to get it under the loop of the eye, and then can twist it free. The fat wheels of the trolley are on excellent bearings; in wrenching out the hook I lean my left shoulder against the stern of the boat, enough to start it slightly rolling; *perhaps* becomes the answer to Lydia's question.

Celeste's turn into the cheerful has been short-lived, "What *now*?" she complains as I still show no sign of coming aboard. Carefully up the ramp, back to the winch, start the motor; the cable comes trailing up, clatters loudly over the threshhold. Centre the lever, now close the big door from the inside, once more go out by the self-locking side door. I understand Celeste's peevishness; it can't be more than thirty or forty minutes since we carried the baggage aboard, but the fiddling, one-damned-thing-after-another nature of the process makes it seem like hours.

So far the drone of an approaching helicopter has remained in my imaginings. Grabbing the clattery rope-ladder I swarm aboard. "Is this going to work?" sober Lydia repeats, choosing to believe I hadn't heard her the first time. Don't snap, we are all, what's that juicy vogue-word? *stressed* — further example of the American genius for making new vocabulary stand in for fresh thought; our parents and grandparents felt exactly the same, though with less self-pity, when they were *on edge*.

"We'll try our best," blandly, swallowing tart questions about how I am supposed to know.

All this would be easier on a warm day in spring, when half the attention would not be devoted to staying unfrozen; my two-hour estimate for our exposure did not take into account the needed preliminaries. The mainmast and with it the mizzenmast, now, using a device like an oversized manual pencil-sharpener, are quite easily cranked upright into pairs of brackets till holes match holes, and a couple of galvanized lynch-pins, hanging on light chains, can then be rammed and tapped (with a fisted screwdriver handle) through each to hold them firm.

Lydia is kneeling to free the mainsail in its sack, and start snapping in the dangling halyards.

"Have you sailed?"

"Not for years. When we were first married."

As my friend Pavel used to say, echoing one of his beloved *films noirs*, I was about doo to catch a break (American, fifty, sixty years ago, was a livelier, more economical language); Lydia can work the mainsail, watch it, at least; I intend to do what I can with the foresails to supply rudimentary steering. "Ah, yes," nodding, "We have no rudder."

Smile notwithstanding, she is feeling the cold; she may be borderline anaemic, not an observation I'm going to risk relaying to a bio-chemist. Nor, once bestowed, can I take away her job and tell her to shelter in the cabin.

The breeze, now comes time to consider it, while freshening, has indeed shifted a little, but if anything helpfully, coming more from the southeast; I hadn't been keen on sailing, if that's the word, close-hauled, and tacking, on small fat wheels that point rigidly in one direction, is out of the question.

Together we haul the mainsail up; nylon halyards in the cold have a strange, half-stiffened feel, more like soft metal than rope. Secured, the sail trembles, and starts to swell as we set it to catch the wind.

"We're *moving* — " Celeste's jubilant shout surely gives aftervoice to an unexpressed scepticism — for which she can't be blamed, I'm incredulous myself. The sail bellies, and we are rolling in a miraculous silence; looking very much like an adept, Lydia slides down in the cockpit aft of the cabin, and leans back against the edge of the afterdeck, sheets and the line for the boom in hand, eyes on the swelling sail. As I clamber forward, Celeste emerges carrying a blanket to wrap over her mother's shoulders.

This is a drunken or dreamlike sensation, enough like sailing to emphasize the oddity, absurdly high above the surface, no eye on the wake and hand on the tiller, and altogether without motion but for the steady glide with a few minor bumps; sidling forward past the cabin to see what can be done with the foresails I have no need to brace myself against pitch or roll.

Our heading is somewhat north, I judge, of true west, out into the heart of the smooth lake. a course I want to correct, so as to sail nearer to the north-easterly shore, where I'll feel less conspicuous, and have greater trust in the solidity of the ice. To do so we must pass inside the first low treeless islands now on the starboard bow — marine terminology stubbornly lingers — and I find that with a jib in place, judicious handling of the steady wind brings a slow but predictable response. Trundling into the broad channel between islands and shore, where a slight coating of snow is undisturbed over the ice, running rough for an unpleasant moment amongst what must be banks or shoals barely breaking the surface, I have clear sight of the point where the lake narrows and, on the shore, of large white uprights with red chevrons, still distant, but surely attainable.

"Is that the border?" restless Celeste demands, scrambling forward for the umpteenth time to offer her unneeded help.

"Must be — " and I have to fight down the leap of hope to maintain a sober concentration. Along the shore the low, blue coaches of a passenger train are gliding, necklace windows catching the sun, till they trickle into a cutting or tunnel.

Perhaps twenty minutes pass; the red-striped pillars are perceptibly closer; we leave the line of islands astern, and are looking into the broadening of the lake beyond the nipped waist, a matching marker now visible on the farther shore.

As I fight to bring us nearer the wind so as to be sure of clearing the headland, I hear at last outside my mind the distant drone of a helicopter, and looking back can see it, coming rapidly from the east like a skimming mosquito, but one no well-timed clap of my hands can reduce to an impotent smear.

No question they have seen us; our hybrid contraption defines the conspicuous in an empty icescape; have I mentioned that to draw more attention amidst prevailing white, the mainsail has broad lightning-zags in brilliant orange and purple? Quickly, I lash down my jib, and go aft where an anxious Lydia has already spotted the helicopter. Her task, and the hope of success, have weatherproofed her, but abruptly she is colder and older, grey-lipped and deflated.

Celeste is in the cabin, at the spoked mahogany-and-brass wheel, apparently pretending to steer, and I tell Lydia to join her, both to stay out of sight. The patrol is certainly coming for a closer look, and sight of the mother and daughter is too instant a confirmation of our identity. Yes, but I have only straws to clutch at; the relative speeds — not to say, manoeuvrability — of our conveyances ridicule any idea of pursued and pursuer; I have no hope.

As if casually, the helicopter descends in a long bend, swings overhead at some sixty feet, hangs tilted well aft, and swoops lower to snarl along our port side; leaning where Lydia was, I try a cheery wave. The nearside door is open, and the uniformed passenger answers with a more purposeful gesture, signalling stop, as if to a speeding car. Sail flapping in waves of wind from the rotor, my piggyback craft is shuddering unpredictably.

There is, in counterpoint to the thwack of the rotor, a squirt of sound like fiercely trilled Spanish *r*'s, and on the starboard side a flurry of flying ice-chips; using a nasty little machine-gun they are literally firing across our bows.

Traditionally, though with more massive ordnance, understood as a warning that the next shot, unless you heave to, will be to kill, and from the open door of the helicopter something to that effect is probably being shouted; the words are unclear amidst the racket. The craft circles us, and again comes up on the port side, even closer to the ice.

Struggling to keep control of sails rippled and rattled by gales, I hang on, also, to the belief that strict orders have been issued not to shoot at anyone — not, at least, in the open, and not where there is a chance of hitting Lydia; that at a range of mere feet (say, a tricky but not prodigious putt) not a bullet has struck the boat bears out my conviction, although a fresh burst of firing still makes me cringe.

"Don't worry. They won't fire at us — " for those below.

"Don't you have that gun?" Celeste, crouched in the doorway.

I shake my head. "Left it in the car." Not by oversight; I was reminded of its existence at a time when I was contemplating acts, minimally a trespass, that only the demands of survival could excuse. If, however improbably, we were caught while B & E, my (unauthorized) possession of a firearm would cancel out all the blizzard's mitigation; before emerging from the Packard I tucked it away in a lidded compartment which, notwithstanding its capaciousness, contained no gloves. There was, I recall, a mysterious jar of something called, in Russian, `Stomach Ointment.'

Looking up from below, Celeste stifles comment, but the quick shuttering of large eyes and the long-suffering twitch of the mouth sign that of all stupid things I have done so far, my disarmament is the dumbest. She may be influenced by cinematic adventures, in which our lone hero, armed only with a pistol, wins duels with multiple machine-guns, blasts aircraft from the sky, and knowing their soft-spots can even cause tanks to erupt in slo-mo blossoms of flame; advanced weaponry seems a silly waste of money where a single clip in an automatic (even Hollywood grew sceptical at last of unreloaded revolvers that became eight-shooters, ten-shooters, sixteen-shooters) can defeat an armoured brigade.

I have lost sight of the border-markers, having been blown off-course by the helicopter; the hunters could, if only they thought it through, bring us to a standstill (even a retreat, if I was slow striking sail) by hovering low just ahead. Perhaps the idea comes to them; rising slightly the craft surges forward. Only to circle once more and come up closer still on the port beam; the uniformed man perched at the open door is still bawling at us, gesturing with his nasty little sidearm.

The rapid confusion of breezes has defeated my attempts to keep some sort of order in too many places; the boom swings wildly, out of my control; struck broadside by a fresh wave of wind we heel dismayingly on two wheels. I dive for the gunwale and lean out, almost beneath the helicopter, trying to counterbalance to port, still fighting to trim sail, but it is too much for me to correct, and we broach to, and all-but capsize. That, I mean, would describe it if we were in water; in icelubber terms even the low centre-of-gravity of the undercarriage is unequal to the leverage exerted by the boat itself and the sails above; we tip over; Celeste gives a short, loud shriek, but it is, by luck, impossible for us to go all the way down. Our conveyance is immobilised, resting, at a guess, on wheel-hubs and the edge of the trolley — the strain on the clamps must be immense, and the boat is sure quite soon to break free and crash on its side.

Like a gratified vulture watching lunch expire, the helicopter describes a triumphant circle preparatory to alighting.

Fresh thunders; looming rapidly from nowhere, a second, bigger helicopter is here. The new arrival is a far more formidable-looking machine, camouflaged (though not for winter), humped at the middle and bristling with projecting devices, some of which might well be lethal. Broad across its nose are the red-and-white Polish colours, and it hovers to confront our pursuer like a large, confident and well-trained dog staring down a smaller, more excitable one.

Equipped, also, with a voice like the voice of God, which speaks unto them, saying (in two languages) that they are now over Polish sovereign territory and in Polish air-space, and are to land forthwith.

As I duck into the skewed doorway to see that Lydia and Celeste, though shaken and apprehensive, are evidently uninjured, our harrier, flouting instructions, turns tail and bolts for home. Its swift retreat is very briefly seen off by the Polish craft, itself reciprocally shy of invading alien air-space; instead it returns to hover just over the surface, stirring up swirling waves of loose, granular snow, a statistically unjust proportion of which finds my cheeks and eyes, then settles slowly on the ice to our starboard, or low side. Celeste, her breath so noisy it almost sobs, clambers awkwardly out of the cabin, but has sufficient resource to turn and stretch out a hand to help her mother, who mutters, "My God," many times.

There is nothing to add to that. We are alive, and in Poland, but I have no delusion of victory. A burly, absurdly young officer in a fuzzy, head-hugging cap descends from the cockpit, joined by two armed others from the sliding-door amidships; all approach in the crouch (under the still-revolving rotors) of inquisitive gorillas.

Down on the ice I face them with what I am trying to make an appropriate face, welcoming but not unearnest. All wasted; the leader is undeflectably set in his own official and officious mode, and not to be delayed.

"You are not under arrest, but you are detained pending enquiries — " galloping through what must be a mandatory legal formula. "I will take charge of your passports, both, all three of you — " as Celeste and Lydia come successively into his view.

I start slapping at my chest as if to locate my passport, though I know very well it is in my valise.

"Not now — " he is brusque, but more recognizably human. "Get into the chopper, and let's get off this fucking ice."

"We have baggage — " recognizing belatedly that the hesitation in their landing was not drama, but nervousness about whether the ice would bear them. Probably for that reason, to facilitate, if needed, a fast getaway, the big rotor has never completely stopped, and is still thwacking laboriously.

"Bring it."

"What about the boat? It has to be righted, before — "

"We'll take care of the boat. Move!" forcefully.

When, as an undergrad, I made my first visit to eastern Europe, there was still, we didn't know how precariously, a Warsaw Pact, whose member states were still referred to as the Iron Curtain Countries. Into one of which, in all innocence, I tried to enter illegally, having failed to obtain (knowing nothing about it) a needed visa; travelling by train from places where the Roman alphabet and an easygoing student internationalism prevailed, I was grimly checked on the threshhold of Slavonia, and made to shuttle back to where, next morning, a consulate readily provided the needed authorisation, not asking me any hard questions. Absurd enough, but the point I want to make is that so far as possible, I actually was prevented, at the first attempt, from penetrating the forbidden country, my passport snapped up, my movements restricted to those needed to leave one train and board another.

Not so now, all these years later; we are flown not to a forlorn frontier shed where, at a gesture, we could be said never to have entered Poland, but some distance roughly westward, to an apparent regional headquarters just outside what may very well be Lublin. What effect, if any, this may have on our prospects of instant extradition has yet to be determined.

We are hardly in chains, scarcely guarded at all, though the bare room where we are installed is reached by way of a whole larger room full of uniforms, and the impounding of our passports and baggage is restraint enough. Still, the general tone has been courteous, and we have been brought coffee and offered sandwiches; a young, attractively smiling officer twice brings us her — what? apology? regrets? — that Captain Kerczy is still tied up, and is a sort of all-purpose response when, with her and other passer-by I enquire about our current status, how long we can expect to be held here, whether we are or are to be charged with anything, in desperation, whether I am to be permitted to ring the local consulate or the Warsaw embassy; all these points Captain Kerczy and only he can clarify. This dismal place with the hard chairs and bare table, devoid even of outdated magazines, is evidently the ante-chamber to his office, through whose unmarked door there is moderate traffic, various minions bearing sheaves of documents or less visible oral information, requests for instructions. It may be megalomania that I deduce from their passing glances in our direction, appraising, curious, at least one friendly, that much of this activity has to do with our case — a case we certainly are, and have been, I would guess, ever since over-zealous pursuers used their firearms over Polish territory.

Our mainly taciturn original detainer, who did uphold tradition by taking charge of our passports, ceremonially buttoning them up in a wide side-pocket, informed us during the flight that a 'political' decision would govern our near future, but if he knew more (which I doubt) he kept it behind a rigidly uncommunicative expression, and answered, "Perhaps," when asked whether I would be permitted to make a phone-call or two.

Not that I know who to telephone, but derive comfort from the abstract idea of communicating with a larger world. Gossbrooke, when briefing me (I never *felt* briefed, but that would certainly be his term for it) hinted at the warning, classic (in fiction, anyway), about being on my own, not to be officially acknowledged, far less helped, if things went wrong; I do have a contact number for him in London, but it is, he made clear, only a kind of robotic *numéro de convenance*, where nothing more informative than my name and a call-back number is to be recorded, and which I am emphatically not to use in any context but that of a final report on my mission. I was not, however, issued a packet labelled (e.g.) 'Smarties' containing cyanide-laced chockies, the sweet-toothed gentleman's way out.

What about Brussels? thrusting aside my desire, stronger than ever, to hear Carina's healing voice; there could be no worse time for such self-indulgence; to tell myself she'll be worried is no excuse for worrying her more — putting that, I say, out of bounds, there is still Babel; Nimrod, under the mantle of rough-hewn bonhomie, is an influential man with drinking, yachting and skiing buddies in high places (metaphorical ones, I mean, not only his Innsbruck retreat) — bloody hell, I'm influential myself, with a broad conduit to public opinion, never used in my own cause before, but temptingly available; the seediest Fleet Street hack who ever got drunk in Riyadh and put his hand on the forbidden knee or sacrosanct bottom of Saudi near-royalty counts on the influence of his journal to save him from the extremes, extreme indeed, of Islamic retribution. My case is less dubious, but to make it I have to expound my reasons, and that means exposing Lydia to the sharks.

Till now I have not questioned Gossbrooke's vision, eyed, too, by Lydia at our initial meeting, of a feeding-frenzy, the scramble of competitive governments and non-governments to possess the fabled Protein Bomb once they hear of it — but its non-existence, or, at most, its merely conceptual, never producible existence, was something Lydia easily convinced me of. If she could bring to a well-attended news conference that same unemphatic, pragmatic, use-your-common-sense tone to a denial of feasibility, she could surely convince almost anyone not blinded by Galek's stubborn need to be right.

Yes, but then in Moscow, probably Beijing and, God-help-us, Pyongyang, somebody is sure to say, `Well, but that Galek is no fool' — echoed, since my side of the tale would have to come out, by, `That Gossbrooke is no fool,' in Washington, Jerusalem and Paris. Another slogan comes to mind: `There's probably nothing in it, but there's no harm in checking,' which leads swiftly and inevitably to, `There must be something in it after all; the Yanks (the Ivans, name your nation) seem very interested in the woman — ' hence, to Lydia under permanent siege. As with the Curse of Tutankhamen, or the Mysterious Events at Roswell, there are legends which once established are invulnerable to logic or common-sense, undisprovable for those who can't acknowledge that quite often, where there's smoke, smoke is all there is.

I'm more than a little hazy about why this should be my concern; I probably ought to look for another profession, if, not even counting the chance of saving my own neck, I'm willing to give someone's (Lydia's) individual wellbeing priority over what, besides everything else, is a marketable story, and one I can tell without any direct betrayal of Gossbrooke. A journalist ought to be bloody, bold and resolute, and, as Pavel likes to say, chips must fall wherever.

Lydia, who of course grew up and lived adult years in the toils of a bureaucracy with patiently perfected talents for delay, misinformation and petty officiousness, putting to shame the worst that even Whitehall had and has to offer, is more resigned than patient — and not optimistic, I judge, as to the eventual outcome of this clogged process — but her daughter is aggressively bored, expressing it in exaggerated, noisy, virtually rhetorical changes of position, from chin propped on one fist to sprawled forward on the table, forehead resting on clasped hands, from one leg cocked over the arm of her chair to legs impatiently crossed, each new pose heralded by a heavy, cheek-puffing sigh — Celeste, I say, has asked me in a couple of different ways why we can't march into that inner office and demand action.

Why not, indeed? having reminded myself of my arsenal, I stand, pulling out my leather-clad notebook, which is also a case for my press credentials, but before I can beard the lion, the door opens and Captain Kerczy, all courtesy, is inviting us into his den.

"Kearns," he says, indicating seats and sidling back behind his desk (many-functioned telephone, computer-monitor, antique inkstand). "Lydia Solyitnova. Celeste. I would like to say, welcome to Poland, but — " he juts a doubtful lower lip.

"We are, you appreciate, only in transit," I offer.

"Are you? We'll see — you understand our Polish?" — to Lydia, who nods. Celeste, perhaps, does not, not fully, but she is warily watchful, chin drawn in.

Riskily, I have begun to like Kerczy almost on sight; he is in every fleet expression or cock of his head quite confident of being liked. The long neck (adams-apple prominent) and spare, linear frame make him appear taller than his actual height; with the jutting ears and heath-grass hair he looks, beyond youthful, actually childlike, but at the same time is a man in whose face, at forty-eight or so, can be precisely seen the familiar elderly chap he's going to be, dark, observant eyes, prominent curve of narrow nose between long vertical creases, quick, alert movements — one of those birdlike old gents, a local oracle with an adoring but sometimes ironic wife, and a penchant for twinkly teasing of otherwise criminally overindulged grandchildren, an undiminished appetite for ogling the neighbours' pretty daughters — a character falling somewhere between Dickens and Daudet, still miraculously reproducing itself through the generations.

"Is that K-E-R-C-Z-Y?" — poised over my notebook.

Not picking up, but bending up a loose page on his desk, he makes a show of studying it. "There are serious charges, you should know."

"I don't know, but I can guess. They come from a former colonel of the KGB." The portraits on the wall behind the desk — an indigenous pope, and the founder and hero of *Solidarz* — encourage me in this red-baiting ploy.

A semi-shrug. "Many prominent people in what was the Union have a past they now find embarrassing — this is regrettable, but to be expected."

"Some have gone on to equally dubious futures. Kvitka's New Nation party, of which Galek is a prominent member, has been a serious concern for both the European parliament and the United Nations — even more, I would think, for his country's next-door neighbours."

A distant half-smile. "Mr Kearns, you speak our language very well."

Lydia, at our first encounter, used this same gambit (as it surely is) to encode *Who are you really, and what are you doing here?* In this case, I start to explain, and at the mention of my Dusatian mother he snaps his lean fingers, and points the unsnapped one between at me.

"You are the Kearns in Dusatia, when the fascists were torturing Christa Rasch."

"Detaining her," I modify. Evidently the story is beginning to be muddled with stuff from one of Christa's early, kinky films. But the sudden recognition is a small and probably harmless pretence; when we came in here he already knew exactly who I am.

Standing, he extends a hand to be shaken, and tells me his name is Stanislaus.

I seize the moment. "This business with Galek is very much the same thing."

"Not quite, ha?" he murmurs. We are practically nose to nose, and only I can catch the meaningful, half-lidded slew of the eyes that comments on Lydia's unfamed form, or Celeste's underage lack of any.

My involuntary frown must be accusing him of an unPolish lack of chivalry; he hastens to correct course. "Oh, me — a policeman, it's all the same to me; if a woman is drowning, or in a burning building, I don't wait to ask `Is she famous?'" Or a babe, he might add, and he almost sighs, "Still... " unable to dismiss his regret at the absence of Ms Rasch.

"How, the same thing?" recovering.

I give him the generalized version, already discussed with Lydia, that Galek was trying to force her to work on biological weapons, which she for conscientious reasons declined to do.

"Is this true?" Kerczy abruptly brings Lydia herself into the debate.

"My opposition to weapons and war — " she is splendidly dignified — "is a matter of record. I was arrested more than once, lost my teaching post protesting Soviet actions in Afghanistan, and am one of many scientists to sign open letters calling for a complete renunciation of chemical, biological and nuclear weapons — "

"Yes, yes, certainly — " all this, for Kerczy, is too abstract.

Lydia sees what is required. "Galek was using my daughter as a hostage, to force me to work on his obscene weapons."

Kerczy considers this with the judicious face of a wine-taster, and finds structural flaws. "But Mr Mark Kearns is well-known as a journalist. If what you tell me is so, well, there are legal remedies, in your country as in mine. Who better than Mr Mark Kearns to make this matter known, to make it famous, notorious?"

The question of questions, and Lydia hesitates. Without a satisfactory reply, we may be handed over, eventually to Galek, but to expose the real reason makes freedom meaningless; other Galeks will be waiting for her wherever she goes. Her large and troubled eyes seek mine, and I know her thoughts; she is wondering whether I am going to seize this chance, perhaps my last, to sell her out, try to save myself by talking about the Protein Bomb — and if not, whether she has the right to keep silent and condemn me to probable prison.

To Kerczy, I suggest he and I must discuss these points privately. Gratifyingly, his assent is immediate; he may even be flattered (or does he hope that man-to-man he might hear more and more intimate stuff about Christa Rasch?); he presses a button, and like an actor stranded lineless on-stage when another misses an entrance, fills in by remarking on the unusually severe weather for the time of the year.

The young and pretty officer appears, and Kerczy suggests 'these ladies' might be taken to the canteen; the soup today, for a change, is really not bad, he tells Lydia.

Who does not like this; her in-the-end abrupt decision, just the night before last, to attempt this escape, must have implied final renunciation of having her future decided *in absentia* by the deliberations of others.

I face her, very close, and say, "Don't worry," trying to convey my resolve not to betray her.

"Tell them — " she is murmuring very softly, but doesn't really care if she is overheard — "That if they send us back, I shall do all I can to kill Harry Galek."

And when we're alone Kerczy lets himself react. "Madame Solyitnova has strong feelings about this Galek. The daughter, too, I judge."

"Lydia believes, as I do, that it is not only as a hostage that Galek desired Celeste."

"She is a child."

"Fifteen," I supply. "But that she seems younger may be all to the good as Galek thinks — if you can call that thinking."

"Mother of Christ! — " not the wearied response I would have expected from a senior rozzer, nerves numbed by the botox of experience. "If there's one crime I could never forgive — I would like a law to let us castrate such beasts."

Like the related and sometimes overlapping question of fraternal, paternal, avuncular incest, this is an issue which doth often bring, methinks, that suspect excess of protest; such terms as *monster* and *fiend*, as well as *unimaginable* and *inhuman* are deployed, it seems, to defend not only society against predation, but our own self-assay against what we cannot admit is very human, only too imaginable. This is as it should be; the myths by which we live require strong hedges, and could not survive a general recognition that *unnatural* is a term through which humans taboo for themselves what happens everywhere in nature; the fastidious cat often is both father and uncle to his offspring, has no qualms about mating with a niece; our own near-cousin chimpanzees do not ask for proof of age before responding to the preliminaries of coupling.

"I have daughters of my own," Kerczy explains. "If ever — it would be the end of my career; I would kill the man."

"How old are your girls?"

"Nine, no, ten now, and twelve. There are two boys, older." His eyes stray towards a desk-drawer, but he decides this is not the time for a show of snapshots.

"You have any evidence for this?"

"Ask the girl."

He sits down and with a spread palm rubs at his faintly stubbled cheek. "No, I mean *evidence*."

"Physical evidence? For intent?"

"I know. I don't doubt you, I would like to crucify the sod, but courts, prosecutors, too, are getting cynical about the abuse defence. Every young punk selling drugs on the street in Warsaw, every teenage whore spreading AIDS, was sexually abused. Some bitch cleans out the joint account and runs off with her lover in the family car, `my husband was abusive.' — we know it happens, but these opportunists are making it like the shepherd boy and his cry of *Wolf!* I expect to see someone soon explaining that Frank was abused by his parents."

(Note for a footnote: general recognition might be enhanced if I pretended this reference was to Heinrich Himmler, or even Adolf Hitler; Kerczy's parents — or a priest — must have passed on bloodcurdling tales — and there are plenty to tell — about Hans Frank, the sadistic Nazi governor of occupied Poland,

hanged at Nürnberg in 1946.)

"Also — " Kerczy keeps me on my toes, with a new flanking movement — "I must ask myself, where is your connection with Solyitnova — how does Kearns come into it? If you're looking for a story, you don't have to get involved in helping her escape, not to this extent, an assault, they say, stealing a car — "

"Borrowing without leave," I amend. "There was no attempt at conversion; it ran out of petrol and we left it by the road."

He makes a wry face. "And we know about the boat you *borrowed*. But what brought you to Yekhalets in the first place? How did you come to hear of Solyitnova?"

All excellent questions. "An English acquaintance told me about it, and I thought I'd come and have a look — I had met Harry Galek a few years ago, and knew he would see me." Feeble, feeble and deplorably vague, but the best I can do.

"An acquaintance? Who would this acquaintance be?"

"I don't believe you would know him."

"I know very few British, but you have a reputation here. When I began, when, *Christie eleison*, I worked for the atheists, I was in counter-intelligence at first. Our bosses had a peculiar reverence for British intelligence; it was their all-purpose poltergeist. Everybody knew the Americans were spending ten, twenty times as much money to spy — shit, our noble but suspicious Soviet brothers had more men on the ground than the British, but anything that went wrong that we could not explain — a document lost, some propaganda initiative gone astray, aha, British intelligence strikes again. My director, he fancied a couple of nights out a week with hired companionship, you know? and when he had to have a month off with penicillin to take care of a nasty little rash, we all knew he would be sure to find British intelligence was responsible."

Dutifully, I laugh. Kerczy is the most skilled of interrogators, but if the lack of any hostility, the apparent desire to help me, is nothing but part of his technique, he approaches genius as an actor.

There is something I am stupidly missing, some supplemental page in the conspirator's handbook I haven't read — not meaning those cryptic utterances, sign and countersign (`*The mulberries flowered late this year*' `*True, but my grandfather's sciatica is very painful.*'), something else. It may be that what's needed here is my unstated, indirect half-assent to his circumindicated deductions, a mutual recognition, even a bonding, of worldly, shrewd and above all discreet fellow-professionals — but leaving aside the fact that I'm not one, there is too much risk of a sudden turn into steely officialdom, of finding that I've taken the bait in what is at base a sentimental trap.

"You see, anything I do," he resumes with another change of key, leaning back in the chair, hands clasped behind his neck. "If I sent you back without an extradition hearing, as your former hosts are demanding, or if I said, the suspects were only in transit through Poland, you must apply to London, or wherever it is you are going, if I held you for a formal hearing — no matter what it is, I am going to have to answer to the under-minister, who has not yet seen fit to give his opinion, and politically — "

The telephone gives a quiet but peremptory warble. It takes me about fifteen seconds to decide that it is to the under-minister that Kerczy is addressing, in a careful but not cowed tone, his salvo of *sirs*. "Yes, sir," he says, "The British man, Kearns, is with me now." A long listen, and, "As I suspected, sir; I have been pursuing that line — of course." So far, so guessable, but now the audible portion of the exchange, a small fraction, loses me in a series of grunted and spoken assents, incomprehensible queries. At last, the functionary's *sine qua non*, "Shall I have written authorisation for this, sir?" then, "Ah. I see. Very well, sir, but — " The reasons why not occupy several seconds, and are far from satisfactory; very formally Kerczy announces that he intends to memorialise his reservations. To what, my summary execution?

They finish. Putting the receiver back very deliberately, Kerczy regards me with what might be an unhostile rue.

"It appears we are losing you. A man is driving down from Warsaw to take charge of you."

"And the Solyitnovas?" That we might be split up for separate treatment comes to me in a wave of dread.

"Yes, yes, all three, that is the arrangement."

"Who is this man? Another of your departments?" Counter-intelligence, for example.

"One of yours." blandly. "Raymond Lippett, perhaps you know him. He is working with your embassy."

While noting the rather careful choice of words, I'm no nearer solving the mystery. Kerczy does not believe in my stupefied visage, which must indeed have the look of wild over-acting.

"In Poland, we keep our main roads open — " the tiny emphasis on the pronouns implying a contrast with other, unnamed countries. "Mr Lippett should be with us quite soon. Till then, while we have the time, perhaps you would like to discuss your understanding of the sort of work Madame Solyitnova has been doing for Galek."

"You had better ask the lady. I believe it is nutritional research, but as for understanding, I'm no sort of scientist." *Oh, God, I sound just like Gossbrooke disclaiming what isn't his bailiwick, and about as believable.*

"Nutritional research?" His tone is go on, pull the other one, but the looked-for rapport, though I am simply telling dull truth, has arrived.

"The government built a new laboratory for her, in the Zmin region - not far from Galek's place."

Yes, yes, this is the stuff. Kerczy is making a note. "Such a remote location."

"As you say."

"This is just personal curiosity," he assures me. "I keep my bad habits, but it is no longer my department."

VIII

From the moment he bustles in, plainly of consequence in his own estimation, and introduces himself to me with a vigorous handshake, inventories Lydia and Celeste, thrusts documents at Kerczy, I understand why Lippett is `working with' rather than `for' the embassy; he is, at a second glance, one of those shady hangers-on that used to plague and exasperate my father, who thought that spookery and other dark dealings should be given an establishment separate from the honourable (if also at times surreptitious) business of a diplomatic mission. Joust away; Sir Matthew, Dad, astride one of his hobby-horses, cannot be unseated; useless to point out that spies, of their nature, depend on the possession of alternative, more respectable, identities, and that to have, adjoining the embassy proper, a second installation, labelled *British Secret Espionage*, would be self-defeating.

But Lippett would not belong there either, he would visit by night, through the side-entrance; no, that's unjust; whilst the somehow devious manner puts me in mind of Minghela, the car-hire factotum, he would with a few modifications pass without comment at an official reception, dressed as now in good off-the-peg suitings, light hair razed very short, emphasizing the flat-topped, chalice form of the head, outsized ears suggesting the handles. He might be a couple of years either side of forty, pale-eyed, concavely semi-circular nose over a wide mouth with full, feminine lower lip. Not tall, startlingly slender in side view, his necklessness. the square shoulders and frontally square frame make him rather like one of the rose-painting gardeners in *Alice*, though with none of their obsequiousness.

"They tell me you wanted to see me," to Kerczy, in unblemished Polish, but with an uncourteous look at his Rolex.

"If you can spare me a few moments." The irony is lost on Lippett, who really sees it that way.

From the outer office where we have emerged, they vanish into Kerczy's sanctum, giving me a first opportunity to bring Lydia and Celeste up to date. The daughter is delighted not to be on the brink of repatriation, but the mother's relief is quickly clouded. "What does this mean?"

"Gossbrooke, I suppose. But if it gets us out of Poland –"

It is not likely Kerczy would have liked Lippett in any case — even without, I mean, the plain disagreement with his under-minister about the policy Lippett serves and represents, without the obvious and self-important wish to be done with the formalities and on his way. What else has passed I can't tell, but as they re-emerge, Kerczy is reiterating (obviously) the reminder that the erstwhile detainees must be out of Poland forthwith, or else subject to arrest and probable deportation whence they came. He comes near an old-fashioned bow as he takes Lydia's hand, smiles paternally on Celeste, and with a return of the warmth so notably removed from his exchange with Lippett, wishes that he and I had met in nicer circumstances, and that he and his department will not be treated too harshly in any account I produce. For that, Lippett has a quick, sidelong look, but must know any power he has to silence me ends with the discharge of his stated function.

It is an Audi, probably a real honey, like noo; Celeste earns herself a shrivelling glance from Lippett, asking, "Is this a Polish car?"

She has used her cradle-language, and I note a faint delay in comprehension before the grimace, and succinct retort, "*Deutsch.*"

No linguist, then, and sitting up front beside him I learn he is as much Polish as I am Dusatian, exactly as much. His maternal grandparents got out of Poland in 1946, the brief interim between imported tyrannies, Lippett's mother then being a small girl; growing up bilingual in London she later worked for Lot there, and so met Lippett's father, a travel-agent. Like me, their son was brought up speaking his mother's original language as well as English; unlike me, his chosen field was political economy. I am unable to discover when he became our handyman in Poland, since he of course does not acknowledge any formal affiliation with any of those dark doings to which Gossbrooke also denies all connection; exoterically in his father's footsteps, Lippett evidently runs some sort of small private agency in Warsaw.

We have it seems been exchanged for a biscuit-factory — not as arcane as it sounds; Lippett explains: one of the leading British biscuit-makers, desiring readier access to the eastern European market, has been seeking a site for a factory nearer the samovars, either in Poland or one of the Baltic states, in any of which unemployment is a nagging problem. With the help of a British 'economic advisor and trade negotiator' (for whom one can, I think, supply a name), the choice, till today, had narrowed down to either Kaunas in Lithuania or somewhere in the region of Gdansk, now the lucky winner. We're not in Kaunas any more, Toto, making our munchkins.

Undeniably impressive; this is, I suppose, how countries do business, but one would expect such negotiations to occupy months, with the Labour Minister, let's say, all for the swap, and the Foreign Minister and his security people dubious at best; merely internally within Poland there is enough difference of interest to consume a small forest in advisories and counter-memos, benefit studies and reminders of international law, threats to put it up to parliament.

Beyond that, or rather before it, there is the question of the starting-point. Making a question out of flattery, I tell Lippett, "You couldn't have wasted much time."

Complacency. "It was obvious you would make for the Polish border. I had a message yesterday morning concerning your sudden take-off from the Yekhalets place."

"From Dominic Minghela." Who else?

"That's need-to-know; the source was one I trust."

Yes, but that still meant that Gossbrooke, when briefing me, Minghela when offering me a stick-at-nothing 'team', both chose not to mention, as is obvious, that they (*we*, it should have been) had one (at least) of what Minghela would call his guys up at the château. Welcome to the Smiley world; the informant was no doubt instructed, when I left Brussels, to keep an eye equally on me, and render a full report.   Minghela, I suppose, could effortlessly suborn one of the young Sergeis with the kind of erotic free-for-all he offered me. Or Evgenia, who could as easily *be* or have been one of his anything-goes doxies; surveillance would supply a better reason for her fascination with me than my irresistible charm. And then my conjectures summon back the parting smile of the young ice-princess, which I decline to call inscrutable, but was certainly knowing; she was obviously aware Celeste and I were making a run for it. More than possible she is the mole, but I'll never know; we can waste a lot of effort with meaningless post-mortems on unique occurrences, arming ourselves for a 'next time' that will never come.

More germanely I am puzzled by the near-surfacing of Gossbrooke, after his reiterated warnings that I would be on my own, not to say his general determination to deny all association with spy-stuff. Having seen his style, I suppose this intervention came with his full apparatus of implicit distancing, `a bloke I know in the F.O. is interested,' `the intelligence bods seem to think' — not a mask that could be used very often before even the most obtuse ally or adversary would see through it. Which is the point I am groping for: for Gossbrooke to risk his carefully-tended image as innocuous authority on trade questions is a measure of the importance London is assigning to *Fall* Lydia; more than ever I see myself as potentially hastening her from one Galek to another, better-tailored but not less tenacious. Which is unacceptable. I am as relieved as the next man to be rescued, but with Lippett feel like the gingerbread man, borne across the river on the fox's nose.

We have been told that snowfall on Warsaw, not 250km from where we almost died in a blizzard, was light, but the excellent road for the capital though indeed open, is far from clear, and in cautious traffic our progress is dogged rather than speedy. Lippett's headlamps have been needed from the start, and the advance of night is a process invented merely to plague him.

"We'll never get you on a flight out tonight," he grouses. "Well, it's their own bloody fault."

"Whose?"

"Poles, the Poles. See, the deal was, they would release you so long as I got you out of Poland toot sweet, but Jasinski, the under-minister, who had to sign off on it, was stuck in some endless bloody meeting, otherwise I could have been in Lublin early afternoon, and you'd be on your way to London. And that windbag captain — there was absolutely no reason for him to be involved; I had all the paperwork signed and stamped. What, Korczy?"

"Kerczy. A good man," I rebuke him; Kerczy was captivity, Lippett is liberation (or something along those lines), but there is no doubt which of the two I prefer as a human being.

"As it is, I suppose we'll have to put you up in a hotel for the night, get you on a plane in the morning — well, they can't say I didn't try, it's their delay, not mine." Defensive grousing; after the prima donna performance with Kerczy he is swiftly redefining himself as mere *comprimario*.

From the back, Lydia leans forward to ask what is being said; she follows English reasonably well where the acoustic ambience is favourable and the speech moderate in pace, neither present here. I translate for her, and test Lippett's command of her language by adding, " — so he believes," to our projected destination. As expected, though listening, he misses it, and warily seeks out a mode common to all by asking if she speaks Polish.

In that language, with an attempt at friendly joshing, he informs her that she should feel flattered by the priority given her case by London. It comes to me that he has not the least specific idea what her importance is. Obvious, once seen; he himself has already used the defining label, need to know. His job, and his obsessive concern, is simply to keep his part of the bargain, and get miscellaneous persons out of Polish territory, so that Warsaw can tell the Galek faction, `too bad, it's out of our hands.'

With a cautionary look for Lydia, I say, "We have to stop in Frankfurt on our way to London — Frankfurt am Main, it's right on the way. Madame Solyitnova has some financial business there."

"My instructions — "

"What difference can it make? Lot has direct flights for Frankfurt, and from there, there are plenty of planes for London; it would only be a couple of hours."

For travel, I know this beat at least as well as Lippett; back in the days when I was chiefly in print, I came to Warsaw, and found that the chap I wanted to interview had gone off to address the European assembly in Strasbourg. Whither I pursued him, discovering that the Lot flight in question, in the odd, meandering way of airbus service, before zagging back to its end destination, Frankfurt, first touches down, mainly for the benefit of the Eurocrats, in Strasbourg. To leave the plane there might mean abandoning some of our luggage to an unpredictable fate, but besides putting Lydia in the real home of her nest-egg would get us out of the process, perhaps beyond tracing.

Lippett is worried. "I would have to get clearance for that."

"I had no idea Ian was running such a tight ship."

Silence, lips pressed together. Lydia is baffled (Celeste lolled sideways, asleep), and I don't dare explaining tactics in a language Lippett to some imperfect extent can understand.

"I'm completely an independent contractor," he says, readopting English, with the tone of one introducing an unrelated subject. "They ask me to do a job from time to time, and they seem to think I do okay."

"That would be my impression, if I could do a piece on this."

"A piece?"

Oh, come; you do know I'm a journalist; it was in the description by the Polish police, the document you signed as a kind of receipt.

"Should I not have mentioned Ian?"

"I don't know who you're talking about — " this beginning in stolid denial, ending almost in nudge-nudge, wink-wink, know what I mean?

"I did promise him there would be no publicity, but that was on the basis of Madame Solyitnova being offered British asylum; it changes the whole story if she is going to be treated as if under arrest. I'm not one of his forelock-tugging lackeys." After a second, I append a clause more telling for Lippett; "I still have a living to earn, after all."

"You will be under arrest, by the Poles, if you don't stick close by me." He tastes and does not like the menace in this, and, shaking off the wholly intended implication in my protest (i.e., that he is one of those lackeys), decides to become more matey. "That's the job I signed on for, and to tell the honest, if you want to go to Rio, for myself I don't give a flea's fart, once you're on a plane out of Poland.

"Don't make too much of that," he backtracks, worrying whether, after all, I am authentically on untitled first-name terms with Gossbrooke. "Anybody will tell you, I don't give short weight; what they hire me for gets done. I'm only saying, for me, it's not some great crusade. They already know that."

Have I done enough? As discovered when taping my series on secret governments, I have no access to the mind of a spook — whether Lippett is authentically one of them can't be said, but he shares with the breed the habit of living inside layers and layers of seeming; I never quite found out what made old Zuylen tick, not money, only marginally boastfulness, and he was extraordinarily open, in general past caring what was thought about him; whether in the midst of Lippett's vanity I have tapped a genuine vein of insubordinate rancour, whether he's susceptible to the small conflicting dash of anxiety over Gossbrooke's predictable anger if I decide to go public — none of this can be judged; I am certain only that he is not going to see us onto a plane for London, and the reception-committee that is sure to be waiting.

Not a hotel I've stayed at before, old-fashioned, in a quiet little side-street, called *Nocturne* by the management, affordable by the package tour's brochure-writer, seedy by the discerning guest. We have been left here by a palpably uneasy Lippett, repeatedly exhorting us not to go wandering, and to be ready first thing for the drive to the airport. Though I would have liked a meal more piquant than the dismal *pierogi* we stopped for, wandering indeed seems inadvisable — for one thing, Lippett still has our passports, although the pretext on which he retained them, that he needed the information for booking our flights, no longer exists; he called in at his office and used a computer to secure not tickets but exchangeable vouchers for an early flight to Frankfurt, where we are permitted four or five hours for business before taking a mid-afternoon plane to Heathrow — and, I don't doubt, the welcoming arms of Gossbrooke. The vouchers, too, remain in Lippett's possession.

Yet there is, surely, more than a dash of the fatuous in this illusion of control, which rests solely on what the Poles can do to us, and ends once we're out of Poland — because I am not on the payroll, but a dangerous professional blabbermouth, Gossbrooke has to disguise his real plans for Lydia, maintaining the pretence of a flight to asylum, otherwise he might have hemmed us in a phalanx of Sergei-equivalents all the way to London. Without that, he's dependent upon my naive acceptance of a done deal.

All this I am beginning to explain to a gravely attentive Lydia, while Celeste is having a bath. Our quarters are a sort of mini-suite, a main bedroom with shabby wallpaper, large bed and little else, a brief vestibule with a clothes-hanging alcove opposite the bathroom door, leading to a very small additional space with a single bed, mine.

"What alternative do we have?" she laments.

At some length, I tell her, and when Lydia succeeds her daughter in the bathroom, and I return to my own space, Celeste (most improperly, in only a peach *après-bain* robe) follows me there.

"I could sleep here, instead of you," she offers. "Then you can do sex with my mother."

I shake my head with an asininely tolerant smile. Hands up, everyone who knows what *vicarious* means; any amateur soul-reader would guess Celeste is moving her own altogether natural desire for initiation onto the safer ground of her mother's supposed deprival.

"Well," she persists defensively, "You were on the bed with her. Why didn't you make a move?"

"We had other things to discuss."

"You could do that and still have sex," nothing if not tenacious. "In books, in films, also, people discuss things much better after they make love."

God, yes, all that pillow-talk. "In real life, too, but this wasn't that kind of discussion."

"Couldn't you pretend you're with Carla?"

"Carina." An unintended twist of the knife; I have been trying to obliterate
the painful prudence of not telephoning her. But Celeste here becomes a startling match with Evgenia, instructing sullenly unuseful me to close my eyes and envisage a lurid catalogue of doings with the Other.

"Carina — " impatient with her own lapse. "You're in love, but that didn't stop you doing sex with Evgenia."

"True."

My borderline forbidding tone has its effect. "That isn't any business of mine," flustered, she concedes. "But I want to understand. Is it because she's young and all that? I hope I get breasts like hers." (unlike American, and other globally privileged girls her age, she does not mean, hopes she can afford to instal them).

"Partly — " once again her impossible innocence — speaking of breasts she even caressed herself speculatively — has drawn me in to genuine discussion. "When a woman like that knows what she wants, it's not easy for a man to say no. We have no tradition of refusal to help us — " *au contraire*, such coy male violets are seen as ridiculous; besides, there's residual chivalry.

"If you are in love? Your responses — "

She is back, I think, with her Russian researcher's obsessed glands. "It's more complicated than that. There's no merit to fidelity if it always matches inclination, if it's all endocrine predestination."

Challenge. "Is there any merit to fidelity? I know the kind of chocolate I like best, but that's because I've had a lot of other chocolate, and I still *like* other kinds."

Very up-to-date reasoning, to turn sexual experience into just another of the pleasures expected (in the amount due), and containing a very up-to-date (and lonely) flaw. "How does the chocolate feel about you?"

A blank moment, but Celeste is really a quite intelligent

child. "Well, but you can only feel for yourself, can't you? Should you be some particular way because of what you think somebody else might feel?"

This, astoundingly, is not in the least a defiant re-utterance of the hedonist creed, but still a genuine request — for information I can't pretend to have. The best I can do is, "It depends what you're looking for."

"No, really."

O, Celeste, Celeste; I became serious about mating at about the time you were born, and since then old ways have changed beyond recognition; anything I tell you will be from the wisdom of the ancients, no longer certified as to validity; I used to think some parts of human nature were unchanging, but it's only words (not their connotations) that are; when Jane Austen used *faithful*, it meant steadfast in an unconsummated attachment; after, and for a long time, up to, say, Iris Murdoch, the same word meant *electively monogamous*, and now, though it's still used, I have no idea what its implications are; having vaguely exclusive intentions but able to rationalize the departures (`He was never *there* for me'), perhaps. "It's going to be your life; you'll have your own rules to work out."

As ever in talk with Celeste, I have had the feeling that the real subject is somewhere else, touched, circled near, but yet to be uncovered. In this one case horribly confirmed. She says, "Anyway, I can't be all that selfish. I really wanted you and my mother to do it and be pleased — " gulp of air, break in the voice — "even though I am in love with you."

She leans over me seated on the small bed, and very quickly, firmly, kisses me on the lips (nudging her glasses askew), retreating into the other room with a flaming face, before I can say a word about pubescent self-delusion (no, of course I wouldn't have). Her mother, bathed, pokes her head in to convey her provisional concurrence in the first part of my plans, and say goodnight.

Very early, we find the breakfast-room yawning into half-life; ours is the only occupied table, and a non-waitress, on loan from other dawn duties, apologizes for the aging baked things, fresher ones not yet arrived.

When first contact was re-established this morning I thought that last night's declaration — as it was for Celeste, no matter how ill-founded — had passed with a flutter of peach-coloured wings, leaving no alteration, but now I perceive she is

being, though with poker-face, lovingly attentive, as if I had —
well, never mind as if what. She unnecessarily tidies my place at
table, pours my coffee, chooses a doughy bun for me to butter,
asks if I would like jam.

Lydia doesn't fail to notice, with a lift of the bold
eyebrows, and after I decline a further ministration, says quite
tartly that she would like more milk, "if it's not too much trouble."
Celeste puffs resignedly and pours.

As maliciously anticipated, our absence from the rooms
has given Lippett a nasty moment when, quite soon, he arrives,
wondering accusatively why we couldn't have told the concierge
where we would be. Keeping in close touch with his Rolex, he
accepts a hasty cup of very milky coffee, gulp, glance, gulp.
glance, and herding us along, throws away the traffic-ticket he has
garnered by double-parking right outside.

At the airport, too, we are running ahead of full staffing;
of the many Lot stations on the long counter, only two are manned,
fed from a common queue. When, quite soon, there is only a
single trio ahead of us (a couple from Buffalo, speaking a horrible,
clogged, virtually grammarless American Polish to a rediscovered
autochthonous cousin), as prearranged, Lydia indicates an urgent
need for a loo, and marches off, Celeste shortly drifting after her,
leaving a quietly frantic Lippett wishing he had at least one
auxiliary with him.

"They shouldn't — " he mutters, and decides he has to
follow, to stand sentinel by the door while they are peeing. I
extend a hand for the vouchers and passports in his, and he gives
me brief, unnecessary instructions, then hastens after Lydia, who
has just vanished round a corner.

All this, riskily, is for the sake of getting our baggage to
Strasbourg — Lydia's two hefty bags, actually; we may well be
able to hump Celeste's tall one aboard as carry-on, and against the
possibility of losing the others, mother and daughter have
redistributed their packing, so that the duffel contains a selection
for both of most necessary stuff; when I mentioned that my own
small case, certainly cabin luggage, was far from full, I received
from Celeste a worn hardback Pushkin, and, with a pinkening of
ears, manner nonetheless challenging, a provocative sheaf of not-
particularly-provocative underpants (Lydia made a tongue-and-
teeth noise).

At the counter, the girl accepts the first voucher, and with a glance — at me or my passport — goes into English. "Three for Frankfurt?"

"No, no — that's a mistake. The flight is the Frankfurt plane, but we're only going to Strasbourg."

She is annoyed, worries away at her keyboard, and confirms that this is the booking made last night. In English, the problem might be almost insuperable, but in her own language we can agree on the ridiculous ineptitude of travel-agents and the folly of not checking every detail, while she rattles more keys, makes a notation on the voucher, and asks if the same seats will be all right, middle, aisle, aisle. From my cart I load all three soft bags on her conveyor, all the while tingling, neck and shoulders, anticipating Lippett's return.

My ticket and boarding pass are handed over. Not the other two; Lydia's passport lies on top of those. "Mother and daughter, travelling together. Where are they?" She has to compare them with their photos.

They return, Lippett impatiently harrying their heels like a dog being kept from his dinner by recalcitrant ewes, and as they present their faces for approval, I wheel on him. "Do you want me to ring you when we reach Frankfurt?"

"No need — " i.e., absolutely not, in this spyworld, where everything not compulsory is forbidden. "Be sure to get back to Frankfurt airport in plenty of time for the London flight. It's Lufthansa."

"You have the voucher for those tickets?" Just outside the small circle in which I am keeping his attention, the word *STRASBOURG* is everywhere; such intermediate destinations on a longer flight are always given particular prominence, of course, and it is being positively shouted from the baggage, which has not budged since its labelling.

"I gave it you."

I shuffle the miscellany of documents in my hands. "Did you? No — oh, yes, here it is," unfolding it. "Sixteen-forty-five, we'll be in London for dinner."

" — and there are your boarding passes," I can hear the Lot girl telling Lydia, with the gate number. "A Continental breakfast will be served before Strasbourg."

"When Madame Solyitnova's business is done with — "
still flaunting its destination, the baggage is at last gliding for the
hungry hatch — "We should have plenty of time for lunch in
Frankfurt. Plenty of time." Seldom, I hope, have I sounded so
fatuous.

And of course Lippett, as through the sinuous waggle and
flap of rubbery skirts, one, two, three bags vanish beyond the
hatch, once more cautions me about allowing ample time for
catching the London flight. If he overheard mention of the other
city, it did not strike him as particularly significant; he almost
comically relaxes as we head for the departure gates, Lydia alertly
following my example, keeping boarding pass, its bold caps
destination, upside-down under the ticket.

The new mood lasts for the entire fifty-pace distance to
the security checkpoint, beyond which unticketed Lippett cannot
pass; knowing that, he has I think still pictured himself watching
us right onto the plane; I turn to shake his hand and thank him, and
anxiety has returned to the pale blue eyes. Lydia, and then
Celeste, also express gratitude, and that he never says a word
about getting in touch with unmentionable but indicable
Gossbrooke when we reach London only makes me surer about the
welcome waiting there for that Lufthansa flight. Had he spotted
the change of destinations, I don't see how he could have
prevented our departure, but don't doubt the reception committee
could be swiftly mustered in Strasbourg. "An unpleasant man,"
Lydia confides as we find our gate.

Beyond Alsace, our journeys are to continue, I have
decided, by rail; it is altogether possible that some counterpart of
Minghela or Lippett was alerted, and waiting for our Frankfurt
landing, not necessarily to meet us, but to confirm our arrival, and
perhaps to shadow, surfacing only if we seemed ready to do
something other than getting on the London flight.

But with our boarding of the plane readily confirmable,
our non-arrival in Frankfurt, unless we acquired parachutes and
baled out over Saxony, points straight and solely to Strasbourg,
and any attempt to trace us must begin with the airport here,
probably planting a watcher against our likely return.

Only twenty-four hours ago I would have dismissed as
paranoia (megalomania's depressive twin) the idea of such an
elaborate, persistent and above all expensive hunt, but being
swapped for a biscuit-factory makes it difficult to over-estimate

one's importance (anyway, Lydia's importance) to the potential trackers: a shadow-world I've written and telewaffled about often enough, where practically unlimited funds and teeming human resources, equipped with every conceivable technological aid, are devoted to seeking, watching, overhearing, a nightmare of observation inescapable, has at last achieved personal reality for me, and once concede that they know more than you like to admit and nothing will impede your free-fall into what would be authentic phobia, if it weren't likely to be plain truth.

Agonizingly, when at last I call Brussels, the same revised estimate of unfriendly capacity and will makes me avoid ringing Carina (Saturday, she's likely to be at home, unless she's gone out, as we often do, for a leisured lunch); if any line is tapped, that will be.

Brussels is, in fact, my second call, not using my mobile, first at the tram station where the airport coach dropped us, and with the same phone-card that Celeste used to break us into the dacha; whilst I was making that lengthy contact, a complicated and harrowing business, Lydia was ringing her friend, the personal banker. Having at last concluded my tricky negotiations I asked if it went well.

"Yes, yes, he is home; I can see him, he has the money in his safe." But there was still a frown, and when I pressed her she said, "It was a little strange, Georg recognized my voice at once, and he didn't seem at all surprised — it must be seven, eight years since I last spoke with him, so — almost as if he was expecting me."

Sketchily as I know Strasbourg, when she showed me Georg's address, I knew just where it is, the secluded section behind the main hospital; I have stayed more than once at a pleasant hotel in the same small street, its name claiming association with a fire-breathing monster, although it could as easily refer to a heavy cavalryman (historically rather more likely); the location, within three minutes' walk of a bridge crossed by the big, new double trams that can take us straight to the train station, is otherwise reassuringly obscure.

But with my new consciousness of encircling danger, where even that dowdy matron, pausing to audit the contents of her jumbled shopping-bag, needs to be regarded with suspicion, I felt like telling Lydia, if she had any misgivings, to let the cash (an undisclosed amount) go — and did not, for a cluster of reasons. First, that I can see no way Gossbrooke could know about Solyitnov's buried treasure, and that it was, still is, too soon for his people to be here in any force, no matter how swift the reaction upon our failure to materialise in Frankfurt; the process would have to be, Frankfurt guy reports to Gossbrooke — not Lippett, about whom he has not needed to know — Gossbrooke or his equivalent calls Lippett to confirm we were on the plane, Strasbourg is deduced; optimally this could not have happened more than half an hour ago, and more probably has not reached that stage by now. Second: last night I mooted for Lydia a possible course for her future, whose feasibility I have now confirmed; she listened and pondered, no doubt discussed it with Celeste, and appears, on the legal principle that silence gives assent, to be resigned to that hard choice, one which is going to take her into some lean or leanish years, for which even a moderate windfall would provide a touch of comfort, a small sliver of free will. Moreover, and I suppose this muddle counts as third, she was and is accepting without demur my order of business here in Strasbourg, an ascendancy I am embarrassed by, not wishing with excessive guidance to push her into revolt, feeling at the same time that I have interfered with her existence quite enough for one day — for one lifetime.

Still compliant, she agreed it was wise to tram first to the railway station to secure tickets and reservations (charged on my company card, with no notion of who, eventually, will pay; no one calls Nimrod cheese-paring, but he did not make two separate business fortunes being feckless about expenses); with Celeste Lydia is now installed in the café, which, though fogged with sour smoke, has far better croissants than those provided (under gleaming film) by Lot (the airline, not in a raffle), and generous cups of the fragrant but near-lethal Strasbourg coffee.

Now, at last, I can dial up Brussels, once more mortifying my urge to try Carina's number. For the same reason, fear of surveillance, I do not try to raise Nimrod though it would be comforting to alert and perhaps enlist all his political pull.

I dial Lise's number; bugging must have a limit, and my friendship with her, if known, would hardly seem important.

"Hello, boss? I hear you had some weather. Are you snowed in with the Cossacks?"

"No." My confidence in being uneavesdropped is wilting away.

After waiting for me to expand, she gives a little grunt. "*All* right."

"Is Carina — ?" Is she what?

"Yes she is, yes she does, though she's never one to say

so. I'm doing a meal and a movie with her later. According to Enrico, she fluffed lines all over the shop yesterday — " (Enrico, a writer for Italian and Spanish, a zealous nursemaid to his precious copy). "You better get back pretty swift. You okay?"

"So far. I should be back early next week. You remember that place where you rang me back last year, just before you went down to the Gulf of Genoa?" My virtually unused Paris hotel, when I went to find Katherine of Oregon.

"Oh, shit — " recognizing the conspiratorial mode. "Didn't I tell you?" Not to involve myself with cloak-and-dagger, she means. "Yeah, I remember."

"Do you still have that number?"

"Somewhere. I can get it."

"Can you ring me there tomorrow night? Eight, or thereabouts?"

"From here?"

"Well — "

"Okay, okay. I'll be seeing Charlie, I'll ring you from there."

"That'll be fine." `Charlie,' most ingenious; that is our own nickname, only ours, for Marc Droueicx, the square-moustached, slightly splay-footed *patron* of our beer-drinking place; he is too genial, his trousers too unpressed, for `Adolf,' our first thought, to stick.

"When you see her, would you tell Carina I — " what?

"Okay, like I say, so does she. Christ, what a pair. Would you fire me if I told you you're nuts about each other? Oh no, that's right, I have told you. Would you fire me if I said you're just plain nuts, both of you. Losh — " and on that Glaswegian interjection, we rest our farewells.

If everyone keeps faith, I can permit myself a sliver of hope. I go to find Lydia, and find her unexpectedly puffing inexpertly on a cigarette, evidently bought or begged from a nearby weary rail worker, whose fleshy face, under the grime, is an amazing array of sunset-and-roast-beef shades.

"Only once in a blue moon," she explains, unasked. Celeste's look contrives to combine disapproval and fascination.

Now Lydia suggests she can take a taxi and go alone to see Georg, saving the need of bagging the luggage, or rather, the other way round. Which has become a traveller's millstone ever since murdering and maiming at random became a popular expression for shabby and otherwise-impotent oppressees, blowing away the golden age of left luggage and lockers, quick carefree sorties into town between trains or planes (understand that as a westerner, I regard as an altogether different case the inconvenient devastation and slaughter caused in huddled, of late mainly Asian cities by the dropping of bombs, the launching of rockets, by uniformed and well-groomed young men from state-of-the-art aircraft, at the behest of duly-imposed governments, and never think of asking how many September Elevenths go to make up a Dresden, a Hiroshima, another liberation, peace in the region).

However. For Lydia the oddity of Georg's unsurprise is coming uppermost once more, causing nervousness, and Celeste counter-proposes that I go with her mother, she stay and guard the bags. No doubt there are further possibilities, where Lydia leaves the fox with the bag of feed and goes back for the hen again, but whilst Strasbourg is ostensibly kind and welcoming — bright under a high, diaphanous overcast, at least as many Celsius degrees on the positive side as Zmin on the negative, two days ago — either of these plans that leave someone solitary makes me uneasy; we could load everything into a taxi, and some of us wait outside while Lydia makes contact with Georg (still burdened by the luggage question, I wonder whether, with a couple of hours in hand before trains, we can manage a late lunch at a place I know in the Petite-France section, where they do chicken — like a *coq au vin*, but cooked in riesling rather than a red — with incomparable home-made egg-noodles; that with a bottle of gewurztraminer leaving no regret over omitting the ubiquitous sauerkraut).

The *patronne* here is smugly conscious of her competence, maternal in a manner peculiarly Gallic, motherly-with-a-shrug; I approach her to hope that it will be no inconvenience if Celeste, with our luggage, remain in possession of our table for an hour or so, and that she can keep an eye out for the girl, see that she is not pestered. The woman looks me over like Mme Defarge sizing up Barsad, nods, and quite pleasantly says, "No problem," then tells me what I owe, the twenty euros I laid down on and she scooped up from the counter thus remaining intact as her honorarium.

In the short, quiet street; substantial four-storey buildings put up some time after Daudet's indomitable schoolmaster, *pour outrager les boches*, chalked a forbidden *VIVE LA FRANCE!* on his blackboard (but well before *la révanche*); these are, as I understand, normally divided each into eight substantial apartments, and Georg has a ground-floor front; the taxi obediently crawls till Lydia spots the number.

Getting out, she examines nameplates by the alcoved front door, presses a button. At the same time, a young man crosses the street behind the taxi to come up behind her.

Everyone, I suppose, has experienced it, fleeting inability to identify the known in a changed context; I have stared, perplexed, at that woman on the next court preparing to serve, and must be all-but dragged into the recognition she has sold me my morning newspaper a hundred times; she nods, having of course instantly recognized me — as she might not if I turned up on her doorstep, vaguely familiar, to read her gas-meter — describing it seems to make too much of the delay, but since recognition of those we know is normally as near instantaneous as clicking a switch, a half-second lag is like eternity — and my delayed illumination, says, Leonid, as it is, the thug tenor for Galek's opera, whom later I induced to quit his post at the door, and charge upstairs to the rescue of his boss. Here, in Strasbourg, when our rescue from extradition in Poland has caused me to dismiss the Galek operation as a spent force.

Too late to tell Lydia to get back in the cab — the front door has opened, and she is vanishing inside, Leonid just behind — I repersuade a dubious taxi-driver to wait by giving him his fare so far and a substantial advance. Unarmed and probably impotent, I reach the large front door before it closes on Leonid. An unlighted foyer with a strip of carpet; on the right side stairs go steeply up, leftward the dim hallway where Leonid is shepherding Lydia, going more-or-less backwards, as she turns to protest. With all the authority summonable, I bark out the man's name, and have surprised him.

His bewildered swivel is very brief satisfaction; at my left elbow, from what I took to be the hidey-hole for a concierge, another of the château's security-clones is emerging — this one, I think, is the authentic original Sergei, unobtrusively but lethally armed with a small black automatic. At the same time, farther up, now immediately behind Lydia, a door opens, and dark against the light behind, Galek says, "Let us keep the violence to a minimum, yes?"

Lydia glumly silent, I doing my not-very best to portray wearied tolerance of trivial delays, we are ushered through a carpeted entrance-hall into a not large but enormously old-fashioned room somewhere between study and snuggery; panelled walls, brown, maroon and dark blue spines of what could as easily be fake books in flush shelving to either side of the tall window behind a dark, substantial desk, top finished with a fancy pie-crust frill over ornate underpinnings; the high-backed chair, with black leather cushioning, would do very well for a Spanish cardinal in a Greco portrait. Beneath a writhing brass chandelier, an oaken central table, slender on a slablike central support, is more like an oversized bench from a mediaeval monastery; we are neither bidden not invited to occupy any of the miscellaneous chairs clustered round it; Galek stands straddled in front of the desk, and regards Lydia with a twinkling pseudo-sternness that puts my teeth on edge.

"I am sorry to detain you, but we had not finished our discussion."

He has, to be sure, no authority on French soil — except that which belongs to the ruthless, behind closed doors anywhere. But it is hard to see how he means to proceed, how he can spirit us out of Strasbourg, back to where his power is secure, and the absence of a third fugitive must trouble him — in several senses; Galek is in one of his dark turtlenecks, and I can see the outline of substantial bandaging over the left shoulder and winding up his neck; he carries his head rigidly, cocked at a slight angle.

Celeste is indeed his first concern. "But where is your dangerous daughter?"

"Quite safe," I assert, before Lydia can say anything, and get a frowning look from Galek. Upon maturer consideration, the question of jurisdiction is not one to be pursued, not by me; not even imagined to possess any valuable information, I am ostentatiously dispensable for one who might conclude that my death would be a neat solution to one part of the dilemma, cadavers being less hazardously smuggled into oblivion than the live and unwilling. Some pressure-point is needed independent of my survival, and I fear it is time for Lydia, the one wanted alive, to step forward. With a push from me: keeping the temperature low, I observe that this is a meaningless exercise, when Mme Solyitnova still has nothing whatever to tell him.

Need-to-know raises it head; Galek tells the two Sergeis that all is under control, and tells them to mount guard outside the door, adding pointedly for the Leonid-Sergei that this means, remain there till he (Galek) orders otherwise. They sidle out, and Lydia, cued, unleashes her assault.

"Let go, you silly man. Discussion? Any useful discussion between us was finished the week after Andrei died, when I told you, as I have told you a hundred times since, that there was not and could never be any Protein Bomb. Can you be so stupid as not to know how Andrei mocked you?"

Galek must have heard this many times before, but it's clear the vehemence is new, new perhaps in Lydia's whole life. "Andrei," she expands, "was an arrogant man — he was from the first, but after his Nobel, much worse; arrogance was the peak side of his manic-depressive personality. It was not only himself, but science; he regarded all non-scientists, all who did not think scientifically, as useless fools — as often they can be, but so, too, can scientists. His Protein Bomb, as I have told you over and again, as he told you if not in so many words, was his joke on the fools — on you."

"So he tried to convince me," Galek concurs. "In so many words. But you still believe his death was no accident. A man does not kill himself over a joke gone wrong."

"Andrei's death had nothing to do with that — oh, your badgering deepened his depression, without those four-hour interrogations he might have found the strength to recover."

"Badgering?" Galek's wounded air could easily be comical. "We had many long talks, and I wanted to get information from him, but a Nobel-prize scientist is not badgered."

"Well, that is how he saw it — " Lydia, on some other track, and having got away with calling Galek a fool, is willing to concede the point. "Andrei — " a deep, resolving breath — "was convinced I was having an affair, and with someone not a scientist, an unworthy idiot in his view. As it happens, he was wrong, but that alone would not have killed him, true or false. But he discovered, by miserable chance, that he could not be Celeste's father — she was born, you know, before we had been married a year."

"This was true?" Galek, all at once genuinely fascinated.

"I was very stupid — I was doing some work that touched on human genetics and needed some fresh DNA data. Gender-linked inherited tendencies came into it, and I was not funded for proper sampling, so for testing I sent material from the three of us, Andrei, Celeste and me — my work was very rough and preliminary, the sample size had no bearing at this stage. Of course, when Celeste was born, eleven years before, I was aware

Andrei might not be the father, but had put that out of my mind —
he had been as much her father as humanly possible, granted his
preoccupations, his greatness, if you like; nothing in life could
displace his work for more than an hour or two. The woman at the
laboratory was a friend of mine, we were at university together,
she knew what my work was attempting, and after the tests were
done she sent back the results with a teasing note to say, in effect,
'Stop wasting your own time and mine, you can't show anything
with these samples. There's not a tenth of one percent chance that
Sample A has any relationship to either of the other two.' It came
in the post, and Andrei opened it. Of course, he saw at once what
it meant — even how we had labelled the samples was a small
joke, Roman A, B, C; Andrei, Bio-chemist, Celeste."

   Without an overt symptom I can name, Lydia seems, yes,
dishevelled. I put in, "Before that, he had no idea?"

   Shrug. "I was a coward, but you have to understand how
frightening his moods were for me. Even then, with the evidence
in front of him, I *chickened out*, the Americans say; I told him
there had been some mistake, obviously, and I would have the
tests redone. He seemed to accept that, half-accept, but he was
very silent in that midnight way of his. But I thought it would
work if I collected three other parent-parent-child samples,
labelled them as before, and made sure my friend at the labs never
mentioned that they were not the same — how could I know that
Andrei would, without a word, have his hair and Celeste's tested
elsewhere? with, naturally, the same results as before, no match.
Those test results I discovered amongst his papers after his death;
he never said anything about them. But then, he said scarcely
anything to me for many days before the crash."

   Wintry smile. "That was how it began, too, when those
silent weeks were new to me; I found someone who talked to me,
oh! it is so long ago, now — and when he wanted more I didn't
want to appear ungrateful — no, that's not fair, I really was
grateful, more than enough to let him have his adventure. He was
not a good man, not anyone to love, but having someone to talk to
is important, especially to a girl — a girl! I was past twenty-seven
when I married, but not experienced; I knew much about biology
but nothing about life."

   Not the details, I imagine, but the process for Andrei must
be a fairly common one, depression breeding the causes for
depression; the sufferer becomes such unrewarding and eventually
impossible company as to guarantee solitude, so that future

episodes will have ample reason to brood upon being forsaken by friends, passed over for promotions, betrayed by a lover.

As when, before dawn and shortly before Celeste bashed him, he changed from wine-soaked buffoon to hard-edged operative, Galek produces a new metamorphosis to astonish me, saying (as Andrei should have) with what could easily pass for compassionate affection, "Lydia, why did you never tell me this before?"

"Shame." She means it, but with all the pain and embarrassment, Lydia is at some level luxuriating in the confessional experience — savouring, it may be, this exposure of a new persona with a capacity for passion. Or, if you'll excuse these Jamesian shadings, enjoying the startling of us; practically anyone alive is aware of possessing hidden depths of emotion, and has fondled the thought, *if only they knew.*

"Celeste," Galek says. "Does she know Andrei was not her father?"

"Not unless he told her, and he would never do that — he was her father in any sense that matters; biology is all accidents, being a parent is choices, many of which he made. So I would have told him, but he would never discuss feelings, which, since they were not covered by the laws of physics, had no objective value. He believed I was sleeping with an unimportant academic administrator, he knew I had slept with someone not more than weeks after we married — I suppose he came to think I had a lover or lovers from start to finish — that I had, as they say, made a lifelong fool of him."

The newly human Lydia, for all her candour, is distressing me by conceding nothing to the newly human Galek, where I perceive a hope to be nurtured. It may be she has some trace of Andrei's scorn for the unscientific mind — or perhaps, more traditionally, she inherits through generations of doctors, teachers, persons of provincial consequence, a contempt for the rural housekeeper's grandson, who can claim distinction only by way of an unprovable bastard descent — there was surely a hint of this, back in the snowbound dacha, when she recounted her understanding of Galek's history, a prim disdain in her tone.

He shakes his head. "He was a difficult man, Andrei, stubborn."

"And vain, too vain to have a wife who cuckolded him, too vain ever to be wrong. You are exactly the same, Galek, but without his black moods — is it men? Sooner than recognize he fooled you, you will go on making a bigger and bigger fool of yourself, chasing unicorns, the fountain of youth, the philosopher's stone — that is what this is, you know, a dream that exists only in dreams."

There is no expressing how glad I am that Galek sent away young Leonid and the other, in whose presence he could surely have never tolerated such *lèse-majesté*; among the three of us he remains impervious to insult, seems to thrive on it. "But, Lydia," genially, "it is not the same, cannot be. Whether he was attempting to hide scientific secrets of his own, or, as you now say, shocked by secrets of yours, Andrei was pig-headed only on his own account. I represent a government."

(Not strictly accurate; he may be a leading supporter, even a bosom friend of President Kvitka, a virtual dictator in the Yekhalets region, but he has no formal national rank; if still in parliament he would be in opposition; the majority party, therefore the government, is so far still Liberal Democrat.)

"Harry Galek, the individual, can say, yes, of course, Harry Galek has been a stubborn mule, Solyitnov told him, Madame tells him, it is all ridiculous. Fine, but what if next year, the year after, the British, the Americans, anyone, has this weapon? A pity, Galek made a mistake, he believed what he was told? For my government, you see, I have to be pig-headed. The old story, Kearns — you see only what you would call the rights of the individual, I have to consider the needs of the many."

Not politic to display amusement for the idea of a Galek putting the needs of any number ahead of his own; nor is this anywhere I can deploy my one defensive weapon, the threat of publicity. I don't doubt that Galek has killed in his career, and would regard my death as no more than another element of strategy, usefulness the only measure of its desirability, the chance of detection (not very strong) its sole contraindication. No, one doesn't flourish that *muleta* in the face of one with the power and no doubt the will to decree my final, farewell disappearance, from television and anything else.

Instead: "I believe unreservedly that there is no such weapon, but in any event, the British, far less the Americans, are not going to have the chance of interrogating Mme Solyitnova — "

"And you are not working for British intelligence? Goosebrook has interfered with your extradition from Poland for what reason? His goodness of heart, I suppose."

"He believes I am acting on his behalf — or believed so until today." Explaining how we have given him the slip, I dig out and proffer Lippett's vouchers, the one altered from `Frankfurt' to `Strasbourg,' the other for Frankfurt-London. "It isn't going to take them long to guess Strasbourg, but I hope to be gone before they can do much about it."

Studying my evidence, Galek thrusts his lower lip, making a Mussolini face.

"*Hope* or *hoped*?" he taunts, then, "Shall we have a drink? Georg has some good malt whisky — from heaven, so he says."

"Where is Georg?" Lydia, not in idle curiosity.

An uncaring wave. "Somewhere; he did not wish to meet you."

"You have not harmed him?"

"Harmed Georg? No, no — why? I have known Georg for several years now — we first met not long after Andrei made his interesting purchase of dollars, currency, in Oslo, and brought them here; Georg and I became quite close; my people had made some discoveries about his private life that really he could not allow to be more generally known — I am not making moral judgements — we even helped supply his unusual needs, which provided us with some so-explicit photos, and when he was shown those, he could hardly decline to co-operate with us — I tell you all this so you won't think too harshly of Georg, who had no desire to betray a friendship — he really had no choice."

(Perhaps not, considering his origins, both of time and place; born later and farther west, exposure would have held no threat; he could have taken all his kinks, whatever they were, onto American television, paraded them, hurling, `It's my bleeping life, I'll do whatever the bleep I want with it,' in the faces of a hostile audience; I suppose blackmailers must still exist on that side of the Atlantic, but wonder what conceivable secrets they trade in, where incest, bestialism, compound treachery are served up as big top entertainment — and by their practitioners.)

Lydia is gloomily silent as Galek finds bottle and small glasses on the dark archaism of a Germanic sideboard-and-cabinet. The heavenly provenance of Georg's whisky (which Lydia doesn't taste) is mistranslation and inappropriate translating (we don't say `White Horse' when we mean Château Cheval-Blanc); it is a single malt from Skye. actually pretty good, peatier than I prefer.

"Andrei's money — " Lydia says at last.

"We let Georg keep a small commission on those dollars, which otherwise were forfeit after Solyitnov's death. They came, after all, from an illegally-held foreign account, never documented for home consumption, not for tax purposes, not even, as you know, in the will. I should, perhaps, have informed you of this, but there might still have been criminal charges once it was known, it was better kept in the family." (ingenious, but I have small doubt the money was `forfeited' no farther than Galek's own pocket) "Besides, I thought you might attempt a hasty departure, and knew that as long as you believed the money was still waiting, you would make straight for Strasbourg — without that, you might have been much more difficult to trace."

It strikes me, with a dislocation of what's real, that we have morphed into a threadbare cliché of filmed and printed romance; what Galek tells is cogent enough, but his self-satisfied air suggests that obligatory scene in which the vain arch-fiend, with our more diffidently conceited hero unmasked, outmanoeuvred, defanged, captured, served up on toast, rather than simply shooting him, seizes the opportunity for some suave swank, boasting in indiscreet detail about his masterly plan, and how effortlessly he has remained a step or two ahead of his bungling adversaries.

The moment, all absurdities intact, is more attractive as a clumsy and transparent plot-device: in real life, Galek's performance is not informing me precisely how I can abort the doomsday machine, not allowing me surreptitiously to wriggle free of my bonds or covertly arm myself with the carelessly-overlooked Uzi lying on the coffee-table. Neither is any rescue at hand; he can talk on indefinitely, without the smallest chance of being interrupted by the benificent arrival of lithe and deadly black-suited anglo-ninjas (whether rubbery frogpersons or jerseyed spiderfolk), allowing me to say, with inexhaustible aplomb, `I thought you were never going to get here.' They're not.

"Andrei's will," he says, a sudden break in tone, a descent from those masterful heights into living perplexities. "It was altered — that is, he made a new will, just before the accident. That seemed to bear out your — " Lydia's — "belief it was suicide, but you yourself were surprised when the new will was produced — you thought the one in your possession was final. Yet the differences, I believe, were slight? You and Celeste were still provided-for in the later will?"

"Except for his manuscripts and papers — " to my astonishment, Lydia is taut with unrelieved fury. "Those he willed instead to the Institute, since he had no descendant, and his wife had shown herself unworthy."

"None of that was in the will, was it?"

"He knew how I would understand it."

My second-best bed.   No doubt (once we decline sentimentally to explain away that slap in the face as meaning something esoterically else), Shakespeare, if he had entertained the smallest belief he still owned them, would have willed *Hamlet* and *Othello* and *Lear* and the rest to Heminges and Condell, or Lady Southampton, or beloved firstborn Susanna — and Anne, whatever her failings, would similarly have got the point.

"But any income has been yours," Galek cheerfully observes, and is, uniquely, something very like intimidated by Lydia's glare.

In which, extraordinarily, or in the authenticity of feeling conveyed by which, lies salvation.   Galek, pouring himself a second and larger whisky with correspondingly slighter water, is shaking his head ruefully. "Why you could never say this — you asked me to believe I had, what is it, badgered poor Andrei into killing himself — didn't you realize that I knew there was no badgering? My dear Lydia, I was there. I questioned Andrei long and often, yes, and he became impatient with my refusal to let go this question of the Protein Bomb — but mainly he laughed at me, and offered to teach me some elementary science; there were no instruments of torture on the table, no use of the kind of persuasions available to me, since if ever there was to be such a weapon I needed a willing Solyitnov who would not avenge himself by screwing up the project — which he could do, with no one able to say he did it on purpose; if he couldn't say what he was doing, who could? So, can't you see? No badgering, therefore something else is bad enough to kill himself over, what else could I think but that the Protein Bomb is real and possible? he often said, when denying that, that if it could exist, it would be too terrible to imagine — and now, only now, you tell me another thing he could not contemplate; he was not the father of his daughter, finding that out was what killed him — and because I remember the will, I believe that is how it was."

In justice, it must be reported that Lydia is now near tears, "I tell you, Kearns — " for no suggestible reason he adopts his bizarre English — "This is for me no-win job. Why does Galek waste such time with ridicularity? Kvitka now says, enough, *basta*, we must have a resolving; somebody at State Television wishes to make a new programme about Solyitnov, Nobel winner, tragic end, sad family, too much prying."

Got it; President Kvitka wants to tidy his house against unexpected visitors, before the parliamentary elections. "Cut your losses," I suggest.

"What is this, `cut losses' — " making a chopping motion with his hand.

I tell him in a language he knows better, adding in English, "Stop throwing good time after bad."

"*Facile à dire* — " (showing off). Perplexed, he frowns (though without bowing his head), and even ponderously silent is so completely in control I can think of nothing to break the spell.

"Kearns," at last. "This is most ways a pain in my neck — " hand going to the unmetaphorical one. "Kvitka, you know, does not believe in Protein Bomb, but says, like me, Galek, no one else must get this; resolve, but make certain — we spend so much money, use fifty good men chasing this — unicorn, eh?"

This sounds like a plea for my sympathy, but with an instant surge of righteous anger he turns on Lydia. "You, you stupid woman, you deserve to lose Andrei's money, go beg beside the road; you have cost us sixty times as much, a hundred times. Four years ago, you could have told me what you tell me now."

Tearful counter-fury. "Four years, yes, four-and-a-half— you prevent my teaching, cut me off from my friends and colleagues, hold my daughter hostage — "

"You have only yourself to blame — " with the contemptuous wave of a street-brawler for someone not worth fighting. She shoots back the withering look of a large-hatted lady for an ill-mannered ostler in a Merchant-Ivory film.

"Okay — " with the air of a magistrate who has reached a verdict, for whom any belated evidence is mere noise. "You lose your British — how? You lose them for now, but I, I must know there is to be no refinding, not for British, Americans, Chinese, Islami — how do you do this vanishment?"

The one question I may not answer in any useful way. Curiously, though, dazed as I am by the mere fragile hope of a hope, my very evasions turn out to be professionally acceptable; Galek very well understands that to be concealed, Lydia's future whereabouts must be concealed, also, from him, and that to say just how is in itself too much information.

Like the familiar afterthrob of sexual completion, his anger returns. "I should enjoy to telephone up your Lord Ivan Gooseshit, tell him, what ho! we have Solyitnova here for you in Strasbourg, allow him to afford next five years of badgering — "

wheeling stiffly on Lydia. "You have no Protein Bomb, you promise, only lovers."

"Only a lover," Lydia virtually agrees, having at last seen, grindingly acknowledged, the value of tactful acceptance. With the ample, backward Slavonic consonants, her English sounds almost like Lise's Glasgow.

"You — you can do no story, eh?"

"Of course not. This whole business must vanish."

"You are strange — person. I know some ace hotshot journalists to drink sometimes with. Many would risk — *risk* is correct? — risk their lives to get story. You could be killed for no story, this is most weird, man. So, no story."

His hand has gone again to neck and shoulder, and I guess that of all things he does not want it known that Galek was felled by a featherweight girl. Yet the absence of any vindictiveness over that dawn assault — equally, over my part in it — is remarkable. Perhaps, though irrelevantly, if I do challenge both copyright and authorship with a new version of *Nevertheless*, I'll leave open the possibility he was his late wife's collaborator.

"No story, not ever — " a promise I am not to violate; none of the persons or places in any account I may write will be identifiable; not news, but fiction,

He finishes his whisky, contemplates the depleted bottle, and turns — because of the injury, his whole upper body must be swivelled — to see what else Georg has to offer. "Your taxi is left," returning without new plunder.

Has left is the meaning I divine. He would, of course, have sent it away.

"We can catch a tram — " casually, meticulously casual. My mind bustles off to the station, to a glum Celeste, still waiting, please, in the café; that vulnerable solitude has been a dark shadow under all the more proximate and personal dangers. I left the tickets with her, but did not want to sharpen anxiety by issuing her explicit instructions in case we had not returned by train-time; instead I spoke as if in general about Brussels as a reserve destination of last resort, but when I wrote Carina's number on the ticket-envelope, large eyes behind the bifocals understood perfectly, and feared.

"Your train — what time?"
I tell him, and it is getting rather near.

A gingerly nod. "You will be in front of the British, by

far. I have kept watch on Goosebrook's main man here, I would learn, bing-bam, if he has gone to meet reinforcement, if there is, um, crisis." Tacitly, he acknowledges the inadequacy of his English for complicated precisions, going back to his own language to say, "I was obsessed by Solyitnova — " speaking as if she were absent, or stone-deaf — "Then today I was interested in a different way, and now I am officially bored. You must make sure I stay bored."

"Count on it."

We are dismissed, not even shepherded; I'm far from certain Galek, in his new conviction his time was wasted, doesn't more than half mean what he said about Gossbrooke getting a taste of the same. Not enough, surely, actually to tip him off about us — though Gossbrooke will be waiting for me, somewhere, and my job now is to make him too late. It has been a long time since Lydia has spoken a word; beside me, making the short walk to the river-bridge where the trams go, in a very low, a veritably meek voice she says, "You still want to help me?"

Still? Since what? The only imaginable answer is preposterous; I lean to kiss her on the cheek.

IX

Perhaps, after all, I should have rung Gossbrooke's leave-a-message number to convey official word of what he won't call my success; my entire reason for flying in to Heathrow is to give him the opportunity to intercept me, and when, with no need to mount watch over the jumbled circulation of luggage, carrying all my stuff — still carrying, it abruptly occurs to me, much of the underwear of Celeste, who forgot to reclaim it — I emerge into Arrivals, it is disappointing not to see his face amongst the throng of meeters, greeters and name-displayers.

Running that gazing, gesturing gauntlet, I at once spot and am spotted; tall, somewhat stooped, hatless in an unimpeachably genuine, almost pristine Burberry trenchcoat, Gossbrooke, flanked to the rearward by what look to me like a couple of youngish coppers in ordinary, acceptably soiled macs. With an agenda of my own, I set a course leftward of the group, for the centre of the large, busy space, and he with his attendant myrmidons moves quickly to intercept, calling my name. I radiate back his insincere pleasure, but his greeting hardly pretends not to be preoccupied.

What he wants to know is obvious, but he can hardly jump the gun without betraying his surveillance; I help him out with, "It's done. Lydia Solyitnova — "

"What have you done with her? — " pettish, so soon.

"Not congratulations, thanks very much, your gong is on its way? *Done* with her? I'm not a government department, I don't do things with people."

"But I expected you to bring Solyitnova to London. Dammit, you must have known we wanted to interview her. I told you — "

"As you know, I got her out of the country. She's a free woman; I thought that was the point of the exercise."

"What have you done with her? Another of our disgusting pimps — " no, Gossbrooke doesn't actually say that, but it is, to me, implicit — "One of our people spotted you with Solyitnova and the child in Strasbourg — " clearly, a lie — "and we know you were on the train to Paris, yesterday afternoon." That part I believe, but it was learned, or rather, deduced, retrospectively.

"While spotting, your people might have spotted Galek in Strasbourg with his people."

"We did, of course we did — " the lies are becoming more flustered.

"And when he had us trapped in that house near the covered bridge — " it wasn't, not anywhere near, but I'm owed a bit of entertainment. "I suppose you had your people ready to move in."

Forced to abandon omniscience, his temper worsens. "Are you trying to tell me Galek has recaptured the Solyitnova woman? Because — "

"No, no, as your people spotted, we went on to Paris. Galek probably went home; did you happen to spot that?"

All the same it was quite close; there must have been a chance sighting at the Gare de l'Est; if they'd read my mind or been swifter, the reception-committee might have been waiting for the train. I could congratulate myself on the celerity and deviousness, excessive-seeming at the time, of my movements in Paris, making our way from one to another terminus by the least-obvious of routes, and alone earlier today to Charles de Gaulle, making eccentric use of surface and sub-surface transport. Not that my interception would have meant all that much, once Lydia (troubled but grateful) and Celeste (inconsolable) were no longer with me. Of course, I guessed that once I booked my flight I (though I didn't know by what means) was back on the radar screen, but after plotting with Lise when she duly rang me at the Paris hotel last night, I was determined that my reunion with Gossbrooke would occur here, exactly here.

"Where is Solyitnova now?" Gossbrooke harps, ignoring what must have been news about Galek.

"I haven't a clue — " a Clintonesque non-lie, dependent on that *now*; I last saw newly reflustered Lydia and weepy Celeste boarding a TGV; it is probable but not nearly certain that they are still on French soil, but their further fate and indeed their identities are in the hands of a man I introduced at the start of this account, calling him Ariosto, who has safe places where people may go, awaiting their rebirth. For any useful purpose, at this moment, Lydia Solyitnova has ceased to exist, and the woman that emerges from seclusion will have no connections back to her. A metamorphosis miles beyond my means, done mainly as what is (without much geniality) called a favour to me, meaning that Ariosto did not need reminding I still have the power to expose him, either on television, or to the French police in the Mirré case.

I have no idea — nor do I want to know, nor would he tell me — what Ariosto will turn her into, but her nationality, her antecedents, all her life, will not be Lydia's, and her new incarnation will be in some place where the possibility of a chance recognition is so remote as to be non-existent.

"Look, Kearns — " what a different, snarling Gossbrooke from my suave host in Brussels. "You may not realize how precarious your position is. Misuse of official funds — "

Threats, so soon? "Would you care to specify, in open court, the purpose for which those funds were advanced to me? In any event, in a day or so you will be receiving, registered post, a complete accounting of my expenditures, and my personal cheque returning the balance to you personally — I didn't know what department budget to repay. I charged nothing for my actual services — " and I have him, of course; whether or not he accepts the registered packet, the receipt is in safe hands, my cheque is dated and I've made a photocopy, no case against me for misprision could be made to stand. Nevertheless, I'm lying; in fact I paid my own way, charging the rental for the Volvo to Nimrod, while the envelope with a thousand of Gossbrooke's twelve hundred conveniently untraceable euros (like a princely tip, the missing two hundred was left behind at the dacha, to cover damages) went untouched with Lydia, to be handed to Ariosto — far short of his normal fee, but a down payment, surely, for out-of-pocket expenses.

For the moment Gossbrooke is chiefly horrified that I would write down and send through the post what he assumes is a lurid inventory of clandestine doings. He calls that unprofessional, and I point out that I've never been part of any craft he might mean, and that the instincts of my profession would be not tamely to send his accounts through the mail, but to put them on the air, or the front page of the *Guardian*.

Stiff already, he stiffens. "I would strongly advise you against the folly of going public with your adventures," he says, with the rigid lower jaw of the ventriloquist's best pal. "Any official participation or foreknowledge will be denied, and you will be laying yourself open to serious criminal charges. This, by the way — " the minion at his elbow, "is Detective-Sergeant Bannister, Special Branch — " less than my age, with a bad shave and wearied eye.

To Gossbrooke's bewilderment, and rudely enough, I am not responding to the introduction, but swivelling left and looking up to where, as arranged, Lise MacNab (née Svendsen), a short way up a spidery non-moving stair to the Departures level, is pointing a very expensive miniature portable camera — actually, a video-recorder. The range is fully fifty yards, but she has a very good zoom lens attached, and the curious, if so minded, will be able to count Gossbrooke's pores when the recording is shown. I also note with satisfaction that Lise has with her the loose-limbed, long-necked Eric, her son, who is aiming a diabolically directional pistol-mike at us.

She waves cheerily, but Gossbrooke allots me a loathing glance, before turning to the sergeant, pointing him to his target. In a purposeful stride which might in an eyeblink bend into a trot, the copper aims for the stairs, but Lise, hardly needing my throat-cutting gesture, has unhurriedly unshouldered the camera, and already ejected the `film' — in fact, a CD (oh, we stay very state-of-the-art at Babel) — dropped it in a carrying case, and now exchanges it for the microphone with her son. Somewhat belatedly backed up by the other officer, Bannister, as Eric comes swiftly down the stairs, does break into a near-run, but Eric, so young, has already broken three-forty for 1500 metres — or perhaps more germanely, now he is carrying his square, black baton, habitually runs the anchor leg for a consistently triumphant 4X400 relay team; he surges into high gear, skirting knots and clumps of customers, and with a somewhat dreamlike effect, vanishes. The sergeant, clearly not a Bannister to imperil the four-minute mile, hasn't a chance — Gossbrooke, of course, has not alerted the ordinary security forces, since a certified Incident could bring in just the publicity he wants to avoid.

With the fuzz dispersed, there is nothing to prevent my wishing Gossbrooke a cheery farewell and sauntering away; equally no reason now not to stay and chat. He says, "I hope you don't imagine we're going to let you make a story out of this."

"No, no," I assure him, as a complacent Lise, camera slung, comes solidly up and nods me a greeting. She is displaying press credentials pinned to her flak-jacket. "This is nothing but insurance, as much for Lydia as me."

"Eventually — " trying very hard to reestablish an atmosphere of menace — "You're going to have to tell us where she is."

"I honestly don't know."

"Your friend Zuylen in Amsterdam can't hide her away, you know."

Zuylen? Gossbrooke is really banging away at random. "Who would think he could — a colourful old scoundrel, but he couldn't make a coin vanish." This has to be dismissive, since there is a faint, tortuous connection from Zuylen to Ariosto, via Katherine of Oregon in Paris, but rather than gone cold, that trail was never warm; I was a journalist and not a player when I made that pilgrimage, and no one was watching. No one, at least, who would be likely to inform Gossbrooke's mob.

"If you think we're going to let you keep her out of our hands, you're insane." He is still attentive to the farther reaches of the terminal, dimly hoping, I suppose, that Eric threw a shoe or in some other improbable fashion fetched up lame.

It might be that, consistent with the reality he inhabits, he believes I have cached Lydia, and plan to sell her to the highest bidder. "When we met in Brussels, you told me the government's only interest in Solyitnov's super-weapon was to see it would never be developed — that his widow would never be used to help develop it. Surely you weren't fibbing?"

A little to his credit, he does grin. "You're no innocent. Do you suppose any government on earth can afford to let such an opportunity go by, knowing it's likely, otherwise, that the weapon may end up in the hands of another, less benevolent state — ?"

I let the benevolence go. "No, I never did suppose it, which is why I made no attempt to bring Solyitnova to London."

"You take far too much on yourself — your actions would amount to treason, if Syria, let's say, or North Korea gets the device."

"Not on. Lydia, I judge, sincerely believes the weapon her husband envisaged can never be made — "

"Of course, she would say that."

"Whether or not it's true, whether or not she believes it, what is certain is her rejection of nationalism, her documented lifelong hatred of war and weapons, her determination not to be associated with either; if her own people, using her daughter as leverage, couldn't shift that resolve, how likely is it that North Korea, or China, or even America, could coerce her? Not that they're going to have the chance; all she wants is to be left alone, and I think she's going to manage that. Just tell your minister the Solyitnova situation has been neutralised to your satisfaction."

"To my satisfaction! Where is she, Kearns? And where is that disc?" wheeling on calm Lise. Like me, he has no doubt spotted the wearied re-approach of the Special Branch, winded, dishevelled, obviously defeated; as they near I surmise that blue-chinned Bannister would very much like to arrest someone, anyone.

Lise looks at her wrist-watch. "That's awfa hard to say —
" exaggerating the Glasgow in her speech out of sheer mischief.
"Gie it a couple of hours, and it'll be in Brussels."

"We don't have to fly it there," I remind Gossbrooke,
seeing him consider having all flights watched. "It's digitalised,
and can be transmitted over a phone-line. Unless I'm in a position
to countermand, it'll go into world distribution, with a cover-story
I filed last night." That part is a little premature; I taped a
commentary last night, and dispatched it to Brussels a few hours
ago.

"Pictures," he pronounces in dismissal. "The sound on
your tape will hardly be broadcast quality; we could be talking
about the bloody weather."

Lisa, technical mastery implicitly impugned, begins to
dispute this, getting as far as, "No, no, these little mikes are a
bloody wonder — " before I put a quieting hand on her forearm.

"You're wrong," I tell Gossbrooke. "But it doesn't matter;
the mere existence of your little reception party is adequate
corroboration for my story."

A long moment filled with dark glances, and then he
begins with immense formality to remind me of the Official
Secrets Act, confirming my consciousness of a winning hand;
British interest in the Solyitnova affair would not necessarily be a
fatal disclosure, but Gossbrooke himself cannot permit his
international persona as a genial, somewhat colourless trade expert
to be revealed as cover for black operations; he would be obliged
to retire discredited from both.

"You know the Official Secrets Act could only be
invoked if the government was willing to admit I was its agent. In
any event, no secrets need be divulged; I'll call the Solyitnova
affair closed the moment you do."

"Will you undertake to surrender that tape, and any copies
that might be made?"

"I'll undertake to put it where it'll never be disturbed, so
long as there are no proceedings against me."

"Not good enough — " the revelatory potential of our
pictures is beginning to obsess him.

"Out of my hands. Unless I'm free to prevent it, the
process is on auto-pilot. You don't in any event have deniability;
you blew that when you rang me at work." When exasperated by
my delay in getting started; he had been circumspect about what
he said, but as with the videotape the mere fact of his call was
enough. Because, mistaken (as Babel often has been) for a

broadcast operation, we could be used as a conduit for terrorist threats and warnings, abductors' demands, anonymous tips, all our incoming calls are, as I inform Gossbrooke, routinely recorded, his voice readily identifiable.

"Look here, Kearns — the last journalist to attempt exposing intelligence operations — "

I liked *attempt*. "Is, last I heard, still walking about in Paris. Spy turned journalist, you should say; he's not much of a writer."

Gossbrooke retreats even farther into the official manner. "Let's have this on the record, then — " I half-expect him to have still-panting Bannister pull out his notebook — "You decline to surrender your unauthorised tape, and refuse to reveal the present whereabouts of Lydia Solyitnova."

"On the record, an accredited news group requires no authorisation to take pictures in a public place — "

"Our Chief Back in London," Lise murmurs. "It's an in-house news item."

" — and the present whereabouts of Mme. Solyitnova are unknown to me."

What now? There must be a limit to the number of times Gossbrooke can ask the same questions, and I don't believe he can risk having me arrested.

At last, "Will you be staying in England?"

"My parents' place in Kent, but I'll be going back to Brussels in a day or two." To Carina, you pompous creep.

"I hope you will be able to," icily, but it's nothing but smoke. "Don't imagine you've heard the last of this. My best regards to Sir Matthew."

My father, and Gossbrooke works to make even this seem like a veiled threat, as if the spotless distinction of Dad's diplomatic years could be charmed into a noose to throttle me. So, with a swivel of his heel and ushering of disappointed coppers, we part.

Or nearly. Abruptly reminded of an untried weapon, Gossbrooke calls me back. "Look here, Kearns — " the tone is positively matey; we're back in Brussels with old brandy and clean hands. "Your family is a lot like mine — we've always been willing to forget personal advantage and so forth, for the sake of country."

"I know. That's just the trouble."

Lise has a square, battered Volvo (borrowed from a former sister-in-law) parked; crouched in the back, Eric does not pop up until we reach motorway, and deem ourselves safe from surveillance; an earnest, lip-pursing youth (after predictable Olympic glory, whether for Denmark or U.K. to be determined, he intends a career in genetics), he requires and receives a detailed explanation of the tape's importance, though having no difficulty (*o, tempore!*) with the part that for me at that age would have been toughest to digest, the idea that government might not be the good guys.

Who are? I have never stopped worrying away at my decisive interference in this whole business; by the time I offered Lydia the chance of a new life, I (together with the unforeseeable attack on Galek by her daughter) had brought her to where there was not much choice left.

It may be all right. With Ariosto, despite his initial annoyance with my ringing him on what he calls his `hotline' — a number entrusted to me exclusively so that (as a favour) I could tip him off if, in the continued probings of my Secret Governments piece, I ran across any indication of curiosity about his operation — notwithstanding his continued citations of reasons why he owed me no counter-favours, made the emptier by his constant awareness that without ever displaying it, I held the trump-card, the lurking threat of exposure, all that said, I have no doubt that his professional integrity will oblige him to treat Lydia and Celeste exactly as if they were another Feyd Mirré, turning him a fat profit. It may perhaps have emerged in this account that on the whole I rather liked Ariosto, no doubt a ruthless man, and one who has seduced public servants beyond numbering from the very moderately rewarded path of virtue, but a crisp professional with no flicker of hypocrisy in his self-esteem. As I told Lydia, he will almost certainly have her sign a note stipulating, let's say, a ten-year repayment plan for his outlay on her, and she can decide whether or not to honour it; it will certainly be unenforceable at law, having been signed either by someone who no longer exists, or by a created someone he can hardly expose in court.

(There was a point when I began to wonder, Lydia began to wonder, whether, with a newly reasonable Galek to face, her disappearance was still unavoidable — but that mood could not be trusted, and if Kvitka ends up with a substantial majority in the elections, the old Galek may be reborn with all the weight of a government behind him. In any case, for the present, he wouldn't have accepted Lydia's change of heart, wanting to be able, like the soldiers in *Alice*, to answer, `Their heads are gone, if it please your majesty,' when Kvitka demanded, `Are their heads off?')

Lydia — well, there's hope for Lydia; besides her own and standard Russian, she is fairly adept in Polish, within a few weeks' coaching of fluency in any of not less than three other languages (follows English, reads German, does well enough in French to obtain a free cigarette); there is a wide range of places where she could practicably be reborn. Her academic credentials, of course, will have vanished with her name and past, but Ariosto will not fail to supply her with some replacement; she'll be able to teach, which she enjoys, and might even remarry, not the improbable Humbertian step-father her daughter might have cast me as, but a choice of her (self-confessedly attention-craving) own. Celeste — with Celeste, sadly enough, there was never any indication of friends her own age, except in certain attitudes — the modification of certain attitudes — which she could as easily have learned from magazines (`*What Teenagers Say About Sex*'), but she's likely to find congenial coevals in a new life, actually going to school, seldom if ever condemned to endless dinner-parties with the tediously mature, never, surely, obliged to divert them with her industrious pianism, finding, soon enough, a more rewarding, more plausible target for her quaint and turbulent, carefully reasoned passions.

It is raining, very lightly, but with the dispirited persistence of an unsuccessful fruit-machine addict, slow moisture dripping from the few, stubborn, splayed yellow fingers still attached to the big horse-chestnut at the gateway to my parents' pleasant dwelling. Before I can sound the bell, the door swings open, we are greeted by my silvered, sweatered father, and just to his left rear, astonishingly, is smiling Carina. After my, in the circumstances, perfunctory greeting for my father, Carina and I kiss, and I say, "How long have you been here?" — which ought to be fatuous; she must (this is to be confirmed) have travelled with Lise, who dropped her here before going to Heathrow — or, first, to collect Eric, wherever he was.

Yet there is an unthought logic behind my question; Carina could never look less than lovely, and today, I note, is quite enchanting enough to break my father's heart, but she's dressed, as I have never witnessed before, in what my vague eye sees as country things, a burnt-orange rugby jersey and a soft, greeny-browny textured skirt, blunt (but by no means styleless) brown shoes. No just-arrived visitor, she belongs, is at home, far more than ever in Brussels.

"I was so anxious," she says, using English, and coming head-on into my arms, and because so much is in its right place we kiss properly, without restraint — through half-a-dozen years, my parents, seeing themselves as boldly on the cutting edge, have without comment assigned one bedroom to me and any *amie de la visite*, but I have never tested their tolerance with open displays of affection — perhaps, at base, because the affection has never before been so unmixedly present.

"I was worried about that terrible man, what he could do," Carina, between kisses, meaning Galek (who for me turned out to be neither dragon nor dragoon), but Lise, a step behind me, still cheerleading, begins crowing about how utterly I had dished the baffled wanker, while simultaneously my father disparages the entire Gossbrooke clan, launching into a reminiscence concerning the impermeable skull of an elder family member, once an envoy in Bonn. We, too, have our bourgeois snobberies, but only upwards.

To Carina, all dark, warm eyes, I suggest, "Let's get married."

Certain quiet utterances, even murmured at a raucous prize-fight when the upstart challenger, against the ropes, is being pulped by our hometown hero, are of their nature heard by all; a miraculous general catch in the breath succeeds my non-sequitur, and it is in a cathedral silence that Carina says, "*Demain, si tu le veux, mon amour* — " striking in intensity rather than volume. Not audible, though it should be, is the great, joyous leap of my heart; not as the most affectionate of private jokes would I ask if her assent, by her stated formula, means that boredom with me has set in. What most astonishes me is my own drastically altered perception of marriage per se; though I can't possibly have abandoned in an eyeblink my deep-seated scepticism about the lifelong sustainability of impassioned pairings, I am not (as ten minutes ago might have been assessed) simply a frustrated bachelor, resigning himself to the only and imperfect resolution between admiration freely given and the fear of loss; to be a husband and to have a wife are all at once the best idea I ever had, so long as the wife is Carina, most cherished of excitements, most beddable of friends: I wish we could be private and unclad together somewhere.

My mother arrives when Lise is thumping me between the shoulderblades, takes in developments at a glance, and understates how pleased she is, my father so soon enthusiastically advocating the advantages of our present location as venue for "the do." Having hugged my smugly smiling mother, ebullient Carina hugs my father, kissing him on — or rather, kissing beside — each cheek, and as he emerges from the ordeal tenaciously elaborating his ideas for the reception, an unprecedented marvel can be seen to have occurred; Sir Matthew Kearns, unflappable veteran of a million deadpan F.O. occasions, is blushing.

He recovers enough, as we herd inside, to mutter that while a bit early, this is a unique occasion, and toddles off to unearth a bottle of the `very special' 1966 Bollinger (a magnum, I hope; there are six of us, one irrelevantly underage, but also in training, say five-and-a-bit) sent to him on his retirement by a French colleague, and said to have come from the cellars in two-churched Colombey: from the Kaiser's cognac and Tito's rakija, I come home to De Gaulle's champagne.

Lise takes the opportunity to offer, sotto voce, some incisive advice; "Great, chief, but if you want to keep her, you better hang that Scarlet Pimpernel turn on a nail."

To be truthful, I'm not likely to be asked; what agency would want to hire someone who, without permission, might irresponsibly go and accomplish their stated objective? But how unutterably luxurious to yield, when circumstances occur, to absolute corn (and I haven't yet had a drop); Carina is across the room still talking with my mother, and all at once her eyes meet mine with an absolute, serene assurance. Life, why have I never noticed, is inexhaustibly precious; the wise but jaundiced French insist, *quand on aime, on n'aime personne*, and I can simultaneously acknowledge its shrewdness, and inconsistently entertain the counter-truth, *car on aime, on aime tout le monde*: I have plenty of spare sentimental affection to splash over onto Lise, to whom I nod a grateful, deal-making assent.

Carina's ties to the church of her fathers are tenuous; that first marriage was a civil ceremony, and she'll probably have no qualms about the thoroughly Anglican operation I see coalescing all about me; bridesmaids, Bentleys, bouquets, there's no stopping it; my mother has already uttered the word *banns*, invoking the name of Jonathan Partridge, the vicar, in connection with a setting of dates. All right, Mendelssohn, I decide, but not *Lohengrin*, a lovely tune as Wagner wrote it, but not with the skip of its dotted 2/4 rhythm dirged by the organist into dogged equal crotchets; dad and my bride (the step-dad, that is, *il simpatico*, if he'll make the journey from Livorno, with Mamma) can process to the livelier march from *Figaro*. And the do here, if do there must be, where better? and my father, experienced proposer of toasts, will take the opportunity to give a speech filled with the jocular bawdy the occasion sanctions, though this time, as undetectable to any but me (perhaps my only sometimes scrutable mother), tapping into a deep, not conscious reservoir of passionate regret for the cruelty of time, the ever-nagging ache of what can't be had. Well, I'm going to be married to Carina, who has curled seamlessly to my side; I'll have to accustom myself to being envied.

Notes

p. 105   *on se fout du basson bruyant*, "screw the noisy bassoon" — a reference to *Rime of the Ancient Mariner* (The wedding-guest here beat his breast/ For he heard the loud bassoon).

p. 134   Daudet: in a famous patriotic story *La dernière classe*, told in the person of an Alsatian child, not long after the Prussian annexation in 1871

p.166   second-best bed: Shakespeare's famous bequest to Anne (*née* Hathaway); vast quantities of ink and ingenuity have been expended trying to convince us that "second-best" had no pejorative connotations for Shakespeare, that he mentioned the specific furnishing at all is a sign of its worthiness, *undsw, undsw* — anything to avoid the plain commonsense implication, that for some reason he no longer much cared for his wife (in an intriguing bit of pure invention, Anthony Burgess conjectured that S. surprised his wife with her lover, disporting themselves on that very bed, and that the testamentary provision was a grim ironic souvenir of that occasion).

p. 170   gong: common British for a medal.

p. 179   *Demain* (etc): "Tomorrow, if you like, my love."

p. 179   French *le dragon* = dragon, but also <u>dragoon</u>.

Two-churched: De Gaulle's home village of Colombey-les-deux-églises

Quand on aime (etc); a French commonplace, "When you're in love you don't like anyone", altered by Mark to "Being in love you (can) love the whole world."

www.ingramcontent.com/pod-product-compliance
Lightning Source LLC
Chambersburg PA
CBHW030254130626
46549CB00002B/522